FATAL COMPLICATIONS

Also by John Benedict

Adrenaline

The Edge of Death

FATAL COMPLICATIONS

A Novel

JOHN BENEDICT

Longboat Key, Florida

ISBN: 978-1-60809-156-0

Published in the United States of America by Oceanview Publishing
Longboat Key, Florida

www.oceanviewpub.com

10 9 8 7 6 5 4 3 2 1

PRINTED IN THE UNITED STATES OF AMERICA

*To my dearest wife, who has taught me the true meaning
of soulmate*

*Lou Ann, you weave the softness of my dreams
Caress the essence of my mind
Love, from my body to yours, streams
By the fiery stars aligned*

ACKNOWLEDGMENTS

My new friends, Kristen Chandler and Kelly Believer Smith,
who encouraged me along the way and were kind enough to add
my books to their awesome blogs

John Dobbyn, superb legal thriller author, who befriended me
and opened the door to Oceanview Publishing

My brilliant editors, Marg Wilks and Patricia Gussin,
who helped take my writing to the next level

FATAL COMPLICATIONS

PROLOGUE

The man staggered out of the garage, coughing violently, a dark form cradled in his arms. Smoke was everywhere and flames spewed from the first-floor windows, lighting up the summer night sky. Red-hot embers danced and swirled skyward like millions of drunken fireflies. The sirens were close now. He stumbled toward his wife at the end of the driveway. "I got him," he rasped. "Poor thing. I found him curled in a ball under the laundry room sink." The man laid the trembling chocolate Labrador retriever on the cool asphalt and knelt to smooth his fur. "I think he'll be all right, Marie."

His wife did not respond—her body was rigid.

The man stood up to comfort her. She remained frozen, her mouth worked, but no words came out. Her eyes were wide with panic. The man whipped his head around. "Where's David?"

Still no response, but she began to shake. He faced her, hands clamped on her shoulders. "Marie, where is he?" he shouted through smoke-filled lungs. "Where's David?"

"He went after you to look for Brownie," she managed to get out before dissolving into sobs. "He moved too fast—I couldn't stop him." She pointed in the general direction of the garage, her arm swaying wildly.

He ran back into the garage. The metal door to the house radiated heat. He touched its surface and yanked his hand away; it was much hotter than it had been five minutes ago. He didn't have time for this safety drill. Ignoring how the knob burnt into the palm of his hand, he twisted it and pushed.

Flames burst out of the doorway, growling like some alien beast. The scorching heat bowled him backwards and he lost his footing and went down hard, hitting his back on his John Deere tractor. The hair on his right forearm was singed off. "David," he yelled from the cement floor. "Come on out! I got Brownie!" No reply other than the roaring of the fire and the crackling of the wood that used to be the frame of his house.

Scrambling to his feet, he ran back out and around to the front of the house. He heard the fire trucks rumbling up the street, sirens blaring so loud it was hard to think. Flashing red lights played on the trees in the front yard, casting strange shadows, lending a sense of unreality to the scene. The flames were spreading quickly to the second floor.

He approached the front door, knowing that it was locked—Marie was a stickler for these things. He shoved his hand under the thick bristly WELCOME doormat for the key, struck by the absurdity as he unlocked the door and opened it. *Welcome to hell, maybe.*

Again a wall of flame greeted him. This time he was ready; he took two steps back, careful not to fall down. "David!" he yelled. "I have Brownie!"

He paused to listen and thought he heard a faint scream. But from where? He was about to back away when he heard a peculiar, musical sound coming from the living room. Was that David playing the piano? Again, the unreality of the situation washed over him and for a split second he questioned his sanity. Then, just as quickly, he realized the piano wires were twanging randomly as the fire set them free.

He ran around to the back of the house, his feet slipping on the dew-slicked grass, and peered in the kitchen window. The blaze was not as intense here, but smoke was everywhere. He thought he could make out some movement through the smoke. *Please God, protect him. Save my boy.*

He tried the backdoor handle—for once it wasn't burning hot, but it was locked and he didn't have the key. He kicked at the door, aiming high, near the lock. Something cracked, but the door held. Backing up several steps, he ran toward the door and sprang forward, hitting it squarely with both feet. The frame splintered and the door crashed inward. He fell backwards onto the flagstone patio, smacking his right elbow. Smoke billowed out of the ruined doorway, but no flames. He pushed to his feet and started forward.

Someone tackled him from behind, knocking the wind out of him and sending him back to the ground. "I can't let you go in there," a deep voice of authority warned. He rolled over and looked up at a large firefighter standing over him. The air tanks strapped to his back and the face mask below his helmet made him resemble a cross between a spaceman and a sumo wrestler.

Painfully, he sucked air back into his lungs and pleaded hoarsely while climbing to his feet, "My boy's in there!"

Another fireman, smaller than the first, ran over and helped restrain him. The big one said, "Take it easy! If you go in there, you'll never come out alive."

"But my boy..." His voice trailed off into an agonized groan. He strained harder against them.

The firefighter put a hand on his shoulder and fixed him with kind blue eyes. "We have equipment. We'll go in and get him." Blue Eyes turned and shouted, "Bill, bring the hose and gear around back here!"

He stopped struggling. As the arms holding him relaxed their grip, he broke free and ran toward the doorway, ignoring their cries of "Shit!" and "Don't be a fool!"

He ran into the house, his sneakers crunching on broken glass. "David—it's Dad," he called out. "I'm in the kitchen." Coughing spasms prevented him from saying anything else. The black smoke was so thick he couldn't see a thing. Breathing was a nightmare. He dropped to all fours, cutting his hands on the glass. Here he could breathe in little gasps and see his bloodied hands on the vinyl brick flooring.

"I'm coming for you, son," he yelled, his voice already raspy from the smoke. More coughing fits. Again, he thought he could hear faint cries coming from upstairs, but he couldn't be sure because the roar of the flames was so loud.

He crawled across the foyer to the base of the stairway and began ascending the stairs on all fours. The heat ratcheted up the higher he climbed, and the smoke thickened. Coughs wracked his chest. He wouldn't be able to breathe much longer. If he turned around now, he could probably make it out the way he had come, to the cool, fresh air outside. He groped for the gold cross dangling from his neck and squeezed it hard, saying a quick prayer. Then he heard his boy crying—no imagining this time—a horrible, high-pitched keening that pierced his very soul. He climbed upward.

Halfway up the staircase, he paused and lifted his sweat-soaked t-shirt to cover his mouth and nose. He took several deep breaths through it, then held the last one and clambered to the top of the stairs. Although the smoke made his eyes burn as if someone had poured acid in them, he forced himself to look down the hallway.

What he saw filled him with a sickening dread. Midway along, a hellish inferno blocked the hallway. The heat pouring off the flames was roasting him alive. He put one hand up to shield his eyes, clenched his jaw, and advanced. As he got closer, he noticed that the wall of flame wasn't quite as dense as he had first thought. There was a spot clear of flames at the end of the hallway, near David's room.

His air hunger was becoming unbearable and his surroundings swirled in his dimming vision. He ran toward the flames, but tripped on some unseen debris and went down hard, forcing the last bit of air out of him. Reflexively, he sucked in a lungful of thick, burning smoke, then coughed painfully. His lungs felt like they were being ripped to shreds; soon the bloody remnants would spill out of his mouth. No air was getting in.

The hallway dimmed again. He wasn't going to make it. As his consciousness flickered, he glimpsed his boy through the smoke and flame at the end of the hallway. David was reaching out to him, crying, "Dad, I'm here! Help me!"

CHAPTER ONE

"I want you to curl into a ball and arch your back like a mad cat at Halloween," Dr. Luke Daulton said. "Or a shrimp. Here, look at me." Luke bent over, demonstrating the proper position so he could administer the spinal anesthetic. He had a healthy respect for large obstetrical patients. Perhaps aversion was a better term, and maybe it wasn't so healthy.

"But you don't have a belly like I do," whined Shirley. She tried to lean forward, but only succeeded in bending her neck—her back remained ramrod straight.

Luke sighed and smiled under his mask. He had forgotten how much he disliked OB anesthesia—taking care of two patients at once was always tricky. He turned and winked at Teri, the anesthesia tech assigned to help him, trying to display more confidence than he felt as he snapped on his sterile gloves.

The delivery room was a busy place and everyone was in close quarters. To his left, two scrub nurses in sterile OR attire counted their surgical instruments, creating quite a racket as they banged them down on the metal trays. Across the room, a neonatologist and neonatal nurse practitioner were readying their pediatric resuscitation equipment. The large radiant warmer above the baby bassinet let out loud screeches intermittently and had to be repeatedly silenced. Two circulating nurses were talking and busily filling out paperwork. Luke could see the obstetrician through a window, scrubbing his hands at the scrub sink.

"That's Dr. Seidle," Teri said, nodding toward the window.

She leaned in close and whispered, "He's pretty cranky for a young guy. Ever since he got sued last year for a bad baby, he's never been the same. He yells a lot—especially when the shit hits the fan."

"Great," Luke said, thinking he knew the type well. He made a mental note to try to keep shit away from the fan today.

Luke searched the faces of the obstetrical team assembled around him, looking for a sympathetic face; he found none. They eyed him curiously, undoubtedly because he was new, but there was no discernible warmth, either. He wouldn't get the benefit of the doubt around here. Plain and simple: this was a test and he was on trial.

There was also an edgy undercurrent present—a kind of dangerous electricity, a palpable tension. Everyone in the delivery room chuckled and talked nonchalantly, but they all knew that things could go horribly wrong in this place. People could die and careers could be ruined in a matter of minutes.

Luke shook his head to dispel these thoughts. Such negativity—Dad would've scolded him, if he were around.

"Teri, can you help Shirley lean forward?" Luke asked.

"Sure, Dr. Daulton." Teri stepped up on a footstool for better leverage. Luke was happy to have at least one ally in the room.

Shirley attempted to lean forward again, but this time managed to arch her back exactly the opposite way to what he had just demonstrated.

"That's better," Luke said with resignation. Time to punt on proper positioning. "Okay, a little bee sting," he said, the words making him smile as they always did. They brought to mind his medical student days five or six years ago, when an old man told him what large bees they had around these parts. He numbed her skin with a local anesthetic.

"Ouch!" Shirley cried. "Sonuva..."

"That's the worst part," Luke soothed. He felt himself relax a little; he had done this procedure countless times. "Try not to move. A little pressure now." Luke advanced the delicate spinal needle, roughly the diameter of a human hair, hoping to hit pay dirt—the CSF, or cerebrospinal fluid that bathes the brain and spinal cord. He kept checking as he advanced. No fluid.

"Got it yet?" asked Shirley.

"You'll be the second to know."

Teri rolled her eyes at Luke. Even though she had her surgical mask on, Luke could tell she was smiling from the crinkling around her eyes. "Bone?" Teri asked.

"No, it's a clean shot."

Finally, Luke had the needle inserted to the hub, three and a half inches in, and still no CSF. "Teri, get me the next one up." This meant the five-inch needle, "the harpoon." Luke hated the harpoon because it was long enough to be dangerous. The aorta and the vena cava ran just in front of the spinal column and were easy targets for the big needle.

He checked her landmarks again. They were difficult to palpate, owing to the size of his patient. Teri gave him an encouraging look. The rest of the team stared at him coolly, fidgeting with their instruments or shooting each other glances.

One inch. Two inches. Three. Four. Still no CSF. Luke began to sweat and felt the droplets course down his arms. For the first time, it hit home that there was a real transition to be made here. Two and a half months ago, he was a well-respected, confident senior resident who knew all the ropes at the Hospital of the University of Pennsylvania. Now, after taking the job at Swatara Regional Hospital, he had thrust himself into the real world of private practice.

At four and a half inches, Luke struck white gold. Precious CSF dripped from the hub of his needle after he removed the inner stylet. Releasing a big sigh of relief, he turned to wink at Teri again. He attached the syringe and injected the spinal anesthetic agent and quickly withdrew the needle.

"Okay, Shirley, all done. Gonna lay you flat now." He grasped her shoulders and pulled her down.

"Wow, my feet are getting warm already," Shirley said.

"Good, good. You did great sitting there. Hope I didn't hurt you too much."

"No, it wasn't bad. I can't move my feet, though. Is that normal?"

"Perfectly normal," he said, although he thought it *was* a bit fast. "Time to check your level." He poked her gently in her groin region with a needle. "Can you feel this?"

"Nope."

He worked the testing needle up onto her sizable belly. "This?" Still no response.

When he got up to her mid-chest, she said, "Yeah, I can just barely feel that."

"Great. You're going to be very comfortable." Luke felt relief and a certain degree of satisfaction wash over him. He couldn't wait to tell Kim about it—the two of them loved to exchange work stories.

Teri nudged him and threw a glance at the blood pressure monitor. It read 90/60, down from 145/80 three minutes ago.

Luke reached around to his anesthesia cart and picked up the ephedrine syringe. He injected some into the intravenous port and ensured the IV was running maximally.

"I feel kinda sick," Shirley moaned.

"I just gave you some medicine to fix that, Shirley," he said, and patted her gently on her head. "It'll work in about a minute."

Dr. Seidle entered the room from the scrub sink, hands held high. "Everything okay?"

"Fine," Luke said. "Ready to go. I'm Luke Daulton."

"Mark Seidle. Nice to meet you." Seidle gave Luke a quick, penetrating stare, then turned to the nurses who were waiting to gown and glove him. "Your wife goes to our practice, doesn't she?" Seidle asked over his shoulder.

"Yes, Kim sees Rob Gentry; he's a great guy."

"Yes, he is." Seidle stepped up to the OR table. "Where are you from, Daulton?"

"I trained at Penn," Luke answered, but quickly wondered if this was what he had meant. "I grew up outside Philly—Media, actually."

"I see," Seidle said, losing interest in the conversation. He peeked around the drapes to look at his patient and said, "Okay, Shirley, let's have this baby."

The BP monitor beeped and displayed its latest reading: 90/60.

Luke scowled briefly at this lack of response to his first dose of ephedrine. He pumped in another 10 milligrams and began to wonder if his spinal was too high, a distinct possibility in an obese patient.

"I think I'm going to—" Shirley let out a loud belch, then showered her pillow with green vomitus.

"You all right up there?" asked Seidle.

"I just yorked all over the place," Shirley said. "Where's my husband?"

Luke groaned inwardly, but said, "You can bring him in now." Having family present in the OR was always a bad idea.

"Okay to start?" Seidle asked, knife in hand, poised to make an incision, not bothering to look up.

"She seems good and numb," Luke said, "but why don't you check her."

Seidle fixed Luke with a hard stare. "I guess we *could* do that." He smacked the scalpel down and demanded a hemostat. "Shirley, can you feel this?" he asked as he clamped her skin roughly with the large instrument.

Shirley gave him a puzzled look. "Nope, not a thing."

"Good. Knife." The scrub nurse handed Seidle the scalpel back.

Luke tensed—he had one more hurdle to clear. There was no such thing as a guaranteed perfect spinal, especially in an obese patient. The spinal block could sometimes range high or low. Luke stared over the drape as Seidle prepared to make the incision. This was the moment of truth. If the spinal was good, Shirley would be unaware of the incision. If not, she would scream.

CHAPTER TWO

Bart Hinkle adjusted his cummerbund for the fourth time in what he was beginning to realize was a futile attempt to rein in his gut. He took another swallow of his scotch, ice clinking, and grimaced. His head was pounding and his back ached—he couldn't tell which was worse. Another fundraiser at the Forum in Harrisburg for Senator Pierce's re-election campaign. Another fucking waste of time.

Bart stifled a yawn and surveyed the large banquet hall. Tables were situated all about the room, but few were occupied during the cocktail hour, when everyone stood talking and boozing it up in small groups. Jazz music came from the far end of the room, where a four-man band played somewhere beyond the haze of smoke. The music was decent enough, and some other evening he might have enjoyed it. But tonight he found it loud and tinny. And he felt as if the bass drum was screwed into his skull.

All the city's high rollers were here, decked out in their tuxes and evening gowns—this included representatives from each major law firm. Lots of younger in-crowd women, staffers, and young trophy wives were strutting their stuff. Maybe the night wouldn't be a total waste.

A young hostess in a black French maid getup walked up carrying a silver platter of hors d'oeuvres. "Would you care for some?" she asked in a high, nasal voice.

Bart was famished; he despised the long wait for dinner at these affairs. He grabbed three chicken-wrapped-in-bacon gizmos and almost spilled his scotch in the process. "Thank you, my dear," he mumbled as he ogled the hostess. She was nice and slim and sort of cute, in a rough, slutty way. He took special note of her black fishnet stockings as she walked away. He imagined her wrapping those long legs around him in some nook in the kitchen.

Mimi tugged on his arm and demanded in a screeching voice, "Bart, are you listening to me?" He had almost forgotten that his wife was standing next to him. The way she spewed smoke and alcohol fumes everywhere reminded him of a diesel bus belching exhaust. She waved her hand holding the glowing cigarette after the waitress and almost burned the gentleman standing beside her. "I guess you were too busy drooling over Little Miss Muffet there." Bart could already detect the slur in her speech—an increasingly common occurrence these days.

Bart took a step backwards. "Mimi, keep it down," he said in a low voice, lifting both hands in a shushing gesture.

"Keep what down?" she bellowed.

"I mean it, Mimi. Don't you embarrass me here." He looked at her closely for the first time that evening and shuddered. Her red lipstick was smudged. And her expensive plaid dress failed to hide a bulging midsection that no amount of liposuction seemed to touch. He made a mental note to withhold the next payment to her plastic surgeon—the joker certainly charged enough money to entitle his clients to results.

Before he and Mimi could escalate things into a full-blown shouting match, Kyle Schmidt, senior partner at Bart's law firm, approached. He slapped Bart on the shoulder and grabbed his hand, pumping it vigorously. "Bart, you old fox—good to see you!"

"Kyle, glad you could make it." Bart disengaged his hand from the older man's crushing grip. Although Kyle was in his late fifties, he was one of those guys who clearly didn't miss many sessions at the gym. Bart was about to say more when a stunning woman appeared at Kyle's shoulder. She had long blond hair, and wore a tight evening gown that displayed an unbelievable amount of cleavage. Bart stared.

"Bart, you've met my wife, Bunny," Kyle said, smiling.

"Of course I have." Bart held out his hand, using any excuse to continue staring. He vaguely felt Mimi elbowing him. He had met Kyle's new, thirty-something wife once before, but it had been at some outdoor function and she had had a coat on, for God's sake. Bart reluctantly dropped her hand and forced himself to turn away from those beautiful breasts toward Kyle.

"Sorry we're late," Kyle said. "Bunny and I had some—uh—things to take care of." He wrapped his arm around Bunny's slim waist and pulled her tight. He pecked her on the cheek and a syrupy grin spread across his face.

"I'll bet," Bart mumbled as Bunny's pretty face blushed pink and she giggled easily. Bart took another swallow of his scotch.

"Mimi, are you enjoying the gala so far?" Kyle asked, dropping the teenage grin.

"Well," Mimi said, "the drinks are always watered down at these things. You'd think they could afford better." She pinched her perpetual look of irritation into one of exasperation. She also belted down her third drink with a fierce determination as if, by God, she'd overcome any silly watered-down effect.

"So Bart, what do you think of our Senator Pierce?" Kyle asked.

"I think he's got a lock on this election," Bart said. "They say he's got the biggest war chest in the history of the state."

"That's true. He is, after all, *the* distinguished president pro tem of the Senate. And of course Schmidt, Evans and Knobe contributed heavily to that war chest." Kyle flashed his bleached-white teeth in another smile.

"Don't I know it. But why are we even here tonight, Kyle? At a damn fundraiser? Barring some major fuckup, Pierce should win in a landslide."

"You know how these things work. Election results are never guaranteed. Polls can be dreadfully wrong—remember the New

Hampshire primary? The party doesn't want to take anything for granted."

"I guess so."

"After all," Kyle said, "the Dems have a real chance of taking back control of Congress this year. The stakes could not be higher. The very balance of power in the US Senate might hinge on Pierce's re-election."

"You really think so?" Bart rubbed his temple and considered making another trip to the bar. The first scotch had done squat to erase his headache.

"Of course I do." Kyle studied him for a moment. "What's bugging you, Bart?"

"It's just—I'm not a huge fan of Pierce. I've met him several times. The guy's a first-rate asshole."

Kyle raised his eyebrows and took a sip of his red wine.

"I can't take his goddamn sanctimonious style," Bart said.

"What do you mean?"

"He kills me with all his environmental crap."

"He *does* own the green position and is crushing his Republican opponent, is he not?" Kyle said.

"Yes, he is," Bart admitted. "But Kyle, I'm telling you, Pierce would support child molesters if he thought it would help him get elected."

Kyle chuckled. "Look, maybe you're right, Bart. He is a piece of work, but he does have a knack for reinventing himself. Could it be you're just a bit jealous of his success?"

"Maybe," Bart conceded.

Mimi yawned. "Bunny, let's go to the bar and get you a drink. We can leave these old farts to talk politics." Politics came out powitix.

"Sounds good, Mimi," Bunny said, breaking into a new fit of giggles. The two headed for the bar. Bunny glided across the floor in her high heels, her silky evening gown hugging her figure, the thigh-high slits revealing titillating glimpses. Half the men in the room watched her, undoubtedly hoping she would lean toward them or, better still, suffer some wardrobe malfunction. Mimi waddled along beside her, looking a little unsteady on her feet.

Bart also followed Bunny's departure with interest. "God almighty, Kyle, you're a lucky man!"

"Bunny, you mean. Yep—she's a real peach. She's teaching me stuff I've never dreamt of." He was all smiles. "How are you and Mimi doing?"

"Funny you should ask," Bart said, shaking his head. "Not so well."

"Is it that bad?"

"Horrible."

"She's a good mother to your son."

"Yeah, if you want an alcoholic for a role model. Perfect for a teenager."

Kyle didn't say anything.

"Listen, Kyle, I need to talk to you."

"So talk."

"Not here." Bart glanced nervously about the room. "Walk with me."

"The wives will be back any minute."

"I know." Bart took Kyle's elbow, almost spilling his wine, and guided him out of the banquet hall and down a deserted hallway, finally stopping at what appeared to be an abandoned cloakroom. The dense carpeting and wainscoting in the corridor seemed to absorb all sound. The air was still and slightly musty, but no longer reeked of smoke.

"What in the world's gotten into you?" Kyle asked. "And why all the cloak and dagger stuff? Is this about the Abercromie account?"

Bart glanced around again and lowered his voice. "No, it has nothing to do with work."

"Okay, good."

Bart took a deep breath, let it out. "Sometimes I wish Mimi were dead."

Kyle laughed and looked relieved. "Yeah, I used to feel the same way about my ex. I don't think you're the first one to have such thoughts."

Bart remained silent.

Kyle's smile dissolved, leaving behind a look of appraisal. "Bart, we've been friends for how long?"

"Twenty years or so, give or take."

"And in all that time, I don't remember you ever mentioning such insurmountable marital problems. What's the big problem?"

"I can't stand her anymore—she's revolting. I'm serious about this, Kyle."

Kyle studied him. "You really are, aren't you? Listen, just have an affair, for chrissakes. Get it out of your system."

"Are you kidding? If Mimi found out, she'd take me to the cleaners. She's got plenty of lawyer friends who'd love to nail my ass." Bart drained his scotch. "Besides, I'm no good at all that sneaking around stuff."

"Well, there's always divorce."

"I can't believe you're saying that after all *you* went through."

"Okay, you're right." Kyle took another sip of his wine. "You're in a hopeless fuckin' jam. Welcome to the human race."

"I've been thinking about this for months."

"And..."

"That's just it, Kyle. I can't come up with a plan that's safe. The news is full of hit men bungling the job or ratting out their employer."

"Whoa—hold on. Did you say *plan*?"

"Yes."

"Are you talking about having her *killed*?"

"I know it sounds drastic."

"Drastic? Are you fuckin' nuts?" Kyle turned to leave. "I don't want to hear any more of this crazy talk."

Bart reached out and grabbed hold of his arm. "Wait, Kyle, I'm serious about taking care of business. I need your help."

"Don't be a fool, Bart. You're way out of your league here—

you'd get caught and spend the rest of your life in jail. These things have to be handled professionally."

"That's the point. I know you *know* people, Kyle."

"Those are just old wives' tales."

"Remember last year when I helped your son beat his cocaine rap?"

"Yeah..."

"And you said if I ever needed anything..."

Kyle looked off into space. Finally he turned and looked Bart squarely in the eye. "I might be able to help you, after all." He set his wine glass down and pulled a business card out of his wallet. "This just might be the professional help you're looking for." He handed the card to Bart.

Bart took the card gingerly, rubbing it gently between his thumb and index finger, as if searching the paper for clues. The card was blank except for a handwritten phone number: *566-3031*. "Thanks, Kyle." Bart tucked the card into his wallet and for the first time that evening forgot about his headache.

CHAPTER THREE

Mark Seidle sliced a foot-long incision horizontally across Shirley's lower abdomen in one quick, uninterrupted motion. Shirley stared off into space, a tranquil expression on her face, completely oblivious to the surgery—the spinal was working well. Luke resumed breathing. Teri gave him a thumbs-up sign and he nodded in response.

The BP monitor chirped, announcing its latest reading—88/58.

"Hang another bag," Luke said to Teri. "I'll give some more ephedrine." Luke turned and bent down to the level of his patient. "Shirley, how do your hands feel?"

"They feel like they're asleep."

"You mean tingly?"

"No, numb." She looked up at him, worry creeping into her eyes. "Aren't they supposed to be?"

"They can be," Luke said, his voice trailing off. The thought of a total spinal—a spinal block that goes way too high—blazed across his mind. *Please, not a total spinal!* It was unlikely, but numb hands were the first sign. If she was developing a full-blown total spinal, her breathing would be next to go, as her respiratory muscles became blocked. He turned to Teri and said in a low voice, "Tube."

Teri raised her eyebrows. Luke nodded and she proceeded to get an endotracheal tube and laryngoscope ready in case general anesthesia would be necessary.

Shirley's husband appeared, led into the room by an OB nurse. He looked like Hulk Hogan's bigger brother. The XXL scrub top looked ridiculously small on him; his chest jutted out and the sleeves looked uncomfortably tight on his upper arms. He was ushered to the head of the OR table and sat down on a little metal stool that looked rather precarious beneath him.

"Hey, Shirl," he said and patted her arm. "I'm here."

"Hi, Bear."

"You okay?"

"I think so," she said uncertainly.

"Are they hurting you, babe?" He threw a threatening look at Luke.

"No." She shook her head.

Luke glanced at Bear's massive, tattooed biceps before turning to Shirley. "The baby should be out in a couple of minutes." It was always a good idea to focus the mother's attention on her baby and distract her from her immediate predicament. "Doing okay?" Luke put forth the question tentatively, afraid of what her response would be. But he had to know.

"Seems kinda hard to breathe."

Shit! There it is in black and white. Unbelievable. Total fricking spinal! First C-section. Difficult OB man. Big, mean, son-of-a-bitch husband and morbidly obese patient.

"She okay, Doc?" Bear asked. His eyes were bulging and the veins popped out on his neck.

Luke ignored him and put the mask from his breathing circuit tightly on her face. "Take a big breath, Shirley," he said, trying to keep his voice steady.

Shirley attempted to suck in some air. "I can't," she said weakly, her voice muffled by the mask. Luke stared at the volumeter on his circuit. *Shit, only 300 cc. Not enough.*

"She can't breathe, Doc." Bear was on his feet, fists tightening and biceps threatening to rip apart his scrub top. "What's going on?"

Teri stood up and said, "Maybe you should wait outside, Mr. Karas."

"I ain't leaving, honey—and from the looks of it, neither of you two twits is gonna make me." Bear puffed his chest out even more and widened his stance, glaring at Teri and Luke.

Seidle looked over the drapes. "Daulton, what seems to be the problem up there *now*?"

"She's having a little difficulty breathing," Luke said. "I'm working on it."

"Deal with it, okay? I'm kinda busy here."

Luke turned to Bear. "Sometimes this happens with a spinal." He hoped that would pacify the man for the moment, because he needed to concentrate on getting Shirley through this. "Shirley, I'm going to help you breathe some. You're gonna be fine." Luke began to assist her respirations with the bag and mask. He glanced up at her oxygen saturation monitor, which remained at 100 percent. *Maybe, she'll make it.* "How's that, Shirley?"

"Better," she answered, but her voice was barely a whisper.

Suddenly the suction apparatus gushed as the amniotic fluid was sucked out following uterine incision. A minute later, Seidle extricated the baby from the muscular uterus and the sound of a crying newborn filled the room. Everyone paused in wonder, and the tension ratcheted down a notch.

"Shirl, it's a baby boy!" shouted Bear. He sat back down and began to stroke her arm.

Shirley didn't respond. Luke watched with horror as her eyes rolled up into her head.

Bear turned to Luke and demanded, "Did you put her to sleep?"

Luke ignored him and checked her respirations. She was making no effort. He was still ventilating her, but now he was doing all the work. He cycled the BP monitor, then shot a look at the suction canister behind him. Moments ago it had been empty, but now it was filled to the top with a mixture of blood and amniotic fluid—hard to tell just how much blood she had lost.

Seidle handed off the large, slimy Bear Jr. to the waiting neo-natal nurse and turned back to the abdomen. "Losing some blood up here, Daulton. Hurry and run the Pit."

BP: 60/35.

Shit! Blood loss on top of a total spinal—not good!

Then Seidle added something that froze the blood in Luke's veins. "Looks like we're dealing with an abruption here." This was truly catastrophic. Luke could barely hear him above the roar of the suction as Shirley's blood was rapidly being sucked out of her body.

"Get some blood!" Seidle practically screamed. "Nurse, see if Dr. Gentry's in house." Seidle's hands were shaking badly now.

Luke figured it was time for action. He had an extremely critical situation on his hands and this lady's life hung in the balance. *Dad was right—sometimes the only one you can rely on is yourself.* The pressure of this situation might have paralyzed him, but he actually calmed down somewhat as he entered his emergency zone. No more thinking, worrying, denying, or in-decision.

He pushed in the Pitocin intravenously and grabbed the ephedrine syringe, but knew this wouldn't be nearly enough. "Teri, mix me some Neo and go get blood fast! Mr. Karas, it's time for you to leave; we've asked you—"

Before he could finish, a steely arm encircled his neck and squeezed tight. Bear's hot breath beat down on Luke's neck. "What the fuck's going on here? I want some answers!"

The circulator ran out of the room yelling, "Red alert!"

Luke clawed at the choking arm and pulled it away enough so he could speak. "Listen, asshole! You got about ten seconds to let me go or she dies!" The arm loosened a bit. Luke pulled harder. "I'm the only hope she's got. You can argue all you want, or put your fist through my face. Either way, she dies. Now get the hell out of here and let me do my job."

Bear didn't move or say anything for a second or two,

then he released Luke and stepped around to face him. "Listen, Doc. Do your thing. But I ain't going nowhere and I'm warning you"—he reached out and repeatedly poked Luke's chest with an enormous finger—"anything happens to her and I'll finish wringing your scrawny neck!"

CHAPTER FOUR

Luke, Teri, and an OB nurse pushed the heavy bed out of the elevator and through the narrow hallways to the Surgical Intensive Care Unit, better known as the SICU. Luke's head was throbbing, his scrubs were covered with sweat and bloodstains, but he had never been happier to finish a case in his life. Shirley lay before him snoring peacefully in a morphine haze. Bear had left to go with the baby and was undoubtedly in the newborn nursery chatting up everyone in sight about how big his son was.

Amazingly, they had pulled Shirley through her ordeal. Though physically and emotionally drained, Luke felt buoyed by a real sense of satisfaction. *Not a bad showing for the new guy,* he thought. This was, after all, why he had gone into medicine—to help people and make a difference in their lives. No more standing on the sidelines, helpless.

While the SICU nurse was getting Shirley hooked up to the monitors, Teri touched his arm. "Good job, Dr. Daulton. I knew you could do it." She flashed him a broad smile. "That central line was really slick."

"Thanks, Teri." He *was* grateful the large-bore, intravenous neck line had gone in without a hitch. "I couldn't have done it without you." He turned to give his report to the nurse.

He heard laughter coming from down the hallway and soon the two obstetricians, Dr. Seidle and Dr. Gentry, walked in. They were all smiles as they reviewed the highlights of the case. Although the two had removed their bloody OR gowns, Dr. Gentry's mask still had some blood spatters on it, a reminder of the frenzied action that had taken place in the delivery room.

Seidle turned to Luke. "Nice going, Daulton—way to pump that blood." He had reverted to his normal, self-assured state, but Luke would never forget the unmistakable panic that had glazed his eyes earlier. "How much blood did you wind up giving?"

"Five units, type specific," Luke said.

"Amazing." Seidle shook his head. "I didn't think we lost that much. Listen, I gotta go check on a labor patient." He turned to Dr. Gentry. "Thanks again for your help in there, Rob. You really pulled my ass out of a sling." Seidle strode out of the room, whistling.

Rob Gentry looked at Luke. "Rough way to start your OB experience, huh?" He glanced over at Shirley, who was still snoring up a storm. "A central line, to boot—I'm impressed. I *wondered* how you got all that blood in so fast." Rob put his hand on Luke's shoulder. He lowered his voice. "You saved her life, you know."

"I don't know about that." Luke gazed out the large window. The sun was making its way toward the horizon, lighting up the meadow just beyond the parking lot. "If you hadn't come in and helped, I'm not sure—" Luke stopped and glanced over at Shirley to make sure she was still out. "I'm not sure Seidle would've been able to stop the bleeding."

"Listen, these cases are always a struggle," Rob said. "Abruptio placenta is one of the most dreaded OB complications, often with fatal outcomes for the baby or the mother or both." Rob ripped off his bloody surgical mask, tossed it in the waste can, and went over to the sink to wash his hands. "Seidle would've done the same thing for me," he said over his shoulder, above the splashing of the water. "Good teamwork between surgery and anesthesia is critical." He dried his hands. "Heck, I feel lucky we were able to save her uterus."

"That was nice work." Luke absently scratched his head

through his cap. "I feel bad about the total spinal business, though—it only made things worse."

"Listen, Luke, you had a lot on your plate and then there was that Neanderthal guy—Butch, Bear, or whatever his name was. You did a nice job handling it all. I've seen others of your crew fold under lesser circumstances."

"Well thanks, Rob. I appreciate you saying it."

"Sure. How's Kim doing, by the way?"

Luke practically cringed. "Great, no problems," he got out weakly. He had no desire to mix his wife into a conversation involving obstetrical nightmares.

"The big day's fast approaching. You all set?"

"Yep."

"Nervous?"

"Nope."

Rob paused. "Hey, we need to hook up for a bike ride soon."

"Sure," Luke said. "I called you several times, but you're always too busy."

"I *have* been really busy recently," Rob said, and cracked a thin smile.

"Oh...hmm..." Luke had no idea where to go with this one. He knew—in fact, Teri had just reminded him—that Rob was getting awfully chummy with the anesthesia billing secretary, Gwen.

The door opened and a serious-looking Dr. Jason Katz walked in. He was large framed, at least six foot two, and still looked trim for a man approaching sixty. "Luke, I was hoping to catch you here. I need to have a word with you." Katz quickly scanned the room, taking in Shirley and her monitors. "I was on my way up here to see what all of the commotion was about and I bumped into Dr. Seidle in the hallway. He filled me in." Katz turned to Gentry. "I understand you assisted with the section. Thank God you were available."

"Yes, as the fates would have it," Rob said, a grin stealing across his face.

There was an uncomfortable silence between the two men and they traded looks before Katz said, "Sometimes, God works in mysterious ways." Katz turned to Luke. "Listen, Luke, finish up here and meet me down in my office." With that he wheeled around and exited the room, the tails of his long white coat fluttering behind him.

"Geez," Luke said, and shook his head. "What was that all about? Just when I thought this day was over." He worked on signing all his papers. "Katz didn't look too happy, did he?" he said without looking up.

"No, I guess not," Rob said. "Special visits from the chief are rarely a good thing."

"I better go." Luke closed the hospital chart and headed for the door. "See you later."

"Call me this weekend," Rob said. "We'll ride."

"Sounds good," Luke said as he trudged out the doorway.

"Hey, Luke," Rob called from behind him. "One more thing. Watch your step around Katz."

* * *

Luke studied the contents of the vending machine and groaned. There was a lame assortment of items ranging from stale sandwiches to artificial tapioca pudding. He patted down his pockets for change but came up empty. He pulled out his wallet and was glad to find several dollar bills inside. He also spied the little piece of paper Kim had given him; he took it out to take a closer look. She loved to make puzzles for him, but this one was special. Ten numbers were arranged in a square.

$$25\ 63\ 24\ 25$$
$$!\qquad\qquad 49$$
$$!\qquad\qquad 19$$
$$00\ 64\ 19\ 61$$

Luke smiled as he thought back to the joyous day when Kim had given it to him, then carefully tucked the paper back into his wallet, retrieved a dollar bill, and fed it to the vending machine.

He punched some buttons and a Snickers bar, aka dinner, dropped with a bang. His stomach growled as he unwrapped the bar.

Minutes later, Luke stood outside the half-open door bearing a brass plaque engraved with *Chief of Anesthesia: Dr. Jason Katz* and finished off his Snickers bar. Inside someone clacked away at a computer keyboard. He took a deep breath, ran a hand through his mussed hair, and knocked.

"Come in," Katz's deep voice called.

Luke entered the small office. Katz didn't look up but continued working at his computer. It struck Luke that Katz's receding hairline didn't exactly fit with the jet-black color of his short hair. He searched the older man's face for clues about what this little meeting was all about. On his way over, it had occurred to him that maybe Katz wanted to congratulate him, but this certainly didn't seem to fit with his earlier tone. Luke just wanted to get it over with, whatever it was. He was tired and hungry and wanted to go home.

"Have a seat, Luke," Katz finally said, gesturing to the only other chair in the room, across from his desk. He turned his computer off with a loud beep and worked on filing some papers. The computer fan took its time whirring down to a complete stop, then left the room awash in an awkward silence.

Luke looked around the office. There were several framed pictures of Katz on the desktop. He had obviously been sightseeing in Italy; Luke recognized the Leaning Tower of Pisa and the Coliseum in the background.

Katz looked up and broke the silence. "So you engaged in a little trial by fire today, eh?" He chuckled.

"Yeah, I guess I did," Luke replied and shifted in his seat.

Katz wheeled back in his chair and surprised him by pulling a pack of cigarettes from the breast pocket of his coat. He lit one up slowly, deliberately, and took a long drag.

Luke glanced at his watch.

"Don't worry, this won't take long," Katz said, exhaling smoke. "I'll get right to the point. As I mentioned, Mark Seidle spoke with me about the C-section." Katz watched the smoke slowly drift upward before refocusing on Luke. "He didn't seem too happy with your performance."

"*What?*" Luke was stunned. "Why? We saved her life."

Katz locked eyes with him. "He said something about a total spinal causing massive blood loss and that she almost bled to death." He paused to let that sink in. "He *did* say you did a nice job treating the hemorrhage—didn't panic or anything—but if you had done the spinal right in the first place—"

"You saw how big she was, right?" Luke interrupted.

"Yes, I did."

"I was lucky to get that spinal in." Luke was vaguely aware of how hard his hands were squeezing the armrests of the chair. "Hey, if Rob Gentry hadn't come in and bailed Seidle out—"

Katz held up his hand. "That may be—"

"Talk about panicking," Luke said.

"You're missing the point."

Luke found Katz's preachy tone extremely irritating and felt his own face getting hot. "Well, what *is* the point?"

"Listen, Luke, it's really very simple. There are two things you must understand here. One—you can't have any bad cases. You almost had one today." Katz flicked some ashes into the ashtray, then took another hard drag. He slowly blew the smoke out to the side. "Two—besides keeping your nose clean clinically, you must also fit in with your colleagues. You must impress the surgeons and please them. Remember, it's a business we're running here and these people, no matter what you might think of them, are our customers. The customer is always right, remember? Even if he's a pompous jackass. Do I make myself clear?"

"Yeah, crystal." Luke felt as if he was back in high school and his dad was lecturing him again. He could see his old man's large, puffy face redden with anger, the tortuous veins standing out on his temples. All Katz needed to add was "smart guy" and Luke would've screamed. He realized Katz had resumed speaking.

"—seem like a nice guy and all. Your credentials are top-notch and your recommendations are all glowing. But..." Katz stared at him again. "Let me bottom line it for you. Your first year here is probational. Nothing is guaranteed. You must demonstrate to the partners that you have what it takes to stay."

Luke didn't reply—he didn't trust himself to say anything civil at this point.

CHAPTER FIVE

"This is crazy," Rob Gentry said to himself, shaking his head as he hung up his cell phone. He tucked the phone into its case on his hip and left the hospital, walking toward the doctors' parking lot. The low sun shone in his eyes, but the blinding light would be gone soon; the fiery ball was rapidly sinking into the gray cloud bank that hugged the ridgeline of the Appalachian Mountains.

He glanced back at Swatara Regional and saw the red-brick building positively glowing, bathed in the orange light. A nurse was drawing the blinds over a window in the second floor SICU complex, in what he believed was Shirley Karas' room. Mrs. Karas was one lucky lady, and so was her baby. That C-section with the abruption had been a real bitch. Rob had seen several over the years that didn't have such happy outcomes.

Luke Daulton had really done a nice job keeping her alive through all the bleeding. Seidle *had* panicked and had clearly been in over his head. That religious nutjob, Katz, had been right, too. "Thank God Rob was there to help," Katz had said. Rob chuckled as he crossed the parking lot to his car. The only reason he had been at the hospital was to see Gwen on her break.

His Porsche 911 Carrera waited for him at the far end of the lot—he had indulged himself and bought it last year for his fiftieth birthday. He never tired of admiring the car's sleek profile and aggressive stance. The aluminum mag wheels and chrome detail work gleamed in the sunlight that set the metallic red body ablaze and made the car sparkle like a precious jewel. Though physically tired, Rob felt strangely exhilarated as he jumped in and turned the key. The 480 horsepower engine throbbed to life, anxious to launch him into the night. Rob goosed the gas and the twin turbos kicked in and the engine roared its deep, throaty growl. He jammed the car into first gear and popped the clutch.

The car roared out of the parking lot and Rob headed west on Route 39 toward the mountains. The sun sank below the clouds, but the sky was still bright. He slipped on his designer sunglasses and cranked up the XM radio as a Dave Matthews song started playing.

What am I doing? he wondered again. Didn't it matter that he had family commitments tonight? What about the promise he had made to his son, that he'd be at his concert? He made a left onto the on-ramp of Southbound 81 and nudged the accelerator; the turbocharged V-8 came to life. The car rocketed forward and he enjoyed the adrenaline rush the sudden G-force always brought on. He merged smoothly onto the interstate toward Harrisburg, the engine burbling happily as the car ate up the pavement. Traffic was beginning to lighten, as everyone had already gotten a jump on the weekend and rush hour was long past. The speedometer needle jumped effortlessly to ninety.

Soon he arrived at his destination—The Rabbit Inn, a little restaurant/bar on the western bank of the Susquehanna River, off the beaten path in Enola. Of course, Enola itself was off the beaten path. Normally Rob wouldn't have been caught dead in such a dive, but tonight The Rabbit fit the bill perfectly.

Once inside, he was forced to stop and let his eyes adjust to the dim lighting. The noise from the jukebox was deafening and smoke hung thick in the air. Rob carefully made his way to a booth in the rear, where the high seat backs would protect them from prying eyes. Risky? Only to those who gave it a second thought.

The waitress came and he ordered a Heineken, then looked up at the oversized flat screen TV suspended above the bar. Senator Pierce was making some announcement. Rob had to smile.

He used to get hot about political issues—he listened to the talk radio stations incessantly and got caught up in the nuances of conservative/liberal bickering. Now he couldn't have cared less—Senator Pierce and the balance of power in the US Senate, Iraq, Afghanistan, war, taxes—who the hell cared?

His musing was short lived as Gwen made her entrance into the bar. At least half the people in the room, men and women, looked up. Conversations paused, even eating and drinking were put on hold as everyone observed the striking woman glide across the room. *Shit*, Rob thought, *so much for subterfuge.* What the hell—he didn't think he recognized anyone.

He stared at her and their eyes locked from across the room. She broke out that dazzling smile, playful and adventurous, and quickly walked over to him. He stood up to greet her. She had on a tight white cotton shirt with a revealing V neckline, and designer jeans and calf-high boots. Her long, dark silky hair flowed down almost to her narrow waist and shimmered even in the low light, framing her pretty face. She touched him lightly on the shoulder as she slid by him into the booth. He caught a whiff of her delightful fragrance.

"You look amazing," Rob said, sitting down opposite her.

"Thanks," she said, still beaming.

"But, did you *have* to wear that shirt?" Rob asked, trying hard to look serious. "Everyone in the freakin' bar noticed you come in."

She cocked her head slightly.

"Remember," Rob said, "this is supposed to be a rendezvous—you know, a *secret* meeting."

"What do you suggest?"

"A burlap bag, maybe."

"Great, I'll keep that in mind," Gwen said. "I think I have several in my closet."

The waitress came over and Gwen ordered a beer.

"Do you see anyone you know?" she asked. "You keep looking around."

"No, sorry."

"And do you always strip the label from your beer bottle? Or is that a guy thing?"

"No, it's nothing." He deliberately removed his hands from the bottle.

"I'm impressed that you got free on a Friday night," she said. "How'd you manage that?"

"Nothing special. I told Cindy I had to work late—bad C-section. She's used to my unpredictable hours by now. And the bad C-section part is true. I helped Mark Seidle with a truly nasty one."

She rested her chin on both hands and affected a doe-eyed, adoring expression. "I heard you're the best."

Rob had to laugh.

"So, how did the phone call go?" she asked, dropping her silly look.

"Great. Well, I didn't actually talk to her—I left a message. She must be at one of her meetings."

"Meetings?"

"Cindy sits on the board of the hospital Women's Auxiliary and co-chairs the Dauphin County Breast Cancer Awareness chapter. And there are half a dozen others—I can't keep them all straight. She's very involved."

"So you've said." A thoughtful expression crossed Gwen's face. "You know, in all the times I've heard you talk about your wife, I've never heard you say anything bad about her. Don't you guys ever fight? Jim and I fight constantly."

"That's just it. We don't fight. We don't even argue. She has her activities and friends, and I have mine. It's a very peaceful arrangement."

"Arrangement? Did you say arrangement?"

"Yeah, but it's not like that," Rob said quickly. "I mean, Cindy and I get along fine. And we're just as happy as the next couple."

"Are you?"

"Yes. It's just that now our lives revolve around Steven and

Jessica and *their* activities. We trade a lot of notes and phone messages—you know, who's picking up who, where and when, that sort of stuff. And, like I said, we never fight."

Gwen just nodded and gave him a thin smile.

"All right," he said, "maybe the sizzle has gone the way of the woolly mammoth—but that's just the way these things work. You're too young to understand."

She smiled and pushed the hair out of her face. "So, what about when it's time to swing from the chandeliers?" she asked, her eyes twinkling. "What happens then?"

Rob looked across the room and took his time finishing off his beer. Finally he turned to face her and said in a subdued voice, "Gwen, we don't even know where the chandeliers are anymore."

"That's sad." She took a long swallow of her beer. "I've always dreamt of being married *and* being passionate. Do you think that's possible?"

"Maybe," he said.

"They say you can tell from a kiss when the fire's fading," she said.

He found himself staring at her mouth as she said this, marveling at the way her lips and tongue moved as she spoke. Just then, a haunting song came through the bar's amped-up sound system; the bass was so powerful that Rob felt the vibrations in his chest. "I like that song," he said.

"So do I. Rihanna sings it." Gwen tossed her hair aside. "But I'm guessing you won't like the title."

"Why?"

"I'm pretty sure it's called 'Unfaithful.'"

"Ouch," Rob said. He looked away as Rihanna soulfully delivered the refrain, "Might as well put a gun to his head and pull the trigger/end it all."

She reached across the table and took his hand. "You okay?"

He nodded and gave her a half smile.

"You don't look it," she said.

He pulled his hand from hers and sat up straighter. "It's

just...we've never met outside the hospital." Rob was vaguely aware that he had crossed a line here—a significant one—but he didn't want to think about it now.

"I know," she said, then glanced at her watch. "You could probably still make Steven's concert, if you left now."

"Hmm." Rob looked at his own watch and thought for a moment. "You know, I almost didn't show. Out in the parking lot, I almost turned around."

"What stopped you?"

"I don't know. I guess you're just too damned irresistible."

She smiled back at him. "So, basically, you have no self-control."

"Actually, I do. I'm usually very disciplined."

"I see." She leaned across the table, looking intently at him. "What happened?"

"Some evil witch put a spell on me," he said, trying mightily not to focus on her shirt; the V-neck afforded him tantalizing glimpses of her breasts, nestled securely beneath the stretchy fabric.

"So, I'm a witch, now?"

"Okay, I take it back. A sorceress."

"That's better." Her smile slowly faded and she took another sip of her beer. "Do you want to go?"

"No."

"You sure?"

"Yeah."

They stared at each other in silence for a long time.

Rob finally disengaged from her eyes. "It's getting hot in here. Want to take a walk?"

"Sure." She stood up and reached across the table to scoop up her purse.

"Do me a favor there, Esmerelda—don't bend over like that again. That shirt of yours is killing me."

CHAPTER SIX

Luke pulled his aging Camry over in front of his apartment on West Areba Avenue in Hershey. The sun had set an hour ago, but the western sky was clear and ablaze with the ephemeral hues of twilight. He hopped out of the car and grabbed his briefcase from the back seat. There was a definite nip in the evening air. A striking orange harvest moon was rising in the east, appearing unnaturally large on the horizon; the days were getting shorter. Across the street rose the giant cocoa bean storage silos at the Hershey Chocolate factory and to the northwest, the Hotel Hershey stood guard on a hill like a medieval fortress overlooking the town.

Luke crossed the porch and stepped inside and was immediately attacked by their golden retriever puppy, Colby. The dog was five months old now, but still had sharp puppy teeth so you had to be careful. After crashing into his leg, Colby rebounded and started running in tight circles on the carpeted floor in the living room. The puppy almost knocked over the small table holding Kim's marble chess set. The smell of roast chicken, one of his favorites, hung delightfully in the air. He heard Kim moving about in the kitchen.

Luke bent over and snapped his fingers. "Colby! Find Froggie!" This stopped the dog in his tracks and he stood motionless with his head cocked to the side as if to say, "Did you say what I think you said?" You could see the wheels spinning in his head. After a moment, Colby sprinted toward the bedroom. Luke smiled to himself and shouted toward the kitchen, "Hey, anyone home?" He took off his light coat and hung it up on the coat tree near the front door.

"You poor thing," came his wife's reply. "I was beginning to wonder."

Luke glanced at his watch. "Sorry it's so late."

"No problem," she called out. "You like your chicken well done, right? Uh, make that blackened."

Luke walked through the dining room into the cramped kitchen and came up behind Kim, who was busy stirring the gravy and didn't turn around. Luke wrapped his arms around her, encircling her big pregnant belly, and snuggled up close. He lowered his face to the long, strawberry blond hair that flowed down her back, then nuzzled her neck, breathing in the delicate fragrance of her hair and skin. "Guess who," he said playfully.

"Um...Mike the plumber?"

"Naw."

"Shucks. Um, Jim-Bob the carpet man?"

"No."

She squirmed around in his embrace and turned to face him. "Oh, it's my long-lost husband, L-something." She giggled and crinkled her nose. "Luke, that's it. What're you doing home so soon?" She couldn't help breaking into an enormous grin.

Luke kissed her and tried to hug her tighter, but her belly wouldn't allow it. Colby made a wild entrance into the kitchen, his clumsy puppy feet clattering across the worn linoleum floor. He tried hard to hit the brakes, but his hindquarters squirted loose and skidded out from under him. He slid across the floor rump first until he thudded into the cabinets. But Froggie—a beat-up old rubber squeaky toy—remained clamped in his mouth. As soon as he regained his footing, his little chest jutted forward with pride. Luke and Kim laughed together.

"Good boy, Colby," Luke said. He knelt down and patted the dog on the head. Colby worked his jaws and Froggie squeaked in response.

"You've really taken to that dog," Kim said. "I knew you would."

"Right as usual," Luke said as he scratched behind the dog's ears. "I have to admit, though, I thought it was a big mistake, getting a puppy with a baby on the way." Colby sank down onto the floor and rolled onto his back. Luke obliged him by rubbing his belly. "But you pleaded so nicely."

She smiled and reached down with one hand to caress the nape of Luke's neck.

"And you know I can't deny you anything," Luke said, looking up at her.

She slid her hand up onto the back of his head and continued to rub gently. "Just think what a great dad you're going to be."

"I hope so," Luke said. He stopped petting Colby.

"Of course you'll be." She studied him and her expression turned serious. "What's the matter?"

"Nothing."

"I know what you're thinking. You're not your father, Luke."

"You didn't know him." He stood up slowly.

"But I know you. You'll be the best father ever."

"Do you really think so?"

"I know so." She reached over and gave him a big hug.

He hugged her back. "I love you."

"I love you too." They held each other for a few moments in silence, then she went back to stirring the gravy. "Don't beat yourself up over the past."

"You're right. Hey, anyway, sorry it's so late. Bad case at work."

"Everything turn out okay?"

"Well, not exactly. All the patients did fine. Their anesthesiologist, on the other hand, lost about five years off his life." Luke forced a weak smile.

Kim turned around. "What happened?"

"Let's talk about it over dinner, okay? I'm starved."

"Okay. Will you carve the bird?"

"Sure." Luke grabbed some potholders, turned, and opened the oven door. The aroma of roast chicken overwhelmed him, smothering all troubling thoughts of his father and work.

"I hope it's not too dry," she said. "It never fails that when I try to surprise you with a nice dinner, you get stuck working late."

Luke sampled a piece of chicken as he was cutting it—dark meat was his favorite. "It's delicious." Food or no food, though, he couldn't wait to share his tale with her. "Remember this morning, how I said I didn't like OB anesthesia?"

"Yeah."

"Well, you should've seen this big, muscle-bound dude named Bear."

* * *

Twenty minutes later, Luke pushed his plate forward and sat back in his chair. "I'm so full. Thanks for making it."

"Sure." She rose. "Do you want some apple pie and coffee?"

He patted his belly. "Just coffee, please. Decaf."

"I'll go make some," she said, gathering up the plates. "That was some scary delivery story. I'm glad it turned out all right." She started toward the kitchen.

"Me, too. Although I did have a little run-in with Dr. Katz afterwards."

"What do you mean?" She stopped and turned around.

"He called me to his office and reamed me out for the total spinal thing."

"You're kidding," she said, returning to the dining room.

"No," Luke said. "And I got pissed."

"No way."

"Yeah, really. I mean, we saved her from bleeding to death."

"I thought you said Seidle kind of panicked?"

"He did. I'm telling you, if Rob Gentry hadn't come in when he did, the lady would've died. I told Katz that, but he didn't want to hear it. He seemed to take Seidle's side."

"Sounds like a rough end to a rough day," Kim said softly.

She set the plates back down on the table and moved around behind his chair. She began to massage his neck and shoulders.

Luke let his head hang forward as she worked on him. "And Rob said to me earlier, 'watch your step around Katz.' I have no idea what he meant by that."

"Sounds like they don't get along," Kim said. "Do they have a history?"

"I don't know. They've both worked there awhile. But, speaking of Rob Gentry, I'm afraid he might be getting involved with one of the secretaries."

"What? That's horrible," Kim said. She stopped rubbing his shoulders. "Are you sure?"

"That's the word around the hospital."

"You know how gossip spreads," Kim said. "He seems like such a nice man."

"He is."

"Does he have children?"

"Yeah, two."

"That's such a shame. Who is she?"

Luke turned to face her. "Her name's Gwen. She actually works for our group as a billing person."

Kim raised her eyebrows.

"I think she's also married with kids," Luke added.

"That's so sad. What in the world are they thinking?"

"Maybe they're in love. Teri, the anesthesia tech, says she's seen them making goo-goo eyes at each other in the hallway."

Kim frowned. "Is she pretty?"

"No way. Gorgeous, maybe, but not pretty."

"Very funny," she said sourly.

"Almost as gorgeous as you."

CHAPTER SEVEN

From the parking lot, the picturesque skyline of Harrisburg was visible across the Susquehanna River; countless reflected city lights sparkled in the roiling water. The green dome of the capitol building appeared majestic, lit up and silhouetted as it was against the night sky.

Rob took Gwen's hand and they strolled closer to the river, neither saying a word. Sounds from the noisy Rabbit faded, replaced by the chirping of crickets. Stepping over a low-hanging chain barrier to a more deserted gravel lot, they were close enough now to the river to hear it gurgling as it flowed. A full moon hung over the city in the east; the rest of the sky was starlit and disturbed only by a few clouds. A faint breeze stirred, bringing cooler air, but Rob barely noticed.

"Want to sit?" He gestured to an old, crumbling cement block.

"Okay."

They sat down side by side and looked across the river, taking in the view. He turned to face her. "Pretty, isn't it?"

"Yes," she said, still gazing toward the city.

Rob pointed across the river. "I heard they put new tiles on the dome—replaced the old, faded ones. That's why they're so brightly colored."

"They do look nice," she said, turning slightly to get a better view.

The mechanical buzz of an approaching pontoon boat's engine interrupted them. They watched the boat, adorned with festive party lights, pass by them and head upstream. Slowly the drone of the engine faded into the background.

Rob refocused on her. "Do you remember meeting for the first time?"

"Yes, in the cafeteria last year, right before Christmas."

"What do you recall about it?"

She started to say something, then stopped.

"I remember it like this," he said. "I could tell you were something special when I first saw you. I was behind you in the lunch line to pay."

"I remember it, too," she said, her eyes drifting as she thought back.

"This is gonna sound silly," Rob said, "but I felt an amazingly strong attraction—like a physical force grabbing hold of me."

She didn't say anything, but looked up at him with a questioning look.

"It gets worse," he continued. "I knew from that moment that you would be trouble for me."

She readjusted her position on the concrete block and her knee brushed up against his thigh. He didn't move away—touching her seemed natural and most desirable.

Neither moved for a minute or two. Finally, she broke the silence. "I felt it, too."

He looked deep into her eyes; he could make out their distinctive emerald color even in the low light. "You're beautiful, you know."

She looked down, an embarrassed smile spreading across her face. "Thanks," she murmured. Neither said anything and she carved out some designs in the gravel with her boot.

"Thanks for meeting me tonight," he said.

"Sure."

"What kind of story did you tell to be here tonight?" Rob asked.

"Didn't really have to—my husband stays out late most Friday nights." A frown creased her face. "He won't stagger in till later." She chuckled at this.

"Who's watching the kids?"

"My mom. I told her I was going out for drinks with co-workers—Friday night and all, I needed to blow off a little steam." She smiled. "Sort of true."

Rob stood. "I should go," he said.

She looked up at him, disappointment clouding her face. Abruptly she rose and faced him. "Okay, but I need a hug first," she said, opening her arms, palms skyward.

"Sure." He took her into his arms and drew her lightly against him.

"Thanks," she whispered into his ear.

Feeling the warm swell of her breasts pressing up against him and her soft hair tickling his face, he had trouble letting her go. His arms seemed to have lost the ability to move. They held each other for several minutes in silence.

She hugged him back gently at first, then pulled him in more forcefully. Rob's resistance crumbled and he matched the urgency of her embrace. Soon their cheeks slid smoothly across one another and he felt her warm breath on his ear again. He inhaled deeply, taking in her magical scent, feeling as if it had the power to stop time. Perhaps he could just stay here in her arms forever, never needing to do another thing in his life.

Slowly he ran his fingertips through her hair, mesmerized by its weight and texture; he felt it play on his face and neck. Her hair was a lovely, dark brunette, long and straight. "Your hair is so nice," he whispered as he stroked it.

She pulled back a bit and looked up at him. He gently pushed her hair out of the way and studied her face in the moonlight. She had told him she was a blend of Native American—Cherokee, he thought—and English. She had a hint of the high Cherokee cheekbones mellowed by the complexion of a fresh-faced English milkmaid. He traced her finely cut nose, lips, and chin with his finger. His gaze came to rest on her full mouth. Her lips glistened with a light sheen of lip gloss. Leaning in close, he very gently touched his lips to hers. He kissed her delicate upper lip first, brushing up against it, then backing off. Then he turned his attention to the lower, fuller, more sensuous one. She murmured and cooed as he did this.

Rob cradled her head and neck in one hand, caressing her silken hair. His other hand settled on the small of her back and drew her to him. He kissed her deeply now, pressing, sliding, all the while amazed by the heavenly smoothness of her lips. She ran her hands through his hair and pulled him in tight.

After an unknowable amount of time, Gwen pulled back and shifted her position on the concrete block so she could face him better. She smiled up at him, looking a little sheepish. She had a dreamy look in her eyes. "That was so nice."

He nodded and smiled. "I wanted to do that for a while."

"Me too," she said. "You do that well—kissing, I mean."

"Thanks. So do you. I wasn't sure I remembered how."

She laughed heartily. "You're a natural," she said and pulled him in for more.

The tender kissing soon gave way to a more heated, passionate exchange. She moaned softly and her body shuddered with pleasure as they smothered each other with kisses. He gripped her all the more tightly, letting her feel the hardness of his body. His tongue explored her mouth and he became familiar with her taste; it was pleasant and unique and became indelibly imprinted on his brain.

After what may have been thirty minutes or an hour, they took a break, each pausing to catch their breath. "Did I mention you were trouble for me?" he asked, his voice sounding huskier than he would've thought possible.

"Yes, you did," she said, another smile surfacing, this one a little naughty, but adorable nonetheless. "Likewise, to be sure."

In that moment, Rob felt bonded to her forever, and the point of his existence had remarkably simplified. Time stood still. As he leaned in to kiss her again, his cell phone vibrated on his hip, but he ignored it.

CHAPTER EIGHT

Luke went to bed around ten o'clock, a little earlier than usual. He was exhausted, but his mind was still strangely alert and he didn't feel all that sleepy. It had definitely been good to talk to Kim about his case today. She had worked her usual magic and put his mind at ease about it. She was such a special person, and he knew he was lucky to have her as his wife.

She was still up reading—in the living room, so she wouldn't disturb him. Yes, it was also nice to be at home in his own bed; he hated the nights he spent at the hospital, away from Kim, in the lonely call room. And the delicious chicken dinner, complete with real mashed potatoes and gravy, was comfort food at its best. But, despite all the cozy warm-fuzzies, he was still too keyed up to sleep.

Too many things were spinning about in his mind. What was the point of Katz bringing up his probation period? Was that a serious threat about his job? Just what he needed to go along with the pressure of fatherhood. He hadn't mentioned this little part of the dialogue with the chief to Kim. No need to worry her about anything, with the baby coming. He knew she would be understanding, but it was time for him to pull his weight around here for a change. She had basically supported them through the four years of his residency.

Luke rolled over in bed and stuffed the pillow further under his head, trying to get comfortable. He also kept seeing that old bus he would pass on his bike route. It was parked on display on the front lawn of the American Antique Automobile Museum on Route 39. He could see it clearly in his mind; *Ride the Red and Tan Line* was painted on its side and a placard reading *World's Fair* was placed in the front marquee. What was so special about the bus? He didn't have a clue. Luke had never been to a world's fair so he couldn't fathom the connection. He pondered this for a long time until he finally drifted off to sleep.

* * *

The next thing Luke knew, he was sitting on his mother's lap, cuddled up close to her. He could smell her warm mother's smell and he felt more peaceful and relaxed than he had been in a long time. She was speaking, but he couldn't quite make out what she was saying. Her voice was soothing, as always.

She was reading him a bedtime story. He looked at the open pages of the book and saw an illustration of lots of old-fashioned cars driving on a busy city street. He looked closer—there at the old-fashioned traffic light was the Red and Tan Line bus. It was leaning forward slightly, and its headlights had been drawn as eyes, the front grille curved up as if smiling. He snuggled closer to his mother, sensing the softness of her body through her warm flannel bedclothes. He felt completely safe, here in her lap.

Soon, however, the cuddly scene dissolved, and he was in the family room watching TV with his dad. They appeared to be watching the History Channel, a program about the Blitz-krieg and the bombing of Poland in 1939. His father asked him a question. Luke couldn't quite hear him; it was as if the sound in the room wasn't working properly. Luke asked him to repeat it, but his father didn't seem to notice. Instead he looked disappointed, then asked another question. Luke leaned forward in his chair, straining to hear this one. All he got was something about Churchill and the Battle of Britain, maybe. He tried to ask him to repeat it again, but nothing audible came out of his mouth. His dad looked even more disappointed and a bit peeved now.

Suddenly his dad was out of his chair, stomping and huffing about the room. He began to take on a bull-like appearance and the brown rug turned to green grass, long and thick, threatening to trip him. He looked quite distraught, and even had a hint of fear on his face, which became bright red; his breathing sounded like a freight train. Smoke trailed out of his ears. Were those horns coming out of his head? Luke was scared. He tried to look away but his head wouldn't move—in fact, his whole body seemed incapable of movement.

His dad approached him and Luke thought he was going to hit him—or worse, gore him with the horns. There was something in his hand/hoof; Luke couldn't quite make it out. There, closer now. He could almost see it. His father's face was no longer red, but was turning deepening shades of gray. Luke's fear was also swelling into panic—if he could've gotten out of his chair and run, he would have, but he remained paralyzed.

His dad was very close to him now. Steam jetted out of his flared nostrils. Luke felt sure his dad would strike him any second now with the object in his hand. His bluish fingers—they were human fingers now—were wrapped tightly around the thing and he was waving it around. If he would just hold still for a second, Luke could make out what it was. Finally his dad's arm came to an abrupt stop; he appeared to be pointing the thing accusingly at Luke. It was a TV remote control. Luke screamed as loud as he could.

* * *

Luke awoke drenched with sweat and shivering. Another dream about his father. Except now, he had to admit, the dreams were becoming more vivid, and scarier. Ghoulish, even. What the hell was going on? His dad had been dead for over twelve years.

CHAPTER NINE

Bart Hinkle pulled out of the law office parking lot, his car fish-tailing slightly on the wet leaves as he made a left onto Front Street. He jammed his Bluetooth headset into his ear and dialed as he wove his Mercedes E-class between cars in the rush-hour traffic.

"Law offices of Schmidt, Evans and Knobe."

"Betty, this is Bart Hinkle. Cancel my four o'clock appointment. Something's come up." He clicked off, not waiting for a reply, then made a right turn onto the Harvey Taylor Bridge, heading toward Camp Hill. The rain intensified, forcing him to turn on his windshield wipers. Damn rain. He was sick of it. He flipped his high beams on at the minivan in front of him and pulled to within inches of the minivan's bumper. "Get out of the way!"

The minivan slowed further.

"Fucker!" Bart whipped his car into the right lane, ignoring the horn from the guy he'd cut in front of, and floored the accelerator. As he raced by the minivan, he shot the driver, a middle-aged woman, a nasty look and gave her the finger.

He drove along several side streets, finally turning into the parking lot of his townhouse. His windshield wipers started to squeak as the rain slowed to a drizzle. He punched the remote garage door opener and pulled in, almost scraping Mimi's Cadillac. The Caddie, he noted with displeasure, was parked crooked, making the tight two-car garage almost unmanageable.

He found Mimi in the family room, sacked out on the leather sofa. The TV was blaring; Oprah was chatting it up with Dr. Oz.

Mimi startled as he walked in; her eyes flew open and she struggled to focus on him. "You're home early."

"My last appointment canceled." Bart reached for the remote control and turned down the volume. "My head's killing me. Where's the Motrin?"

"In the kitchen—corner cabinet." Mimi rubbed her eyes.

Bart retrieved the Motrin and dry-swallowed some. "Any plans for dinner?" he called out from the kitchen.

"I didn't make anything yet. I didn't expect you home for another couple of hours."

Bart walked over to the granite countertop and leafed through a pile of mail. "Right," he said, not bothering to look up.

"I thought maybe we could go out," she said.

"Did you deposit those checks I put out this morning?"

"Oh—"

"I put them right here."

"I had a hectic day."

"What? You forgot?" Bart ran his fingers through his thinning hair. "Jesus, Mimi. I ask you to do one thing all day—"

"I was busy."

"Doing what, exactly?"

"Don't start with me, Bart."

"Driving to the liquor store? Buying cigarettes?"

"And don't use that tone of voice with me." She glared at him.

He threw the mail down on the countertop. "You mean *this* fucking tone."

"Watch your language. Joey might be upstairs."

"*Might* be?" Bart could hardly believe his ears. "Christ, you don't even know where he is, do you?"

Mimi looked down and fidgeted with her hair.

Bart rubbed his right temple vigorously; it was sore to the

touch. "Don't worry. I'm sure Joey's at the football game. His car's not outside." He looked at her closely for the first time. "You've been drinking again, haven't you?"

"No."

He walked over and grabbed the empty crystal tumbler from the end table and held it up accusingly. Several ice cubes clinked before one flew out onto the carpet as he waved the glass at her. "And I suppose this is Diet Coke?" He sniffed the glass. "Jesus, Mimi! It's not even four o'clock."

He spun around and paced toward the large expanse of glass that made up the back of the house. Even on such a gloomy afternoon, the view of the city was spectacular from their perch high above the western bank of the Susquehanna. He took several deep breaths and tried to collect himself.

"It's none of your damn business," she said.

He turned to face her. "That's where you're wrong." He could feel his heart pounding and the throbbing intensified in his head. "It *is* my damn fucking business."

Mimi labored to get off the sofa. "I don't have to take this," she said, breathing hard. She headed for the staircase.

"In case you forgot, dearie, we have a seventeen-year-old son living here. What kind of example do you think you're setting for him, being hammered all the time?"

She whirled to face him, a little unsteady on her feet. "Now look who's calling the kettle black. I suppose you think he doesn't know about your trips to the strip joints and massage parlors on Route 22? Mister fucking good example!"

Bart felt the blood run to his face and his heart pounded even harder. Mimi turned again and stomped up the stairs. Bart went out the garage door and slammed it behind him. Standing next to his Mercedes, he quickly pulled his wallet out, ignoring his car keys as they slipped from his fingers. With hands that were still shaking, he clumsily fished around in the wallet for a business card.

Ten minutes later, Bart was standing at a pay phone on

Second Street in downtown Harrisburg, close to the Hilton. He dialed and waited.

"Hello," a man's voice answered.

"Hi," Bart said, "Who is this?" He jammed the receiver up to his ear, straining to hear above the rush-hour street noise.

"Where did you get this number?" The voice sounded brusque.

"I have a business card with a number on it." Bart waved the card in his hand. "A friend gave—" A Capitol Area Transit bus whooshed by, not three feet away from him, loudly hissing exhaust. "I said, a friend gave it to me," Bart practically shouted.

"Who might this friend be?"

"Look, I have a problem." Bart was never a fan of the twenty-questions routine. "Can you help me or not?" His headache was intensifying and his right eye was twitching to beat the band.

"Goodbye—"

"Wait, don't hang up! His name is Kyle Schmidt—*the* Kyle Schmidt of Schmidt, Evans and Knobe." There, that should impress this guy. "And I'm his partner, Bart Hinkle." He paused to catch his breath. "Now, who am I speaking to?"

"Counselor, you really are naive. No names here. Phones are not always safe. The less you know, the better. Now what is it that you want?"

"It's my wife," Bart stammered. A police cruiser rolled slowly by and Bart could've sworn the cop was looking right at him. He waited until the cruiser was gone, then shot a glance over his shoulder. "I have a problem with my wife." This was tougher than he had thought.

"You sound a bit desperate."

"I am."

"Good. To demonstrate your interest, you must electronically transfer ten thousand dollars into the account number I'm about to give you. When the money arrives, we'll contact you about further steps."

"You must be kidding. Fork over ten grand to someone I don't even know? That's fucking ridiculous!"

Click.

Bart slammed down the phone. Un-fucking-believable! But as he stood there by the phone and simmered down a bit, a smile slowly spread across his face. He was in. This guy sounded very professional. He knew he'd risk the ten thousand—the money was never an issue. Fuckin' Kyle Schmidt—Bart had always known better than to underestimate him, but this connection was the real deal.

A Lincoln Town car pulled up to the Hilton entrance. A beautiful blond babe wearing an ultra-short dress got out and sashayed into the hotel. Probably meeting some lucky guy. Soon he'd be free of that drunken bitch and it'd be open season. Bart would rejoin the hunt. His smile broadened as he redialed the number.

CHAPTER TEN

Careful to tread lightly on the carpeted floor, Rob Gentry walked down the second-floor hallway toward the master bedroom. He certainly didn't feel like explaining his whereabouts tonight. He sniffed his shirt again, searching for any telltale signs of Gwen's perfume. The door to the guest room was closed and he figured that Cindy was already asleep there—this was nothing new; she spent many nights there. Steven's room was next. The door was half open and his sixteen-year-old was sprawled on the bed, softly sawing wood. Jessica's room was across the hall from Steven's, although thankfully her door was closed. Rob was struck with a renewed sense of guilt as he remembered that he had missed Jessica's play tonight. He shook his head and felt oddly like a stranger in his own home.

Rob entered the master bedroom and noticed the light to the bathroom was on. He paused for a moment to listen. Satisfied he didn't hear any sign of life, he studied his face in the mirror over the dresser, searching for any stray lipstick smudges or marks that might betray the fact that he had spent the last several hours parked along a deserted road with Gwen. Everything appeared normal.

It *had* been a very pleasant night, he had to admit. He smiled foolishly at his own reflection. Kissing Gwen was one of the most enjoyable things he had ever experienced in his life. He knew that sounded ridiculous, but it was true. He doubted many people would understand. In fact, he knew if anyone had asked him a year ago, he might've politely agreed, but inwardly would've dismissed the notion as romance novel gibberish.

He paused for a moment, lost in the memory. It all started with her smile. Again, he realized this teetered on the edge of Hollywood hype, but after all, he had been to the mountain, had seen the other side. When she met him and flashed him that smile—that hungry, come-hither smile—he'd been thrilled to the core and already imagined he was kissing her. Her gorgeous eyes would always twinkle just so and he often felt he could read her thoughts—and one of the thoughts she radiated was an unmistakable desire for him. This was what really pushed him over the edge.

"I thought I heard you," Cindy said, coming out of the bathroom. She was wearing her pink bathrobe and slippers.

Rob's heart pounded in his chest. He quickly took a step back from the mirror. "I didn't expect to find you still awake. What are you doing up so late?"

"I'm working on a dumb newsletter—you don't want to know." She paused to look at him. "You look beat. Rough night?"

"Yeah." Rob swallowed hard and looked away. "Tough ectopic pregnancy. Big-time blood loss."

"I'm sure you handled it." She gave him a light pat on the shoulder.

Rob didn't say anything. He smelled her distinctive floral scent—pleasant, but very different from Gwen's.

"Need anything?" she asked.

"No. Just some sleep."

"Okay, I'll leave you be. I'm going to work a little longer." She turned to leave. "Oh, one more thing."

"What?" His heart accelerated again.

"Jessica was a real hit tonight. They loved her."

"I'm sure. Hated to miss opening night. I'll see it tomorrow night for sure, I promise."

"Great," she said and walked out of the room.

"See you tomorrow," he said to her back.

Rob sighed his relief and sat down on the edge of the bed. He ran both hands through his hair and waited for his heart to slow down. How in the world had it gotten this crazy? Gwen's power over him was something he still didn't understand—he couldn't begin to fathom his reaction to her. Gwen and he had been going at it for several months now, meeting every chance they got, twenty minutes here, an hour there, no time was too short. Had it really been almost a year since he had met her? Rob realized full-well things were out of control and it scared the hell out of him. Mr. Precision—always in complete command of the complexities of gynecologic surgery and the art of delivering babies—had no use for this wild uncertainty. And lying to his wife seemed like something someone else would do, not him. He hated himself for it.

He knew he should break it off with Gwen now—before it was too late. A little preventative medicine, painful and distasteful now, but much better in the long run. Although they had progressed well beyond the kissing stage, amazingly they hadn't consummated the relationship. Rob realized this wasn't by accident or due to any lack of passion—God knew he was aching with desire. He had actively resisted taking things to the next level, sensing that having sex with Gwen would undoubtedly carry him well past the point of no return. He clung to this last vestige of reversibility or deniability, like a drowning man to a life preserver. He wondered if it was still even possible to step aside from this path? When had he become so weak?

Rob climbed into the cold, empty bed and began his nighttime ritual. Even though his faith was crumbling all about him, he still managed to get out a prayer. He asked God for the same thing he had asked for every night for the past several months, as he lay down and wrestled with his sleep demons. He prayed that one of them would die. He didn't even care which one. He might lie in his bed for hours staring up at the ceiling as he played his twisted version of Russian roulette with the universe. Interestingly, the well-oiled chambers making up the gun of fate rotated smoothly enough; he never had any trouble imagining any one of them dead.

Sometimes he wished Gwen, beautiful Gwen, would take a bullet. Other times it was his wife Cindy's turn. He was also perfectly willing to take *his* place in the cosmic crosshairs; he would welcome his own ticket out of misery. But the triggering mechanism seemed to be faulty or the triggerman was asleep on the job. He even smiled a little at his own analogy—when had guns and death entered his deepest thought patterns?

For some reason, his prayer kept falling on deaf ears. Or maybe the universe had no ears and he was praying to the cold blackness of space with no real hope of an answer. *God, where are you?* This much was clear—something would have to give soon. The situation was too unstable to hang together for long.

Weariness finally overtook him and dragged him down to the fitful, trance-like realm that passed for sleep these days.

CHAPTER ELEVEN

"I feel sick, Bart."

"What's wrong, honey?" Bart asked, feigning concern. He knew exactly what the problem was. Mimi was sick because of the stuff in the little vial he had poured into her afternoon martini. *That was fast*, he thought.

Mimi grimaced and doubled over in pain.

"Maybe you've got a touch of the flu or that GI bug that's going around," Bart offered.

"I'm going to be sick," she said, and ran to the bathroom, one hand clutching her abdomen and the other covering her mouth.

He could hear her pitiful retching over the television and it turned his own stomach. The local female newscaster with the funny hair was saying there were three hours to go before the polls closed tonight. She encouraged everyone to go out and vote.

"Bart, help me," Mimi wailed from the bathroom.

"I'm sure it will pass," Bart said, glancing at his watch.

"Something's horribly wrong," she said. The flushing of the toilet obscured what she said next.

"What?"

"I have such pain." She staggered out of the bathroom, grasping the doorjamb for support, her face pale and drawn. "I think I need to go to the hospital."

"Seriously? The hospital?" Bart stood and clicked off the TV with the remote. *So*, he thought, *the plan is playing out exactly as prescribed*.

"Yes, right away."

"Okay, whatever you say, dear." He glanced at his watch again, concerned that rush-hour traffic would be a bear at this time of day.

"Bart, I'm scared," she said and started to cry.

* * *

"Just need to draw a little blood, Mrs. Hinkle," the lab tech said as he cinched the rubber tourniquet tightly around her flabby arm.

"Ow," Mimi screeched, and gave the tech a withering glare.

Bart loosened his tie and directed his question to the ER physician hovering over his wife. "What's wrong with her, Doctor?" Bart hadn't quite caught his name—Dr. Najaf, or something like that.

"We won't know for sure until we get the lab results," he replied. He had an accent—Indian for sure, but with British overtones. "Then we will have a much better idea of what we are dealing with." The man had very dark skin and gleaming black hair and seemed to be in an awful goddamn hurry. He spoke rapidly, running his words together. "Did you eat any questionable foods that you can think of, Mrs. Hinkle?"

"No, I don't think so," Mimi managed between moans.

"What're you thinking, Doctor?" Bart prodded.

"Well, it could be viral gastroentcritis or food poisoning or appendicitis. We'll just have to wait and see." Dr. Najaf turned to go.

Bart recoiled a bit from the word poisoning. "How will you tell?"

Dr. Najaf halted and sighed loudly. His tone as he addressed Bart was a mixture of irritation and condescension. "The white count and differential will be very helpful." He promptly left the room.

Arrogant prick, Bart thought. *Typical doctor.*

* * *

A tall, lanky man in his forties with intense hazel eyes strode into the exam room. "Mr. and Mrs. Hinkle, I'm Dr. Howard, the general surgeon on call." He shook Bart's hand. "Dr. Najaf informs me we might have an appendicitis on our hands. Mrs. Hinkle, I need to examine your abdomen. I'll try to be gentle." He probed her briefly with his big hands, eliciting more moans from Mimi. "Is this tender here?"

Mimi practically jumped off the stretcher. "Yes," she shrieked.

"Well, folks," Dr. Howard said, "this certainly looks like appendicitis. However, the lab values will be telling."

An orderly came in with a computer printout in his hand. "I haf lab results," he said in a thick Russian accent as he handed the paper to Dr. Howard.

"Thanks, Nikolai. Perfect timing." Dr. Howard studied the labs for a few seconds. "Well, the white count is 19.6 thousand with a pronounced left shift." He turned to the orderly. "Nikolai, tell the OR I have a case."

"Yes, Doctor." Nikolai took the lab sheet and left.

"Left shift, what's that?" Bart asked.

"A higher than normal neutrophil count in the differential, indicating we're dealing with a bacterial process such as appendicitis."

"I see." Bart turned to Mimi. "They think you may have appendicitis, dear."

"I'm going to need your permission to operate," Dr. Howard said. The rest sounded like a canned talk that had been recited too many times. "Anything that looks strongly like appendicitis must be operated on. Missing an appendicitis can lead to a ruptured appendix and peritonitis, which can be life-threatening—so we always err on the conservative side. The most common risks are bleeding and infection; death can result, but these are really remote possibilities that I'm forced to mention for the lawyers."

"I'm a lawyer, Dr. Howard," Bart said evenly, studying the man.

"Oh, I see," Dr. Howard replied, barely missing a beat. "Well, we won't hold that against you." He gave Bart a thin smile.

"I'll be okay, won't I, Bart?" Mimi looked up at him with fear in her bloodshot eyes.

"Yeah, sure, dear." Mimi looked so helpless and in pain. *Death? Did Howard say death? Isn't that what I wanted?* He tried to recall the sound of the man's voice on the phone. *Was it Howard?* A vague queasiness began to settle over Bart.

He thought about their two children and how Mimi had done a decent job raising them—before the alcohol. Sure, they had their differences and she had a drinking problem, but that's what counseling and rehab were for, right? Maybe this didn't really call for drastic measures. Bart suddenly began to sweat and he felt light-headed. *What the hell was I thinking?*

"You okay, Mr. Hinkle?" the surgeon asked.

"I don't feel so well. All this medical talk makes my stomach turn, that's all."

Dr. Howard gave Bart a brief once-over. Apparently satisfied, he whirled to exit. "You'll meet the anesthesiologist upstairs," he said as he left the room.

Bart steadied himself on Mimi's bedrail. He couldn't believe what was happening—but he couldn't deny it, either. Was this possible, after dropping ten Gs? Could he actually have developed cold fucking feet? "Look, Mimi," he said, "maybe we should just leave. I'll take you home, we'll let this thing run its course." He was sweating profusely now. "Besides, everyone here is so rude."

She looked up at him with a look of pure exasperation. "Bart, you heard him say my appendix is *crawling* with bacteria! It needs to come out."

"He doesn't know that for sure," Bart offered weakly. "It could just be a virus, or..." His voice trailed off.

"You go if you need to," she said, and started to cry. "I'm staying," she got out between sobs.

What else could he say? That he had paid some unknown bastards to murder her while she was on the operating table? He ran his fingers through what little hair he had and tried to think.

What could he do? His head began to pound. He'd just have to let them know the deal was off. It was all a big mistake. He'd even forfeit the money. The only problem was, he didn't exactly know who *they* were.

* * *

Upstairs, in the holding room outside the operating room, Mimi lay moaning on the stretcher while Bart fidgeted at her bedside, taking in his surroundings. The room was way too cramped, he thought, and privacy was nonexistent. He could probably sue the hospital's ass off for some HIPAA violation.

They didn't have to wait long for the anesthesiologist to arrive. An older, sturdy-looking guy walked up to them, confident in his manner. "My name is Dr. Katz," he said in a deep voice, "from the anesthesia department." He shook Bart's hand firmly, then turned to Mimi. "Sounds like you're tired of your appendix, or it's tired of you." He chuckled at his own humor. "How're you doing?" He paused, then answered himself in what sounded like a well-worn line. "Silly question, huh? I know—you could be better." He picked up the chart and began to leaf through it.

"Look, what are the risks to this whole thing?" Bart said, trying to catch his eye, but Katz was busy with the chart. Bart loosened his tie further, then decided to take it off completely. He took a step closer to the anesthesiologist and lowered his voice. "I don't want anything to *happen* to her. Do you understand? She means a lot to me."

Dr. Katz paused in his chart review and made eye contact with Bart. "Look, Mr. Hinkle, we don't want anything to happen to her, either. We'll take good care of her. Now, I just need you to sign here, please, to give me permission to put her to sleep for the surgery." He held out a clipboard and indicated where Bart should sign.

Bart didn't really want to sign, but he felt as if he had no choice. He needed to communicate to them not to kill her. But who? There were more people taking care of Mimi than he would have thought possible. He'd have to make it clear to all of them.

He signed the paper and Katz walked away.

A few moments later the surgeon, Dr. Howard, returned. He was no longer wearing his fancy suit, but had changed into green scrubs. "All ready to go, Mr. and Mrs. Hinkle?" he asked cheerfully, as if they were going to ride the Great Bear roller coaster at Hershey Park.

"Can I speak to you alone?" Bart said, clutching Dr. Howard's elbow. He led him around the corner.

Dr. Howard's cheerfulness evaporated. "What is it, Mr. Hinkle?"

"Listen, I just wanted to let you know that I don't want anything to happen to her. *Anything.*" Bart stared at him. "She's special to me. You got that?"

"Yeah, I got it, Mr. Hinkle," Dr. Howard said frostily. "Like I told you before, this is a minor procedure and she's relatively healthy, other than the cigarettes and alcohol. She shouldn't have any problem. Now, let me do my job."

Bart returned to the holding area in time to see a young man kneeling down at Mimi's bedside, taping something in her arm. He looked like he was fresh out of med school. *Christ, how many people can be involved in her care?* Before Bart could say anything, two OR nurses and Dr. Katz rounded the far corner into the room, apparently ready to take Mimi away.

Katz surprised Bart by shouting at the young man. "Daulton!" Katz hurried over to Mimi's litter. "What're you doing?"

The young man stood up, a grin spreading across his boyish features. "I just started her IV for you, Dr. Katz."

"This is my case, Luke," Katz said, his tone already softening. "I'll take *complete* care of Mrs. Hinkle." He reached down and patted Mimi on the head, throwing her a broad smile. "I see you've met Dr. Daulton. He's one of our newest associates."

Mimi nodded and Bart just stood there, trying to figure out what to do.

Katz turned to Luke. "I'll take it from here, Luke. I've got everything covered." He smiled again. "Why don't you call it quits and go home. I'll beep you if I need you. Okay?"

"Sure," Luke said, and walked away.

The two OR nurses came over and unlocked the brakes on Mimi's litter. "Time to say your goodbyes," the taller one said.

Bart searched the faces of the nurses. The short, plumper one had a kind face and a warm smile. The tall, skinny one looked cranky and impatient. "Please take good care of her," Bart said to them, "and don't let anything happen to her." He bent over and kissed Mimi on the lips, tears welling up in his eyes. Some deeper portion of his brain registered the fact that neither of these things had happened in years. "I love you. See you in a little bit."

"I love you, too."

Their hands were clasped. The skinny nurse began to roll the stretcher away, breaking the link. Bart hoped he had communicated what he needed to. He had never felt more helpless in his life. He reached up with both hands and clutched his aching head.

CHAPTER TWELVE

Rob Gentry walked his last patient of the day to the door. "Take care, Mrs. Janeski. Everything will be fine, don't worry. I'll see you next week." He held the door for the full-term pregnant woman and patted her arm as she squeezed by.

"Thanks for listening, Dr. Gentry," Mrs. Janeski said, her face lighting up with a warm smile. "See you next week." Midway down the hallway, she turned and gave him a little wave.

Rob shut the door and tossed Mrs. Janeski's file down on his desk. He sat down and buried his face in his hands. *God, what a mess.* He tried some deep breathing yoga exercises to relax, but felt himself tightening up anyway. He stared off into space while drumming his fingers on the desktop blotter, trying to collect his thoughts.

His office schedule was unusually light today, although it wasn't by coincidence. He had planned to get done early to meet up with Gwen when she finished up in the billing office. However, after the weekend, his original plans had changed. He got up and started pacing around his small office.

The weekend had been an emotional roller coaster. Saturday he had gone to the high school football game and watched Steven play his trumpet in the band. The fall weather had been lovely—enough sun to keep you warm, but nippy enough to feel like football. Cindy had gone to a garden club meeting at the Hershey Country Club, so he was there by himself. But Rob didn't mind. He always enjoyed a good football game, and the home team actually won.

Later that evening, Cindy met them at the high school for Jessica's play—the second night of the play; he had of course missed opening night. A senior now, Jessica played one of the leads in *Music Man* and sang beautifully. Her acting was not too shabby, either. Afterward, they all went home for a late meal. The dinner conversation was burned into his brain:

"Mmm, good chili," Rob said between generous mouthfuls.

"Thanks," Cindy said. "Not too spicy?"

"Naw—I like it with some kick to it."

"I made it with you in mind." She favored him with a warm smile.

Rob looked down and concentrated on his food.

"Daddy," Jessica said, slipping gracefully out of her chair. She came around behind him and gave him a big hug around his neck. "Thanks for coming to see my play. I knew you'd come."

"Sure, wouldn't miss it for the world, sweet pea."

She took a step back and regarded him with her light blue eyes. "Did you really like it? Did I do okay? What about the high notes?"

"Yes, of course. You're singing was perfect." Rob felt the beginnings of a lump growing in his throat. "I got video of it all," he said, patting the phone on his hip.

Jessica, all smiles, danced lightly back to her seat.

Rob turned to his son, who wore a sullen expression. "The band was awesome too, Steven. You're really coming along with that trumpet."

"I messed up a note on the solo."

"I didn't notice—I doubt anyone else did, either."

"I did better at the band concert."

"Yeah, your mother told me how well you did." Rob looked down again. "Sorry I missed that one." The next bite of chili didn't go down so easily. The lump was growing.

"Anyone up for a movie?" Cindy asked. "We could take our food down to the family room. I know it's late, but it might be nice."

Steven brightened at this idea. "*Talladega Nights*?"

"The Will Ferrell one?" Rob asked.

"Yeah. He's so crazy-funny," Steven said.

"So stupid and crude, you mean," Jessica said, wrinkling her nose. But then she jumped out of her chair again. "I'm up for it."

All of them giggled.

Cindy was smiling at him. Rob finally met her eyes and smiled back. She reached under the table and squeezed his hand.

Later, in bed, Rob had tossed and turned endlessly. Between thinking of his family and Gwen, wrestling with enormous guilt and temptation, and playing frickin' cosmic Russian roulette again, he didn't get much sleep.

Sunday morning he got up early and, despite the lack of sleep and physical exhaustion, he was in better spirits than he had been in a while. He felt like something had changed, as if a fever had broken during the night. The family went to a morning service at the Hershey Lutheran Church. He hadn't been to church much lately, pushing God away, denying his faith to make room for Gwen.

Sunday afternoon the gorgeous fall weather continued, and Rob went for a walk by himself at Schenk Park to sort out his thoughts. For the first time in a great while, he felt that he could think clearly. It was as if he had been lifted up out of a dense fog and could actually see his surroundings—see where he had been and what lay ahead around the bend.

He could see the enormity of his mistake and was left to wonder about his motivations. Several questions taunted him. How could Gwen possibly wield this power over him? What was this strange emotion dancing about his brain that commandeered his rational mind and ordered him about? Couldn't he rise above this with the help of God? He paused in his walk to listen as a breeze came up. The rustling of the trees seemed to be whispering something to him, but he couldn't quite make it out.

The logical part of his brain screamed that all the red flags were up—it was a frickin' flag frenzy. Everything about it was wrong. It would be an end to all that was peaceful in his life. Again, what hold could she possibly have on the rational man? And so before he had completed his walk, he vowed to tell her that they must never see each other again.

* * *

Rob took off his white coat and hung it on the hook behind the door. He glanced at his watch—4:30 p.m. Less than an hour to go. Just one more nasty task remained: to actually tell Gwen. He slowly realized that this might be harder than he had thought. He certainly didn't want to hurt her. Things weren't quite as clear as they had been this weekend; the fog seemed to be reforming. Was that her scent he imagined floating in on the mist? He had the beginnings of a migraine and his gut was doing its familiar knot-tying tricks. He took several deep, cleansing breaths but soon realized the futility of this. His emotions were whipsawing about so violently that they were well beyond the scope of yoga's healing powers. He threw in a last-ditch prayer.

CHAPTER THIRTEEN

Luke opened his locker door and sat down on the bench. He was tired from the long day he'd put in as late guy. He still had time to make it home to take a walk with Kim if he didn't dawdle. The thought of Kim—beautiful, pregnant Kim—waiting at home for him helped him forget his weariness. He checked his watch—probably no time to vote, though.

Although the sun was setting earlier each day and the temperature was creeping down into the fifties, Luke and Kim still both loved to take their evening walk together. They would traipse around the quiet neighborhood, hand in hand, and bounce their dreams off one another. Lately, of course, the conversations centered around the arrival of their baby. What would she be like? Were they really ready? How much would it change their lives? And even though Colby tugged on the leash like a dog possessed, Luke had to admit that he actually enjoyed taking the spunky one along.

The overhead intercom crackled to life, spoiling his pleasant reverie: "Case One, OR Number 7. Case One, Room 7."

Luke jumped up, grabbed his cap, and put it back on. He barely stopped to consider that he had been dismissed and was free to go. Or that he wouldn't get to take that walk with his pretty wife. He was under no obligation to return to the OR. However, someone was in trouble—probably that poor, terrified lady he had just started the IV on—and maybe he could make a difference. This was, after all, why he had gone into medicine, his overriding need to help people. His dad would never have understood this.

Leaving his clothes draped over the bench, Luke sprinted back into the OR complex. He grabbed a mask and tied it on as he ran down the hallway toward OR 7, bursting through the door into a scene of controlled chaos. Dr. Katz was at the head of the OR table, frantically barking orders to several OR nurses, CRNAs, and anesthesia techs. The surgeon, Dr. Howard, who had already started the lap appy operation, looked somehow very peculiar. Luke didn't get it at first, but then he noticed that Howard's hands were uncharacteristically idle as he held the laparoscopic instruments limply, unsure of what to do. His brow was also creased and his eyes were laden with worry. Luke recognized the lady from the holding area, the VIP that Katz was taking care of personally.

Katz looked up and appeared startled by Luke's entrance. "Daulton, I thought I sent you home!"

"I was just leaving and heard the Case One. What's up?"

Katz paused for the briefest of intervals. "I think she's got MH."

"Wow," Luke murmured to himself. Malignant hyperthermia was very rare but also very deadly. "What's the temp?"

Katz pointed to the monitor screen and said, "104 and climbing. We're getting some ice and the techs are mixing the dantrolene."

He seemed to have a good handle on things, but Luke knew you could always use help in these bad situations. "I'll get you another IV," he said, heading to the anesthesia cart.

"Uh, listen, Luke," Katz said, locking eyes with him. "I appreciate your offer to help, but I've got lots of helpers here." He gestured to all the personnel around him. "I really don't need you. You're free to go." He waved toward the door.

"I'm fine, really, Dr. Katz," Luke mumbled as he grabbed a tourniquet and IV supplies from the cart. He knew people in these situations always appreciated help even if they didn't want to admit it. Anesthesia practitioners were no different than most doctors in this respect—they suffered from a touch of machismo, preferring not to show any sign of weakness.

Besides, here was the perfect opportunity to demonstrate to Katz his dedication to the job, and his knowledge. Luke considered himself something of an expert on malignant hyperthermia as he had just given a Grand Rounds conference on it last year at Penn. His knowledge had to be more current than Katz's.

"Where's that ice!?" Katz shouted. "Temp's 104.5. I need it now!"

Luke applied the tourniquet to Mimi's pudgy arm and hoped some veins would appear. He found one in her antecubital space and worked on driving a 14-gauge, large-bore needle home. *Success! There, that should impress the boss.*

"Dantrolene's ready, Dr. Katz," said one of the CRNAs.

"Good," Katz said more evenly. "Bolus it now, then start the drip."

Luke hooked up his IV, turned it on, and taped it into place. It ran like a spigot, and Luke mentally patted himself on the back. He threw his spent needle into the sharps container. "Here's a fourteen for you," he said.

"Thanks, Daulton," Katz said.

An OR nurse came in with two buckets of ice and they packed Mimi's head and body in ice. Luke always hated this part—it was so dehumanizing. He felt like they were packing a mackerel in the hold of a deep-sea fishing boat.

"Anything I can do, Jason?" the surgeon inquired.

"Just get those trocars out of her and close as fast as you can," Katz said. "I had to turn all her anesthesia off. The gas acts to trigger MH."

"Sure," Howard replied, then put forth tentatively, "How's it going?"

"Not so well," Katz said. Just then, Nikolai came in and handed a lab report to Katz. "Oh, shit!" Katz said. "Blood gas is pretty bad. PH 7.09, CO2 is 85."

"Need anything else?" Nikolai asked. Katz shook his head.

The surgeon went to work closing the belly incisions with gusto, as if he thought it might help reverse the MH.

"Run that dantrolene quickly!" Katz barked.

Luke knew these blood gas values were bad—real bad. The body goes to great lengths to keep the blood pH within very tight parameters; 7.35 to 7.45 was the normal range. Mimi's pH of 7.09 represented overwhelming acidosis caused by hyper-metabolic muscle tissue. This was how MH killed. It caused an uncoupling of the calcium channels, leading to runaway metabolism, which in turn caused the temperature to skyrocket. The brain and heart cannot tolerate acidosis or the high fever for very long.

Dantrolene, a form of muscle relaxant, was a miracle drug that somehow restored order to the calcium metabolism and cooled things off, literally. The only problem was, it had to be given early enough in the crisis, when the process was still reversible. Also, it came as a powder that was very hard to dissolve and required several people to mix up an intravenous solution. Luke wasn't about to abandon one of his new colleagues in the midst of an MH crisis.

He studied the EKG tracing. He didn't see any abnormal beats, but she was taching up a storm at 130–140 bpm. That also wasn't good. He searched his mind for something they had missed. "Did you give bicarb?" Luke asked.

"I already gave her two amps," Katz said. Again, Katz was right on the money with his treatment. There wasn't anything else to do but hope the dantrolene worked its magic before the patient cooked. Katz was holding up well. This couldn't be easy on him.

Luke heard the irregularity in the audible pulse ox signal before he saw it on the EKG monitor. Premature ventricular contractions, the first sign of cardiac irritability. He glanced over and saw the ugly PVCs on the monitor. Shit—again a very bad sign.

* * *

The locker room door squeaked open and in walked Dr. Jason Katz. Luke tried to read his expression but couldn't.

"Thanks for your help in there, Daulton," Katz said. "Sorry it didn't turn out better."

"Yeah, me too." Luke didn't know what else to say—he just sat there staring at his open locker. He was mentally and physically drained. They had worked on Mimi Hinkle for ninety minutes before giving up. Luke was in a state of shock. He still believed they should've been able to turn this one around—Katz had caught the fever early enough. Usually it was the delay in diagnosis that cost people's lives.

Luke had no desire to carry on a conversation with Katz at this point. He was still wary of him after getting reamed out. Three months on the job and Luke had already been involved with an obstetrical calamity and now had participated in his first intraoperative death. What would Katz say to him now? Would this turn into another lecture on what he should have done? And how maybe he's just not partnership material? Luke stripped off his scrubs and threw them on the floor with disgust, then changed into his street clothes.

"I'll take care of talking to Mr. Hinkle," Katz said, breaking the silence. "Go home, for God's sake." Katz opened his locker door and tossed something in. "Remember, Luke, medicine is not an exact science. There's only so much you can do—so much you can control. The rest is in the Lord's hands." Katz approached Luke and put his hand on his shoulder. Luke resisted the urge to cringe. "Don't try to play God, son," Katz continued. "You do your best, but ultimately the outcome isn't up to you."

Luke dropped his gaze. "I guess you're right," he lied weakly. Dad would've disagreed, too.

"Are you a praying man?"

"No sir, not really," Luke answered.

Katz seemed vaguely surprised and hesitated for a moment. "Have you heard the words of James from the New Testament: 'Even the demons believe'?"

"No," Luke replied, continuing to stare at the floor.

"Perhaps you should consider that verse—belief can be very

powerful. Well, pray with me now, anyway, for the soul of Mrs. Hinkle." Katz bowed his head. "Please Lord, we pray for the soul of Mrs. Hinkle. Watch over her and keep her safe on her journey. May she awaken in a better place, in your arms; in Jesus's name we pray. Amen."

"Amen," Luke said, feeling his throat tighten. He was genuinely touched—and a bit surprised—by the older man's compassion. He certainly sounded sincere. He hadn't seen this side of Jason Katz before. Perhaps Luke had judged him too quickly, earlier. Perhaps he had just been doing his job as chief of the department.

But Luke couldn't shake the feeling that he, himself, had failed on some level. He didn't want to be a part of any more deaths.

CHAPTER FOURTEEN

Rob locked the door to his office and turned to walk down the hallway. Gwen was suddenly right beside him, wrapping her arms around him.

"Hey, what are you doing?" he asked in mock alarm.

"Finally, you're done." She squeezed him tightly and gave him a quick kiss on the cheek.

Rob could feel his face heating. He looked up and down the hallway to see if anyone was watching—it was empty.

"Sorry," she said. "I missed you."

"I missed you, too."

She took a step back. "How much time do you have?"

"Not much. I promised I'd be home by eight."

"Darn." He could see real disappointment in her face and was touched.

They started walking down the hall. "Friday night was fun," she said with a fresh smile. "Thanks again for the moonlit car ride."

"Sure."

"And the parking part was nice, too."

"Right."

"So, how was your weekend?"

"Not bad."

"Did you make it to Jessica's play?"

"Yeah. She was great."

Gwen stopped walking. "Are you okay?"

"Fine."

She studied him. "What else did you do?"

"Well, we had a big family dinner after the play."

"Oh."

"Cindy makes this chili; it's really good."

Gwen didn't say anything.

"And I took a nice long walk Sunday afternoon to try to make some sense out of this pathetic mess I call my life." He held the door for her, and they exited the building and walked slowly across the parking lot toward Rob's Porsche. The lot was mostly empty and dark, except for some sparse overhead lighting. A buzzing sound came from one of the lights.

"Did you figure it out?" she asked.

He chuckled uneasily. "I'm not sure."

She took his hand in hers and squeezed it gently. "What's the matter, Rob?"

"Nothing."

"No, really. I can tell."

She fixed him with those pretty eyes, and he quickly looked away. He stared at a bright patch of horizon, where the sun had set earlier. The Appalachian ridgeline was beautifully defined, lit up by the delicate hues of twilight.

"Look, Gwen. I didn't really want to get into it here. I'm not sure this is the best place." Rob shot a glance around the empty lot again.

"I don't like the sound of that." She let go of his hand and swept the hair out of her face. "Do you want to take a ride?"

"It's just—there's some stuff I've got to tell you." Rob still had trouble meeting her gaze. He saw her nod out of the corner of his eye. "I've been thinking a lot about my kids lately. This weekend was rough. Saturday was special—everyone was so happy together."

She didn't say anything.

"Then Sunday we all went to church. I haven't been in a while."

"You've said."

"You should have seen it, though. The sun was shining in the window on me like a spotlight. And you won't believe it, but the title of the sermon was Jesus Allows U-turns. I felt like the minister was talking right to me."

Her eyes began to glisten in the dim light. Still not a word.

"I'm not sure I can do this to them. You and me, I mean." Rob swallowed, trying to dislodge the lump growing in this throat. "It's just not right."

She turned and looked off into the distance. They didn't say anything for a long time, both just standing there, staring past each other.

Finally he said in barely more than a whisper, "We probably shouldn't see each other anymore." The lump in his throat was now painful.

No response.

Rob heard the hospital door open, but didn't look over. He watched the tears stream down her sad face.

She turned and began to walk away.

"Aren't you going to scream at me or hit me?" Rob asked after her. "Would you just say something?"

She didn't stop, but slowed and gave him one last look over her shoulder. She mumbled what sounded like, "Don't worry. I get it."

He stared after her, listening to her boots clop loudly on the pavement. More than anything in his life, he wanted to run after her and hug her and comfort her, kiss her, and tell her he didn't mean any of it; it was all a big misunderstanding. They would work it out. Instead, he held his ground. With a trembling hand, he grabbed the handle of the car door and clutched it tightly, as if it were an anchor in a storm.

He heard footsteps approaching.

"You all right?" Luke Daulton asked.

Rob didn't answer. He continued to look off into space.

"You okay?"

Rob turned slowly to look at him. "I'm fine now."

"You don't look it."

"I just ended it with Gwen."

Luke didn't say anything for a moment. "Well, you dodged a bullet on that one."

"It doesn't feel like it," Rob said weakly. "It feels like I got hit by the bullet right through the heart." He tapped his chest. "And I feel like I'll be carrying this slug around for a long time."

"Okay, bad analogy," Luke said. "But I guess what I'm saying is, it could've been worse."

"I'll buy that." Rob took a deep breath and sighed. "I jumped from the moving train before it wrecked. I guess it was going faster than I thought."

Luke nodded, although he looked confused.

"Be careful, Luke. Don't think you're immune."

"Okay."

"You're too young for any of this to make any sense," Rob said. "I know you've got a good thing going—I've met Kim—and I know you guys are all wrapped up in love for each other. Just keep your guard up."

"Yeah, I will." Luke paused. "No offense, Rob, but you haven't exactly been thinking logically here."

"Luke, logic's got nothing to do with it."

"I guess." Luke looked away and an awkward silence followed.

"Well, see you around," Rob said. He opened the door to his Porsche, but stopped before getting in. "Hey, I'll have more time for that bike ride, now. Give me a call." With that, he hopped in and fired up the high-powered engine.

After Luke's Camry pulled away, leaving the parking lot truly deserted, Rob was left alone to face his thoughts and feelings. Breaking it off with Gwen was the hardest, meanest, cruelest thing he had ever done in his whole sorry, pathetic existence, and he knew that look on her face would haunt him forever. But he had done the right thing, he kept telling himself. He should feel better—he would feel better soon. He would've just hurt her—

and himself—worse by prolonging it. What would be the sense? Why drag it out? He said these things over and over, never believing any of them for an instant.

As the pain swelled and became unbearable, he pounded the steering wheel with his fists and howled his distress. Then he buried his face in his hands and cried. Finally, after a long while, when the tears came no more, he drove away with a heaviness in his chest and a hollowness in his soul that he didn't think would ever heal.

CHAPTER FIFTEEN

"How'd she die?" Kim asked softly from the other end of the worn sofa. She lifted a spoonful of her steaming wonton soup and blew on it.

"She had a case of malignant hyperthermia." Luke took another bite of his pork egg foo yung. Colby, who was sitting on the floor, rested his head heavily on Luke's knee. The dog's eyes followed every move of the egg foo yung.

"Malignant hyperthermia," she repeated slowly. "You mean where they get the really high fever from anesthesia?"

"I'm surprised you remember it."

"You did Grand Rounds on it." A grin crossed her face. "How could I forget? You agonized about it for a month. I helped you with your slides."

He lifted his hand to stop her. "Okay, I guess that's the price for being married to a smart aleck know-it-all. Anyway, it wasn't my case, it was Dr. Katz's. In fact, I was changing to go home when I heard the Case One being called."

"You ditched our walk just to *help* someone?"

He cocked his head a little and gave her a warning stare, but he felt the corners of his mouth curling up in spite of himself. He could never maintain a harsh demeanor with her for long. Besides, he knew she was just trying to cheer him up. He suppressed the smile. "I'm not so sure I was much help, Kim—the lady died."

"Oh," she said quietly.

The egg foo yung had lost its flavor. He set the half-full

container back down on the side table next to the sofa. Colby nudged him with a cool snoot, and Luke began to pet his head and rub behind his ears.

"How old was she?"

"Only in her fifties—wife of some VIP lawyer or state government type."

"Yow, that's young."

"Katz seemed to catch it right away. We gave dantrolene—the antidote—quickly enough, but she never turned around. Temp just kept going up, despite packing her in ice. She cooked right before our eyes."

"Sounds horrible." She poked thoughtfully at a wonton with her spoon, slowly dunking it under the broth.

"It was." Luke shook his head. "Reminded me of a kid I once took care of in the PICU whose temp was out of control—very scary. He had flesh-eating bacteria and sepsis. He was burning up, too. I remember even his feet were red hot."

Kim grimaced. "Nasty."

"This lady's blood gas was nasty too. PH was 7.09! Normal is 7.4."

She looked up at him, brows arched. "Wow, no wonder she didn't make it. How did Dr. Katz do with it?"

"He did really well—better than I would've expected."

"Why do you say that?" She took a break from the soup and moved on to her pepper steak. "He seems like a very intelligent man."

"I know he's smart and all, but Kim, MH cases are rare. Maybe you see one every ten years or so—less, if you're lucky. He knew all the dantrolene doses perfectly."

"Maybe he's just really good at his job after all these years."

Luke took a sip of his Coke.

She set her pepper steak down on the coffee table. "Are you okay?" She sidled closer and put her arm behind his back to lean her head into his shoulder. "Was it really bad for you?"

"I'm fine," he replied. Neither said anything for a few moments. "How's Abi doing?" he asked.

Her smile returned. "See for yourself." She took his hand and placed it on her big belly. "She usually wakes up when it's dinnertime."

Luke closed his eyes and focused on his hand resting on Kim's stomach. "She's moving," he said. "I think she's kicking!" Luke loved to feel his daughter move. He grinned at Kim and said, "She wants out."

"That makes two of us."

"And you're sure you're good with Abigail? No second thoughts, I mean?" Luke had to admit he wasn't totally thrilled with the name but he knew Kim was, and that was enough for him.

"I love it." Kim hugged him as best she could and kissed him on the cheek. "And I love *you* for being okay with it."

"I love you, too—and Abi." Luke returned her hug and kissed her gently. They sat there cuddled together for a few minutes, the only noise Colby's breathing.

"I have to tell you something," Luke said, opening his eyes.

"What?"

"Remember a while ago I told you about *your* obstetrician, Rob Gentry, getting involved with another woman?"

"Yeah. With *your* billing secretary, I believe."

"Right. Well, I think he ended it tonight. He told me he gave her the boot while we were in the parking lot."

"Hopefully he's come to his senses." She snuggled closer to him. "Hey," she said, "I think Abi's drifting off to sleep."

"Good," he whispered back.

Kim turned to look up at him, concern clouding her features. "Will *you* be all right sleeping?"

"Sure."

"It seems lately that you toss and turn a lot at night. Bad dreams?"

"I'm okay." Luke couldn't bring himself to meet her eyes, especially when he thought he wasn't being a hundred percent truthful. He hadn't shared the dad nightmare with her yet. He squirmed a little and sat up straight. Colby looked up at him.

"I'll give you a back rub," Kim volunteered.

"That'd be nice, but I'm supposed to be giving *you* back rubs."

"You'll owe me, then," she said, shifting around.

Luke chuckled and leaned forward. He busied himself rubbing Colby's velvety soft ears. Colby purred with appreciation sounding more like a kitten than a dog.

"Maybe I'll even throw in a front rub, if that would help," she added. "Then you'll really owe me."

Luke nodded and smiled back at her and felt himself getting choked up. He couldn't help but think he didn't deserve her.

Later that night, Luke again had trouble falling asleep, even after Kim's all-inclusive massage. What was happening? Sleeping had always been one of his strengths. It was past midnight and after tossing and turning for well over an hour, he was now thoroughly exhausted—and becoming more and more irritated. He really had to sleep—5:30 would be coming soon enough. But the harder he tried, the more elusive sleep became.

The woman's death obviously had something to do with his restlessness, but he knew it was more than that—he was also afraid to have the dad nightmare again. He rolled over once again and saw Kim sleeping peacefully next to him in bed. Her strawberry-blond hair glowed in the moonlight streaming in through the window. God, she was beautiful. Gazing at her was always soothing to him, the balm his mind needed to ease his pain. He joked that she was his antidepressant. She was definitely the best thing that had ever happened to him. And truth be told, if it had been left up to him, nothing would've happened between them.

He recalled very clearly that it hadn't been her looks that had initially attracted him, six years ago at Penn. In fact, when he first saw her, she was wearing a full-length white lab coat and her long hair was pulled back in a bun, and she wore glasses—computer nerd personified. What attracted him was her brains—she was the smartest girl he had ever met.

Luke had been a fourth-year medical student at the time, Kim a graduate student in applied computing. They crossed paths because of an extra credit research project Luke was working on. He was investigating the effects of anesthetic gases on cerebral blood flow in dogs. To this day, no one really knew how these strange anesthetic agents produce unconsciousness reversibly. He utilized positron emitting glucose molecules to tag the blood flow and a PET scanner to track their whereabouts. The PET scans were then reconstructed into 3D images of the brain using high-speed computer algorithms. Kim was in charge of the computers doing the reconstruction and her abilities were nothing short of astonishing. He smiled as a memory surfaced.

* * *

"So, Daulton, how's that research project going?"

"Oh, hi, Kim. I didn't see you come in. Hey, take a look at this graph. Isn't it sweet?"

Luke rolled his chair back to give her more room as she came closer. As she bent over to study the plot on the CRT monitor, he got a whiff of her pleasant scent, but did his best to ignore it. "That PET scanner data of yours is perfect," he said.

She tapped the screen. "I'll bet if you plotted the second derivative you could nail down that inflection point." She adjusted her glasses. "I could add that to the program."

He smiled at her. "You're the best, Kimby."

She straightened and took a few steps toward the door. "When you're done here, why don't you take a break and join us for a little softball," she said over her shoulder. "A bunch of the grad students get together every Friday after work."

"Thanks for the invite," Luke said apologetically, "but I really need to finish this paper, plus I've got a big micro test on Monday."

She turned and put her hands on her hips. "So you're gonna hit the books on a Friday night?"

"Yeah, 'fraid so." Luke scribbled a note in his notebook about the new derivative plot. "I'm not a genius type like you, who aces all her tests without ever cracking a book."

"You're such a nerd."

Luke thought he detected a note of genuine disappointment under her usual bantering tone. He looked up from his notebook to find her staring right at him. It was the first time he noticed how blue her eyes were. "Hey, you know my grades are important to me. I need to get into a good residency program."

"Why is that again?" Her expression was hard to read.

"I need to make a difference."

Luckily for Luke, Kim was persistent. She continued to invite him to play softball or go to parties with the graduate students. Luke never fully understood the reason for her persistence. He knew he scared most women away with his all-business attitude, which was okay with Luke; in fact, it was mostly on purpose. Women were a distraction he couldn't afford.

Finally, one Friday afternoon in May, against his better judgment, Luke relented and agreed to meet Kim on the softball field. She had helped him so much with his project that he felt he owed her—besides, he had to admit he was beginning to enjoy her company. She was such a bright, upbeat person and she always made him laugh, something he didn't do too much of on his own.

When Luke showed up late for the game, he thought for a moment he was at the wrong field. He didn't recognize Kim at first, with her long blond hair down. She was also wearing short shorts and a silky Penn gym shirt. She was very pretty, he realized. From that point on, he always noticed her looks, despite her habit of wearing loose-fitting, sometimes even baggy clothes. Later she confided to him that she didn't dress provocatively because she had been hit on so much in college. She had been asked on a lot of dates, but when the boys found out how smart she was, they didn't call back. She wanted to meet someone who cared about her, not her looks.

Luke had a fabulous time at the softball game—it felt really good to take a break from his constant studying and lighten up for a bit. In fact, from that point on he decided it would be okay to make time for one distracting woman.

And distract him she did. After several more softball games and beers out with the gang afterwards, he soon got around to asking her out for an official date. She told him it was about time and the two quickly became inseparable. After three or four months, he realized he had fallen hopelessly in love with her and couldn't stand to be apart from her. Within a year he had asked her to marry him, and she accepted.

***

Beside him, Kim murmured in her sleep, dissolving the pleasant memory. Luke sighed. It was one o'clock and he was wide awake. The sinking moon still shone brightly enough through the window to illuminate Kim. He looked absently at the shadow lines cast by the windowpane slats, crisscrossing the white bedspread. The rectangular shadows twisted and arced, forming a three-dimensional tableau as they hugged the curves of Kim's body. He lay there transfixed, admiring how the gridwork pattern distorted rhythmically with her breathing. Then he noticed a distinct rippling effect on Kim's belly. He reached out and put his hand on her stomach, ever so gently, so as not to wake her. He smiled when he felt movement under his hand.

"Can't sleep, Abi?" Luke whispered, drawing his face near to his hand. "Me neither." Abi became still. "You okay in there? I can't wait to see you." Words and melody from the song "I Can Only Imagine" flowed through his mind. Kim had taken to singing it recently, as the day of Abi's birth drew closer. Movement tickled his hand. He smiled and kissed Kim's belly. Tears welled up, blurring his vision, and the shadows danced out of focus. He couldn't tell whether he was happy or sad, whether they were tears of joy for Kim and Abi, or tears of pain for himself. Again he felt Abi move beneath his hand. "Are you scared, little one?" He paused for a second. "I am."

CHAPTER SIXTEEN

"CNN just called it!" screamed one of his younger campaign volunteers—the pretty blond one. She had on a tight pullover and her boobs bobbed up and down as she jumped for joy. He had nicknamed her Perky. Her real name was Kristen or Kiersten, something like that.

Senator Russell Pierce looked away from her and settled his large frame back into the chair at his makeshift desk. He was tucked away in the little alcove to go over his acceptance speech. He heaved a big sigh of relief and gazed about the large room in Founders Hall that served as his campaign headquarters. He loved the heavy marble overtones of the place—the rich, solemn atmosphere always photographed well. His staffers scurried about, all with one eye on the multiple video monitors tuned to all the major stations. Operators manned a bank of phones on the other side of the room. The place had gotten very noisy as the celebrations began. Several of his closest advisors came by and high-fived him or shook his hand as they gushed congratulatory statements. He had done it—reelection to the US Senate for a fourth term.

He looked around for his wife. She should be here with him, he thought. Where is she? She needed to be by his side when he gave his statement to the press, which would be shortly.

It was only eleven o'clock. Pierce still had a long night in front of him. He didn't mind—in fact, he relished it. He felt re-energized tonight, more like someone in his thirties than someone who had recently celebrated his sixtieth birthday. *Nothing like a big win in a national election to rejuvenate a man.*

His party had a chance to regain control of the Senate after it had languished in Republican hands for twelve long years. His friend in Ohio, Jim Fox, had a tough battle to unseat the Republican incumbent. He'd have to call him later to wish him well.

"NBC and CBS have called it too!" Perky screamed again, her voice growing hoarse. Pierce shook his head. No two ways about it, he liked her unbridled enthusiasm. And she wasn't too hard on the eyes, either. He always told her she seemed like a smart girl and if she played her cards right, she could go far. No time for that now.

Pierce had to admit his campaign strategist, McGrory, had nailed this one several years ago. *Give credit where credit is due.* Forget tax the rich and universal health care—those were old stick-in-the-mud issues from your daddy's Democrats. The sexy issue of the day was the environment. And just made to order was the threat of global warming. No, strike that—the *crisis* of global warming.

In his thirty years in politics, Pierce had never seen an issue attain such passion and true sex appeal in so short a time. He'd have to remember to thank Al Gore personally for whipping this thing up to a fever pitch. But it was more than that; sometimes you just needed perfect timing—and the planets really had aligned themselves big-time on this one.

Global warming was a godsend to his flagging career, the answer to his prayers. Truth be told, he didn't even put much stock in the whole thing. Too many scientists with their high-tech interstitial glacier measurements, carbon footprints, what have you. You didn't know who to trust. You could always find an egghead somewhere willing to pontificate about anything—coming down on either side of any issue. He didn't care much for the damned tree-huggers either, with their righteous, holier-than-thou attitudes. The only tree he cared about getting hugged was the big woody between his legs. He chuckled out loud.

But polls he trusted, and they were very clear on this: people cared passionately about the environment. Pierce sighed. He missed the good ol' days, when things were simpler and he had a better grasp of them. Sex sells and money talks—these were the basics he understood. Today, it was green all the way. Who'da thunk it?

Well, just because he had missed the fuckin' tuna boat on this one didn't mean he couldn't capitalize on it. Adapt or perish. Survival of the fittest. That was cool, in vogue eco-jargon, wasn't it? And it was so easy—like taking candy, or whatever they fed them nowadays, from a baby. Down with big oil; up with home-grown corn and ethanol production. Who could possibly be against mom, apple pie, baseball, and a Toyota Synergy drive?

A year and a half ago, at his campaign manager's urging, he had fired up the Pierce Eco-tour, crisscrossing the commonwealth in his hybrid drive, ethanol-burning green bus. Placards with slo-gans like *Pierce is Fierce for the Environment* and *Green Peace for Green Pierce* adorned its sides. Simple, but highly effective. Build a green stadium and they will come!

And come they did. Voters flocked to him, donations poured in, and he became the darling of the media. Russ was a quick study and he easily assimilated the eco-lingo, the buzz words and catchphrases designed for news sound bites. Passion was also easy to fake—rather, to project. He simply translated his passion for re-election to Mother Earth and it was a done deal. Anyone listening to him speak on the environment would swear he recycled his very tears for the sake of water conservation for the beleaguered planet.

Bob Kingman, his senior staffer, interrupted his reflections. "Senator, CNN will take a statement in ten minutes." Kingman adjusted his earpiece for a moment. "Wolf Blitzer is standing by."

Russ Pierce smiled, stood up, and immediately doubled over as a sharp pain shot through his upper abdomen—or was it his chest? He put his hand on the chair to steady himself and had trouble catching his breath. What the hell was that? The room spun, his legs wobbled. Perspiration beaded up on his forehead and waves of nausea coursed through him.

"Senator, are you okay?" Kingman asked, voice heavy with concern as he grasped Pierce's arm to support him. Perky was also quickly by his side, looking stricken.

"I don't feel so good, Bob. Here, let me sit down." Pierce collapsed back into his easy chair and labored to catch his breath. "Get me some Maalox," he gasped. Several staffers scurried away.

After several minutes, the intense pain seemed to subside, and he could breathe more normally. "How much time to CNN?"

"Five minutes, sir. Maybe we should cancel—er, tell them you're sick."

"Are you crazy?" Pierce shot back. He massaged his chest and belly, hoping to erase some of the pain. "Just arrange it so I can do it sitting down. I'll be fine." A horrible thought scared the bejesus out of him. *Could I be having a heart attack?* If this *was* a damned heart attack, he'd be furious. *Not now. Not when my time has finally come.* Probably just the stomach flu or too much of that cheese fondue he had gorged on earlier.

Moments later the CNN camera crew descended upon him. They fluffed his hair, powdered his face, and stuck an earpiece in his ear. They told him Mr. Blitzer would be on in sixty seconds and trained the camera and bright lights on him. Pierce put on his best smile and tried to appear thoughtful as he waited for the reporter. There he was now. Pierce listened and then responded, "Why thank you, Wolf. That's mighty nice of you."

Before Wolf could get through his first question of the evening, pain slammed into Pierce's upper abdomen again, taking his breath away and forcing him to gasp and grimace and clutch helplessly at his midsection on national TV. His vision swam in and out of focus and he watched Perky's pretty face distort grotesquely. Soon his vision dimmed and he saw nothing but blackness.

CHAPTER SEVENTEEN

Luke awoke with a start and looked at the dresser clock—2:30 a.m. A persistent thought, or perhaps a feeling, ricocheted around inside his skull. He sat up in bed, his mind shedding sleep like Colby shaking off water after a dip in the creek. He had been dreaming he was on his honeymoon on the Big Island of Hawaii. Except the dream included being buried alive in a lava flow from Kilauea. The frightening volcanic scene was fading quickly, but the sensation of intense heat radiating from the molten rock stuck with him. Something about the heat bothered him.

He struggled to wake up more and let his intuition guide him.

His mind kept getting drawn back to the malignant hyperthermia case. He replayed the part where he had started the patient's IV and touched her arm. She hadn't felt that hot. Her arm hadn't felt blazing to his touch.

But the digital thermometer had read 105 degrees—he had seen it with his own eyes. And the blood gas pH came back 7.09. And to top it all off, she was dead—there was no denying that. So, what was he missing here? Something was still bugging him big-time. And why did it seem that Katz wanted to get rid of him?

Numbers don't lie, do they?

Could he have been mistaken about her arm? He re-visualized starting her IV. He still couldn't recall her arm being hot. A sudden flash of insight made him jump out of bed. Just how *did* Katz know all the dantrolene dosages so perfectly and the MH protocol so well? *Numbers don't lie, but people sure do.* Luke started to put on his clothes.

Kim awakened and said in a voice thick with sleep, "What's wrong?"

"I gotta go to the hospital."

"Huh?"

"I have to go to the hospital." Luke continued to struggle with his pants in the dimly lit room.

"That's supposed to be my line, sweetie," Kim said, more awake now. She propped herself up on her elbows. "Hey, you're not on call."

"I know, I know."

"I didn't hear any phone or beeper, anyway. Everything okay?"

"Yes, everything's fine. There's just something I gotta do. Go back to sleep. I won't be long." He stopped and manufactured a big smile. "I'll have my cell if you need me. Love ya." He bent down and kissed her, then made a quick exit.

Luke headed west down the empty, moonlit stretch of Route 39. Swatara Regional came into view in a few minutes.

Focused on completing his mission as quickly as possible, Luke entered the hospital through the back doors using his ID swipe card and headed to the second floor OR complex. He hoped there were no cases tonight—he didn't feel like explaining his presence to anyone. He went into the empty locker room, pulled on a pair of scrubs, and headed into the OR. The door to the nurses' lounge was shut, probably meaning they were asleep. Good. Luke put on a cap and mask and headed for OR #7.

He flipped on the lights and looked around. The place was cleaned up, all spic-and-span, with no traces of the tragic life or death struggle that had taken place less than eight hours previous. It was all ready to be used again in the morning for the next patient. Ignorance is bliss, as they say.

He walked over to the sharps container and held his breath as he looked in. Had they dumped it in their cleaning frenzy?

Usually the containers lasted a week or so before they got full enough to discard... Bingo! The container was still half full of syringes, needles, IVs, ampules, and various other trash. Luke hesitated. Sticking your hand into one of these would be as dumb as sticking your hand into a snake pit.

Luke grabbed a towel from the anesthesia cart and spread it on the floor. He gingerly dumped some of the contents of the sharps container onto it, hoping to find what he was looking for. There, toward one side—he was pretty sure that was the IV needle he had used earlier to start Mimi's second IV. The plastic cannula stayed in the patient, whereas the metal needle assembly was discarded into the sharps container. He was able to recognize his needle for two reasons—not many people used the older angio catheters like those he'd used at Penn, and even fewer 14-gauge IVs were started.

He picked up the needle and checked to see if its hub was full of blood—it was. Since it was a large-bore needle, the hub actually contained a cc or so of blood and some of it may not have clotted yet. Luke was counting on this; he needed several microliters of liquid blood.

He picked up the towel carefully and deposited the rest of the sharps back into the container and returned it to its place before hitting the lights and making his way to one of the open heart rooms. Here, they had one of the machines he was looking for: a rapid blood gas analyzer. He hoped he was not too late and that enough liquid blood remained in the hub to allow the machine to run.

The little machine hummed to life and went through its warm-up cycle. Luke put the probe in and watched as a small quantity of blood got sucked up the metal probe. Ten seconds later he had a reading: pH 7.05. "Wow," he muttered. He knew the $pCO2$ and $pO2$ readings would be unreliable at this point, but the pH should remain fairly stable. He paused for a second to let the number sink in.

So, she really *was* acidotic. Katz had been right all along and was playing it by the book. In the confusion of the resuscitation, Luke must've been wrong about whether her skin was burning up or not. Now he felt really foolish and wanted to get the hell out of there. Maybe he just felt guilty about not being able to turn the lady around and couldn't accept that someone had died in spite of his best efforts. He knew he was clutching at straws to blame something or someone else.

Luke changed back into street clothes and headed toward the stairwell at the end of the hall. He stopped in his tracks when he saw the light on in Katz's office, midway between himself and the stairwell. *Shit!* He listened carefully and thought he could make out Katz's voice talking on the phone. *With any luck, he's preoccupied,* Luke thought. He walked swiftly and silently toward the exit, passing by the half-open door.

"Dr. Daulton," Katz called out from the office.

Shit. Luke froze and said nothing.

"Is that you?"

Luke heard a phone being hung up and the squeak of Katz's chair. Moments later, Dr. Katz was at the doorway.

"What are you doing here at this hour?" Katz asked, his tone more curious than anything, but he was positively staring.

"I, uh, left some stuff I needed in my locker," Luke said, not making eye contact. "I was just leaving." He checked his watch and turned and eyed the exit stairway.

"Oh...I see," Katz said. "Well, as long as you're here, come into my office. I want to have a word with you." Katz stood there, motioning Luke to come in.

Great. Luke entered the office and sat in the same chair that he'd sat in when he got reamed out after that god-awful C-section. *Probably another partnership lecture,* he thought. Or, maybe he'd be told that sneaking around the hospital at night was strictly forbidden.

Katz sat down at his desk, eyed Luke, but said nothing.

Luke became uncomfortable with the silence. "Are you busy tonight?" Luke asked.

"Naw, the OR's dead." Katz searched his pockets, presumably for a cigarette, but came up empty. "Listen Luke," he continued, "I just wanted to thank you for your help this evening. You didn't have to stick around and get involved in that mess, but you did. I'm sorry it didn't turn out better, but I wanted to let you know that your help didn't go unnoticed."

Luke wasn't expecting a thank you, especially considering the lady had died. He looked up and met Katz's eyes, trying to gauge his sincerity. Satisfied that he was telling the truth, Luke said, "Hey, no problem. I'm here to help people." For the second time that night, Luke thought that maybe he had been wrong about Katz, maybe they had just gotten off on the wrong foot after that OB fiasco.

"Have you ever seen a case of malignant hyperthermia?" Katz asked.

"No," Luke replied. "I did a report on it once as a resident."

"What'd you think?"

"Well, it's funny. I always thought the patient would seem hotter, especially with a 105 degree temp."

"We did pack her in ice," Katz said.

"Right," Luke answered without much conviction.

Katz stood up, apparently signaling an end to the conversation. "Luke, I know it's late. Why don't you head home to that pretty wife of yours."

"Yeah, good idea." Luke rose. "I appreciate your words."

Katz walked over to the door and held it open for Luke. "I have one more thing to say to you—a piece of advice, if you will."

Luke paused to look at Katz, some of his initial wariness returning.

"Be careful of Rob Gentry. He's not your friend." Katz shook his head and a pained look crossed his face. "I don't know what he said to you, but he said some pretty damning things to me about you, behind your back."

Luke was stunned by this and didn't know how to react. Could that really be true? Before he could respond, Katz continued.

"Did you know Gentry is cheating on his wife?"

"I've heard some rumors," Luke said softly. He thought about adding that they had just broken up, but decided not to.

"You'd do best to steer clear of him."

"Okay." Luke glanced around the room, very uncomfortable with the turn in the conversation. He noticed a picture on Katz's desk he didn't think he had ever seen before, next to the Italian vacation shots. It showed a handsome young boy kneeling with his arm draped around some type of retriever dog. He could've sworn that Katz didn't have any children. Perhaps it was a nephew or something? Anxious to change the subject, he asked, "Who's the cute kid on your desk?" He pointed to the picture.

"My son."

"I didn't know you had a child." Luke smiled widely, suddenly hopeful that they might establish some type of connection. But the smile was short lived as he processed Katz's somber tone. Luke looked closer at the picture. The colors were faded and one of the corners was a bit tattered.

"He's dead."

"I'm sorry," Luke stammered. "I didn't know." Sorrow welled up in him for Katz.

"The Lord called him back home fifteen years ago."

CHAPTER EIGHTEEN

Rob jammed down the accelerator and his Porsche's engine roared with anticipation. The car rocketed down Sand Beach Road, tires squealing around the curves. He downshifted aggressively through the turns, ignoring the engine's high-pitched whine as he red lined the tach. The beautiful fall scenery whizzed by. Any other time, it would have been exhilarating, but to him the spectacular colors looked washed out and bland.

He cranked up the volume on his XM radio in an attempt to drown out his thoughts. As he flipped through the stations, he caught snippets of the news. Senator Pierce, who had collapsed last week on national TV when he won re-election, was to undergo gallbladder surgery. There was no heart involvement, so control of the Senate was safe. *Who cares?* he thought.

He settled on easy-listening XM 23, The Blend—something to calm his nerves. Without warning, one of the forbidden songs came on. He would've quickly changed stations, but he was shifting through another sharp turn and didn't have a free hand. Besides, it was such a pretty song; he could probably handle a little of it. Before long, the whole song had played out and an ache that was becoming familiar throbbed in his chest.

Soon the ache became a pain that tore through his heart with a speed and ferocity that astonished him. Tears came to his eyes and blurred his vision, so that he almost drove off the road into a ditch. He slammed his foot onto the brake and pulled the car onto the shoulder, tires skidding noisily on the loose gravel. His heart pounded in his chest.

Catching his breath, Rob released his tight grip on the wheel and stared off into space, thinking again of the evening when he told her he couldn't see her anymore. He absently turned down the volume of the cursed radio, eyes distant as he relived the memory—he couldn't get that look of anguish that had twisted her pretty face out of his mind.

The past two weeks had crawled agonizingly by, each hour creeping languorously into the next as he waited for the awful hurt to subside. Except the pain hadn't diminished—in fact, it had worsened. He had entered a shadow existence where the numbing darkness constantly reached out for him. He felt he had ripped Gwen's heart out that night, and in the process destroyed his own. Would he ever find peace? He thought not—he didn't believe he deserved it. He pulled out his cell phone and stared at it.

The ache he felt in her absence was real, as real as any physical hurt he had ever had. Worse, even, because it went through his whole being, making it hard to breathe, impossible to relax. He was incomplete, torn in half and bleeding, needful. Simple things brought it to the surface, ordinary things—songs, smells, familiar places, anything. He thought of her constantly. He didn't believe he could go an hour without her intruding on his thoughts: What would she think of this? Or that? This would make her smile—one of her big ones. That would bring a tear to her eye.

He realized he had been horribly mistaken the other day, when he thought he was free of Gwen and her power over him. He thought he had emerged from the fog and had used his logic to command his heart to cease and desist. The absence of pain he had felt was a charade, merely a temporary reprieve as the devil repositioned the talons that pierced his heart. Any real or future attempt to remove or resist them would surely shred his heart to useless ribbons. And the rustling of the trees in the park that day, when he had made his plans to end it with her? He now knew that had been the devil's voice whispering in his ear, "Don't think this is over."

His feelings for Gwen surged out of control now, and he felt as if his heart might burst. Tears streamed freely down his face. It took the breaking of his heart for him to finally realize how hopelessly in love with her he really was. He loved her with an intensity he had never experienced before, and perhaps this explained why he had been so slow to recognize it. It was uncharted territory for him—he who'd thought he had known what love was all about.

There was only one thing he could do. Hands shaking, Rob swiped the tears from his eyes and dialed her number, knowing she wouldn't answer. He heard her message and visualized her speaking. At the tone, he spoke. "Hey, it's me. I have to see you— I need to. I'm hurtin' bad, real bad. Please, call me when you can. *Please*."

CHAPTER NINETEEN

Luke shivered a bit as he walked down the driveway to get the Sunday paper. It was a brilliant November morning with high fluffy clouds and a slight breeze that cut through his jeans and t-shirt, but he could tell it was going to be a gorgeous day after the sun had a chance to warm things up. He had to search a little before finding the thick paper tucked under the mugo pine at the end of the driveway. He could make out the headline through the clear plastic wrapper—*Pierce to have Gallbladder Surgery—Senator Suffers Second Attack in 2 Weeks.*

Straightening, paper in hand, Luke surveyed his little patch of front lawn. He wondered if the grass needed one more cut for the season. The weatherman had said the Indian summer was still going strong and it would get up into the mid-sixties today—"So get outside and enjoy it." Luke's dad used to say you could count on one hand how many days you'd get like this for the whole year in central Pennsylvania.

And that memory led to a disturbing thought—this morning was a dead ringer for that awful day in September when his life had changed. Twelve years had done nothing to blunt his recollection—he remembered clearly the video game he had been playing and could still see and hear his dad as if he stood there.

* * *

Immersed in the make-believe world of video games in the third-floor playroom his parents had added to their house, Luke hadn't given much thought to what he would do today. It did look pretty nice out, but first things first—there were castles to conquer and demons to battle. Today he was playing Myth: Soulbiter and the game play was very absorbing for an eighteen-year-old male.

Time slipped by unnoticed until a yell from downstairs interrupted his fantasy world: "Luke! Are you up there?" The voice belonged to his father and he sounded pretty P.O.'d.

"Yeah," Luke called down. He paused the game, irritated that he had to stop so close to beating the level. His dad sure sounded like he was in a yelling mood.

"Get down here! I want to talk to you."

"Coming." Luke sighed, unpaused the game, and saved it. He set down the controller and rose slowly from the chair, reminding himself that he was counting the days until he went to college next fall—although almost a year away seemed like forever.

Luke met his father in the kitchen. His dad was looking out the back window so Luke couldn't see his face to gauge his anger. "Do you know what time it is?" his father asked.

Actually, Luke didn't have a clue, so he answered truthfully. "No."

His dad turned to face him. "Well, I'll tell you, smart boy. It's frigging eleven o'clock and you haven't done a goddamned thing all day!"

Oh, so that's it, Luke thought. The laziness lecture. His dad's cursing didn't actually mean he was extra mad or anything—he'd pretty much fallen into that habit several years back. Luke didn't really feel like having it out with him right now. He'd been perfecting the art of avoiding the old man this past year, biding his time until he made his escape to college.

He used to get sucked into arguing fairly easily. In fact, it seemed his dad actually provoked arguments to serve as twisted training/toughening-up sessions. But Luke eventually figured out that they didn't earn him much other than an occasional grounding. Luke had also perfected the art of sneaker-inspecting—he could describe to you every square inch of the tops of his Adidas Stan Smiths.

He could tell his dad wasn't finished. Best to let him run his course.

"When do you plan on cutting the grass? Can't you see how friggin' long it is?" The big man gestured out the French doors to the backyard and paused to take a breath. He seemed short of breath already.

Luke glanced out to the backyard and had to admit the grass was long. He was also surprised that it was eleven o'clock already. But he had been planning to get to it, just not immediately. Luke played with the tail of his Dallas Cowboys football jersey and re-eyed his Stan Smiths.

"Your mother's gone up to some stupid church thing. One person wasting time around here is bad enough. I'm not going to stand around here and raise a pack of lazy kids, too!"

Luke knew better than to remind his dad he only had *one* kid, not a pack. His dad's face was getting red and you could hear his breathing now. Luke hated when he dragged his mother into it—that meant he *was* getting mad. "Dad, I'll cut it."

"You know what the only thing worse than dumb and lazy is?"

Ow—this one hurt. This one really hurt. Luke could feel his father's stare bore into him. He knew the answer to the question because he had heard it a hundred times before—but it still stung. He also knew better than to say it. That would push his dad over the edge. He just waited, turning his foot on its side, trying to glimpse the cool tread pattern on the sole.

"Well, I'll tell you. Smart and lazy, like you. Now that's a real waste." His dad paused again to breathe, then shook his head and seemed to try to calm himself down a little. "You're a smart kid, Luke. You could really go places. I've spent my whole life trying to teach you stuff about success and how to get ahead and self-reliance." Amazingly, his tone seemed to mellow a bit, the anger replaced by a hint of sadness, almost a defeated quality. "But sometimes I feel like I'm talking to the friggin' wall."

"Dad, I'll get the grass." Luke didn't appreciate the lecture. He hadn't seen eye to eye with his dad for a while, but he hated to disappoint the old man. There was something deep inside him—some stupid, fundamental fiber-of-his-being crap, that longed for his dad's approval. Being an only son was tough.

Luke remembered when he used to look up to his father, wanted to grow up to be just like him. He was impressed by all his business achievements, his knowledge and worldliness and his razor-sharp mind. He had already internalized a lot of the man's teachings. But over these past two years their relationship had deteriorated. Luke didn't know if it was all his own fault—his needing to break away and establish his identity as he made his way out into the world? He didn't think so.

His father's worsening health *had* to be a contributing factor. He wasn't dealing well with the new limitations imposed by his recent heart attack and bypass surgery. It had to be hard on the guy, who had always been a take charge, pedal to the metal kinda guy, someone who prided himself on being in complete control of his destiny. Maybe Luke should cut him some slack. He started to make his way to the garage.

His father stood up and followed him. "Why do you make me yell at you like this, son?" He spread his palms upward, his expression pained. "You know I don't like to. We used to be so close."

Luke didn't relish the heavy emotional turn the conversation seemed to be taking and figured it was time to bail. Recently his father had become more weepy, too, and Luke definitely wasn't comfortable with that. "Dad, I'll get the grass," he said and purposefully avoided eye contact with him, afraid of what he might see. Luke opened the door to the garage.

As he walked into the garage, he realized on some level, he was experiencing a tangled mix of emotions—guilt, love, anger; you name it, he felt it. What a pain in the butt. Killing demons in Myth was a whole heckuva lot easier than this.

Looking around the garage, Luke couldn't help smiling a

little. It was neat and tidy—a place for everything and everything in its place. His dad believed that how you kept your garage was a metaphor for your life. Neat and tidy garage equaled an orderly life. Sloppy garage meant an out-of-control, misfit life. Luke pressed the button to open the overhead door. As it noisily cranked open, he was vaguely aware that he could still hear the sound of the TV inside—kinda loud. He didn't pay it much attention.

Luke grabbed the gas can and sloshed its contents into the mower's gas tank, spilling a little in the process. *Shit,* he thought, *can't even do that right.* When the garage door finally clattered to a stop overhead and things quieted down, he was surprised that he could identify the sounds of Nickelodeon coming from the TV. What was his dad watching that for? *Who cares?* Luke didn't give it another thought as he muscled the heavy rider mower out into the driveway.

The day was spectacular—dazzling bright sunshine, high wispy clouds in a blue sky, and a nice comfortable temperature, to boot. Mix in the smell of gasoline and suddenly the prospect of several hours of lawn mowing didn't seem like such a bad idea. Might even help him clear his head. He sat on the rider and reached for the key. The starter cranked and whined loudly and the engine sputtered but didn't catch. Even out here on the driveway he could still plainly hear the TV—it was ridiculously loud. He went to turn the key again.

Suddenly, Luke sat bolt upright. Something wasn't right—things just didn't add up here. The TV shouldn't be that loud. He went cold and his heart lurched a beat.

He ran back into the garage and into the house. What he saw inside froze him to the core and changed his life in an instant.

His father was sprawled facedown on the family room carpet. The TV was blaring so loud it was hard to think. "Dad!" he screamed.

No response. Luke was momentarily paralyzed as he struggled to process it all. What should he do? What should he do

first? Check his dad? Call for help? Luke didn't really know how
to do CPR—there had only been that basic run-through in health
class. Should he try it?

Then something else grabbed his attention. His dad had the
TV remote clutched in his right hand. Now the TV volume made
perfect, horrific sense—his father had obviously tried to signal
Luke that he needed help. Awful, suffocating questions quickly
came to mind. Why had he, Luke, been so slow to respond to his
dad's desperate cry for help in the first place? How many minutes
had he wasted screwing around with the mower? Was it because
he was mad at his father?

Luke shook free of these paralyzing thoughts even as he
knew these questions would haunt him forever. He clicked the
TV off, silencing the dreadful noise. He knelt down beside his father and searched for any sign of breathing. His father's face was
ashen and had an expression on it Luke was not used to seeing—
fear. There was no sign of movement or breathing. Luke ran for
the phone in the kitchen and dialed 911.

He returned to the family room and started to roll his father
over so that he could do CPR while waiting for the ambulance.
This proved difficult—his dad's massive body was totally inert. It
took him two tries before he finally got the big man on his back.
Luke was now breathing hard.

However, before Luke started CPR, he had one more thing
to do. He grabbed his dad's hand and tried to get the remote out
of it. This part was also hard—the remote was jammed in there
tight. He had to pry his dad's beefy fingers off it, one by one, to
release it. Finally he tossed the remote onto the sofa as if it were
a poisonous snake. No real point in telling anyone about the part
where his dad called for help while his lazy son ignored him. Tears
welled up in his eyes as he started CPR on the big man.

* * *

The side door opened and Colby bolted out and ran up to him,
bumping into his leg.

"You okay?" Kim asked, appearing at the doorway. "I thought you just went out to get the paper. I wasn't sure you were coming back."

"Sorry," Luke said, bending down to pet Colby. "I was just looking around, taking in the gorgeous day. Looks like the grass could use one more cutting, though. I'll take care of it."

CHAPTER TWENTY

The instrument of the devil rang again. Rob Gentry glanced at the number on his cell phone and smiled. Right on time—it was 1:00 pm. She was very reliable.

"Hey-hello," he said, while turning down the volume of his Porsche's radio.

"It's me." Gwen's voice was musical. "I'm just leaving. I'll be on 81 in a few minutes."

His heartbeat quickened. "Great." He could picture her face in his mind and pretended he was staring into her liquid eyes. "I can't believe you called off work, sick! You're crazy, you know."

"I know," she said.

"Certifiably insane."

"Stop it," she said. "You're making me feel guilty."

"I'm surprised you even know the word." They both laughed. "There's only one person I know who's crazier than you—that's me!" She laughed some more; he found the sound adorable. "Where are you?" he asked.

"Crossing the river."

Shit—still a long way. "Hurry! I'm in the parking garage already. Do you know the way?"

"Yeah, I think so."

"Call me if you get lost, okay?"

"Okay, see you soon."

Rob got out of his car, locked the door, then spun around once, almost stumbling on clumsy feet. He laughed out loud—

God, he really did love her, and the feeling was intoxicating. He shot several glances around the Strawberry Square parking garage to see if anyone was staring at the crazy man by the Porsche. He was alone. Still chuckling, he made his way to the main hallway and followed the signs to the Harrisburg Hilton. His feet seemed to barely touch the ground.

The lobby was tastefully decorated with paintings, large potted plants, and an assortment of comfortable-looking leather chairs. Rob plopped down in one and haphazardly flipped through a magazine for a few minutes before tossing it aside and moving over to the bank of elevators. Soon he was on the top floor, gazing out a large window at Harrisburg and the picturesque Susquehanna River. He could make out people walking and biking across the Walnut Street Bridge toward City Island. Just off to the right was the Harvey Taylor Bridge, one of the main thoroughfares to the West Shore and Camp Hill. The far bank of the river was mostly tree-lined; the foliage was past peak, but the colors were still vivid in the soft afternoon sun. His senses always seemed sharper when he knew Gwen approached.

Twenty minutes later, he saw her coming down the hallway from the parking garage, looking trim in a fuzzy yellow sweater, navy-blue slacks, and black high heels. Her long dark hair shone, seeming to flow as she walked gracefully toward him. She'd pushed her sunglasses up onto her hair.

He opened the door leading into the hotel for her. "Staying at the Hilton, madam?" he asked with a phony French accent.

A huge smile lit up her face as she recognized him. She laughed loudly. "No," she said, "I'm here to meet some pervert for lunch." She giggled and put her arm around his waist.

He laughed and started walking, thinking how easy and natural it was to be with her. And yet he was still vaguely uncomfortable, being in public with her. She stood out like a beacon, so they didn't have a prayer of going around unnoticed. And he knew full well he'd never be able to fake this one. No one looking at the two of them would believe for a second they were just having a business lunch, or that they were just friends or coworkers out for a bite to eat. He pulled away from her arm and said, "You look amazing."

"You're looking pretty good yourself," she replied, and wrapped both arms around him in a big hug. She let go of him quickly, but not before he caught her scent; it was intoxicating, as usual.

"This way, madam." He led her along the hallways of the hotel, Gwen's heels clip-clopping loudly on the shiny tile floors or muffled on the carpet, until they came to the Golden Sheaf Restaurant. Rob quickly scanned the small eatery. There were about ten tables and only two were occupied; luckily business was slow at this hour. He didn't see any familiar faces, but still asked the maitre d' if they could have a more private table toward the back.

They sat down and smiled at each other. The waiter, a young man who looked barely twenty, came by and Rob ordered a bottle of Napa Valley Cabernet. Neither said anything for a few moments.

"Thanks so much for agreeing to meet me," Rob said.

"After your sweet phone call, I figured I owed you that much."

"Well, I do appreciate it."

"I'm glad you called," she said.

"Me too."

"Was it really bad for you, like you said—the last two weeks?" she asked.

"Horrible. I thought I would die."

"Come on, be serious."

"No, I am," he said. "I was barely able to survive without you."

She looked away, a faint blush rising on her face. "That's nice of you to say."

"How was it for you?" he asked.

"Rough. But I've been burned by men before. They're not

real reliable. I just figured you were another in a long line of scumbags."

"Ouch. I guess I deserve that."

She nodded.

The waiter came and poured the wine. Rob held his glass out to her and she lifted hers. "We can drink to second chances, then," he said.

"Sounds good." They clinked their glasses together.

Rob took a big drink. The wine tasted especially good. "I promise never to do that again," he said.

"What?" she said softly.

"Break up with you."

She smiled weakly.

"No, I really mean it. I swear to God, I'll never send you away again."

They both sipped their wine, staring at each other.

"You know what? I wish we could do this without all the secrecy," he said. "Wouldn't it be nice to just come and go as we please?"

"Yes, it would. But don't you think that adds to it? Heightens the tension?"

He sighed. "I guess, but it's so limiting. A real pain in the butt."

"For me, it's everything. Without it...I don't know, you'd just be another boring middle-aged man trying to score with a younger chick."

"Thanks a lot," Rob said, laughing.

"You deserved *that*, as well," she said, and joined him in laughter.

Rob suddenly assumed a serious expression. "Hey, who's boring?"

"Don't worry," she said, "I'm kidding—about the boring part, that is. Dull, maybe."

The waiter came back and she ordered a sushi appetizer. Rob grimaced.

"You must try it. It's really very good—you'll like it. Would *I* steer you wrong?" She held his gaze, but her smile had turned playful.

"*You*? Of course not," he said, and chuckled. He had no intention of trying the sushi, though. "You know what they say about girls who like sushi?"

She smiled, tipping her head to one side, and reached out to take his hands. "No. What do they say?"

Normally he would've giggled or broken eye contact at this point. Instead he surprised himself, squeezing her hands and holding her gaze. "They'll eat anything."

She just laughed lightly, and squeezed his hands in return.

A few minutes later, the waiter came back with the appetizer. They continued to hold hands across the table. Rob mumbled thanks, but neither looked up at the waiter. The young man set the food down and left.

She picked up one of the rice-encrusted sushi discs and held it across the table, motioning for him to open his mouth. He obliged her. He had never done this sort of thing, but the sushi was surprisingly good. She fed him some more. He realized the wine must be going to his head and that the business lunch pretense had now gone completely out the window.

Gwen slipped off her shoes and slid her feet up his thighs. One of her stockinged feet found its way into his crotch—surely not by accident. He assumed a puzzled expression, as if to ask, *Do you know where your foot is?* and she wiggled her toes in response. They had gotten good at communicating without words; their new vocabulary consisted of facial expressions, glances, and nods.

"This is nice," she said and sighed. "I told you you'd like the sushi." She smiled broadly.

He returned her smile, but dropped it abruptly. "I just had the weirdest thought," he said. "You'll think bad of me, though."

"No, I won't. Tell me."

"Cindy will be flying home from California tonight, you know."

Gwen recoiled slightly, camouflaging her reaction well with a smile. "I know."

"Sometimes..."

"What?" she coaxed.

"Well, sometimes..." He took another drink of wine. "It just seems that things would be so much simpler if her plane would just crash." He surprised himself for saying it and added quickly, "Is that horrible, or what? Does that make me a monster?"

"Godzilla, I think. But I think I understand." Gwen looked away. "It's sad, really."

Rob shook his head. "Sorry to bring her up. It's just that I feel I can tell you anything, even my deepest, darkest thoughts."

"It's good to be honest," she said, although she was still gazing across the room.

More wine came and he lost count of how many glasses they drank. The rest of the meal was a blur—another hour flew by. This was probably the most enchanting lunch he had ever had. He reached across the table, lifted one of her hands to his lips, and kissed it.

She smiled and looked down. "What was that for?" she asked.

"Just because you're so kissable," he said.

"Save some of those," she said, her voice taking on a husky tone.

He felt the full effect of the wine when they rose to leave—he was light-headed and unsteady on his feet. He left a wad of twenties on the table that would more than cover their bill, and they left the café arm in arm, using each other for support. The waiter told them to have a nice afternoon and sent them on their way with a curious smile.

They made their way down a corridor of rooms. The doors were open to some of them, as housekeeping readied the room for the next occupant. Rob glanced inside one of them, eyes lingering longingly on the bed. When they came to the end of the corridor and ducked into an empty stairwell, he took her into his arms and started to kiss her as soon as the door closed behind them. She murmured and moaned, and kissed him back with equal passion.

"Thanks again for meeting me here," he got out between kisses.

"Sure," she said.

"I love you, you know."

"I know."

They kissed for several more minutes. She pulled back and looked at him, as she slid her hand down the front of his pants and caressed him. He had never been harder. Now it was his turn to moan. All thought vanished from his brain other than the wide-open sensory channel to the only part of his body that counted. Nothing was going to stop this runaway train.

Suddenly he pulled her hand away. She looked at him with surprise, but he took her by the hand and led her back into the hallway. Soon they came upon a housekeeping cart parked outside an open room. The high-pitched voices of two maids arguing in Spanish spilled out into the hall. Rob pulled Gwen into one of the other open rooms across the hall. It was empty. He stuck the *Do Not Disturb* sign on the outer knob and slammed the door shut, then locked it and put on the safety latch. They both giggled uncontrollably. He pushed her against the wall and they began kissing each other.

Shortly, her hand returned to its rightful place in his pants, touching him. Soon she was kneeling down and undoing his belt buckle. He moaned in anticipation. She looked up at him with a mischievous smile. "And you were right about girls and sushi."

The mouth and tongue that he was so fond of kissing were now engaged in other work—indescribable work. His eyes rolled back and he began to pant. She brought both of her hands to bear on him and he groaned in exquisite pleasure, knowing he wouldn't last long. He had never seen a woman enjoy this part as much as she did. Was that possible? Surely he was dreaming. The dream ended explosively, as waves of ecstasy rocked him.

Several moments later, her voice penetrated his stupor. "By the way, I love you, too."

CHAPTER TWENTY-ONE

The pencil-thin beam of light danced about the pitch-black office. Benjamin Harris twitched his head after it, trying to get his bearings in the unfamiliar room. *It's gotta be here somewhere,* his mind, juiced up on adrenaline, repeated for the tenth time in several minutes. Desks, chairs, bookcases, and row after row of squat metal filing cabinets whizzed by at dizzying speed as Ben whipped the beam around. Finally the light came to rest, or at least as still as his shaking hand would allow, on a bulky CRT monitor and a computer standing next to it. "Eureka!" he blurted, and instantly regretted his outburst.

While he pumped his fist in celebration, the penlight squirted out of his hand and dropped to the floor. As soon as his finger left the spring switch, the room was once again immersed in darkness. Ben crouched down and groped around the carpeted floor like a blind man, searching for the penlight. When he found it, he turned the light on and played it on the computer. He noticed the familiar Apple logo and smiled. *A Mac,* he thought. *How nice.*

There wasn't a computer on the planet that was safe from Benjamin, but as a young boy he had cut his teeth on Macs and they remained his first love. It was an older model G5, probably ten years old. *Cheap bastards,* Ben thought, but also marveled that the machine was still in service. He ran his hands over the smooth metal casing. As a boy, Benjamin had shown incredible talent for computers, impressing his father and teachers. After leaving high school early, he had graduated after three years at MIT last spring with a degree in computer science at the ripe old age of twenty.

Ben hit the power button and simultaneously pressed a couple of virtually unknown command keys to silence the start-up jingle. He was on his first covert op and couldn't afford any more extraneous noises or slip-ups like that "Eureka" to alert the bad guys. The old hard drive whirred and squeaked to life and the monitor flickered and came on with the start-up screen. He checked his watch while waiting—4:30 am. He still had about two hours before anyone showed up for work.

He took a big breath. His heart hammered in his ears, but he felt more alive than ever. *This is what it must feel like to be a full-fledged FBI agent, kicking through the door into the unknown beyond.* He had dreamt of this moment ever since he was a teenager. He'd been unbeatable when playing Rogue Assassin or Perfect Dark on his Xbox, something he'd done nonstop.

Ben knew he was a genius at computers—he had understood this from early on. He had parlayed this fact into a job with the coveted Bureau. The FBI always needed highly skilled computer people. So he had signed up and found his niche, working in the Bureau's newly formed Medicare fraud branch. He could've taken a job in the private sector—the insurance industry, for instance—for twice the money, but those jobs didn't have the pizzazz he was looking for. An actuary for John Hancock just didn't have the same ring to it as Special Agent Harris of the FBI. Of course, he wasn't actually a special agent yet; he was still an intern. You had to be twenty-three and go through an extensive training period first, including firearms, before you became a special agent.

Ben looked around the room, which was now dimly lit by the monitor screen. He hoped the faint light wouldn't be too visible through the window. Suddenly, he stopped breathing and tensed, hearing something in the hallway that sounded like footsteps. He listened for several seconds. Nothing further. Just the sound of his heart pounding in his ears, he told himself. *Relax,*

Ben. The Bureau's field manual on covert ops came to mind—Ben had long since memorized all the pertinent manuals—A good field agent must keep their cool at all times. *Be cool, Ben.* Drawing a deep breath, he went back to work, fishing around in his pockets for his flash drive. Where was it? It had to be somewhere.

Ben remembered thinking at first that the whole Medicare billing thing seemed kind of boring—sifting through countless reams of electronic billing records, searching out irregularities. Even the prospect of designing complex, irregular pattern matrix software for huge data arrays was only mildly tempting. However, when his superior threw in the possibility of fieldwork, Benjamin had jumped. It had seemed like a fair trade—they would get his computer skills and he would get his shot at real-life adventure. Plus the stories he could tell couldn't help but impress the babes.

When red flags began appearing in the anesthesia billing records for Swatara Regional Hospital in Hershey, Pennsylvania, Ben pounced on the idea of an inside investigation. At first, his boss had said, "No way, Ben, it's too dangerous." But his pleading finally paid off. He was dispatched complete with Elizabethtown college credentials identifying him as a premed student doing a rotation at the hospital. His mission was simple: gain access to the anesthesia department's billing office, interrogate their computers, and determine if any shenanigans were going on.

Ben had spent several days learning the department's layout and determining the whereabouts of the billing computer. It turned out the computer was not even in the hospital, but in the Medical Arts Building adjacent to the hospital, where the anesthesia billing office was located. By Thursday night, early Friday morning, he had been ready to launch his first field mission—eager, really.

Ben finally found his flash drive in his back pocket and plugged it into the computer's USB port. The tiny drive contained his proprietary virus, which he had dubbed SoftPartner. The virus inserted lines of code deep into the operating system where it would never be found, and essentially deputized the computer. Ben sat back in the chair for a moment and exhaled a sigh of relief. He owned the billing computer now. If he didn't give it regular "all clear" signals, the computer would secretly call for the cavalry and download any and all hard drive activity to the "mothership"—Ben's high-powered computer back at head-quarters.

His buddies at the Bureau made fun of Ben and his active imagination. And of course, they had a field day with SoftPart-ner. "Sure, it's cool code, Ben, but like, you're not being sent to Afghanistan," they would say. Ben usually responded with some-thing like "Never underestimate the enemy" or "A terrorist attack can come from the least likely places." Someday, he vowed, he would show his coworkers, and earn their respect.

SoftPartner beeped like a hound dog catching the scent, bringing him back to the present. His program scanned the hard drive for any levels of limited access, security layers, pass codes, or any encrypted files. Apparently it had already found some. The screen lit up and began flashing *JACKPOT* in huge, colorful letters; a pulsating border mimicking a casino marquee rippled around the edge of the screen. "Hmmm," Ben muttered, "I may have to tone that down a bit." The garish show on the monitor cast flashing lights around the room.

The jackpot screen vanished as quickly as it had come, re-placed by list after list of encrypted files followed by their encryp-tion technique. Ben glanced down the list and smiled to himself. Child's play.

Noting that one of the files was heavily encrypted with mul-tiple algorithms, he concentrated on this one first, following his instinct. After all, what separated a good agent from a mediocre one was instinct. You could train all you wanted, but what hap-pened in the field, sometimes in split seconds, often spelled the difference between mission success or failure. There was just no substitute for boots on the ground.

"Why so secretive?" he murmured as his code-breaker

subroutine sank its teeth into this one. Maybe he was onto an Al Qaeda sleeper cell and this was the dirty bomb file? Or maybe he would uncover schematics for flying a plane into the White House and taking out POTUS? He imagined the beautiful, exotic Mata Hari that he would have to befriend and seduce in order to gain access to the terrorists. Ben smiled again. He didn't think any of these scenarios were very likely, but hey, you couldn't blame a guy for dreaming, right?

SoftPartner beeped and the decrypted file appeared on the screen, revealing several terse email correspondences. As he read them, all notions of Al Qaeda flew from his head. He sat mesmerized and a low whistle escaped his lips. "Holy Mother of God!" he whispered. He really *had* hit the jackpot. This was not boring Medicare billing fraud stuff. This was the real thing—the big leagues. Ben knew protocol dictated he should get on his cell and call this in pronto, but he couldn't resist checking the other files—again following his instinct. Who knew what else he might find?

He jumped as the door flew open behind him. Lights popped on, blinding him. All he could recognize were heavy footsteps thudding through the doorway. Squinting in the blinding light, one hand over his thick glasses, Ben barely managed to hit the abort key with his other hand.

CHAPTER TWENTY-TWO

"Caught you, young man!" a gruff, heavily accented voice shouted. "Don't touch computer!"

Ben whirled in his chair, almost falling off. Though his eyes had not fully adjusted, he peered up at the man: thirty-something—Russian, perhaps—definitely Slavic. "W-what are you doing here?" Benjamin stammered.

"No, the question is, what you are doing here?" Ruskie said sternly. He walked over to stand behind Ben and clamped one hand on his shoulder. With the other hand, he patted down Ben's pockets, finding and confiscating his cell phone.

"I'm Tony Jones, a premed student from E-town," Ben answered, and swallowed. God, his cover sounded lame; he'd have to work on that. And he wished he had completed his firearms training and had a service revolver secreted in a shoulder holster. "Just doing my homework, sir," Ben added weakly. He put on his most innocent smile as he reached for the mouse.

"Don't touch mouse!" Ruskie yelled, increasing the pressure and digging his fingers into Ben's shoulder.

"Ow," Ben said, pulling his hand away from the mouse. He turned and looked at the man, his face now eerily lit by the colors coming from the screen. He could read the hospital name badge dangling from his shirt: *Nikolai Andropov, Hospital Orderly*.

Nikolai's face relaxed, even gave a hint of a smile as he looked at the screen. "Well, well, my boy," Nikolai said. "Looks like you are studying human anatomy."

The stunning nude shot of Pamela Lee Anderson languishing on the beach with the surf foaming about her legs shone forth from the monitor in vibrant 64-bit color. In spite of himself or the precarious situation, Ben suppressed a smile and noted with a touch of pride that SoftPartner was performing admirably.

Nikolai dialed his cell phone and jammed it up to his ear. Seconds later he said, "It's me. We got problem." His eyes darted around the room and his free hand returned to his pocket. "I found this kid here snooping around computer. I came in early and saw funny light bouncing around window." Nikolai paused to listen. "He said he is student doing homework, but I not think so. I do not know how he got through key card lock." Nikolai listened some more while his hand fidgeted with something in his pocket.

Nikolai grunted and shook his head. "He doesn't smell like Fed. No gun. He is probably twenty and looks like big nerd. What you think we should do?"

Ben eyed the mouse. If he could just get his hands on it for ten seconds, he could trigger crisis mode on SoftPartner and send electronic SOSes to multiple law enforcement agencies, including Hershey's finest, the only ones with any real prayer of getting here in time to help him. He inched toward the mouse.

Nikolai was scowling. "Okay, I guess you are right," he said, "but hurry and get here." He paced around in a small arc behind Ben's chair.

Ben advanced his hand until it was about six inches away from the mouse. He glanced up at Nikolai, whose head was bobbing up and down with the phone still glued to one ear. Ben almost had the mouse. Several moments later the Russian stopped pacing and said, "Yeah, okay. I got it."

Just as Ben got his hand on the mouse, Nikolai reached under the desk and disconnected all the cables going to the computer. The screen flickered and went dark and the hard drive whirred down to a stop. The fans stopped as well, leaving only silence.

Shit. The mouse was now useless and SoftPartner had just

been neutralized. What could he do? Without the computer, he was helpless. He wracked his brain, trying to think of alternatives. Maybe he should try to overpower Nikolai before the other guy showed up? Sadly, Ben knew all too well that he had never been able to disable anyone in training—he usually wound up pulling a muscle or hurting his wrist. So he assigned a low probability of success to this option. Maybe he should make a run for it. The guy didn't appear to be armed, although he didn't know what was in the man's pocket. *Orderlies don't usually carry guns, do they?* This option also had a low probability of success, as Ben couldn't outrun many people.

"Who are you and what you doing here?" Nikolai said in a menacing tone, interrupting any further vector analysis of the current predicament.

"I told you," Ben replied. "My name's Tony Jones and I'm an Elizabethtown college premed student doing my senior elective at Swatara Regional."

"Yeah, sure. And I am Saint Nick. What you looking for on computer? Who sent you?" Nikolai's eyes bored into him and sent a shiver down his spine. Ben didn't answer, which seemed to anger the man. In one quick, fluid motion, Nikolai pulled a nasty-looking gizmo out of his pocket and flicked his wrist. With a loud, metallic *pfft* the gizmo came to life, exposing a fearful, serrated blade. He waved it a bit, carving the air in front of Ben for effect.

For the first time, real fear shot through Ben. The switchblade crystallized his thoughts—this was no Medicare billing fraud. He had indeed stumbled onto something big. What he saw on that computer needed to get out. It got worse, though. Whoever planned something like this wouldn't buy his feeble excuse and let him walk out of here.

"I can make you talk," Nikolai said with a cruel smile.

Shit, this thing's going down badly and I've got to do something. Ben's fear amped up exponentially. This wasn't the cool, adrenaline rush of encountering lots of high-level creatures in

Oblivion who were resistant to your magic spells and would likely kill you. This was a sickening, helpless feeling that made his insides feel all squishy and out of control. He felt like he might vomit and have diarrhea at the same time.

"I'll explain everything when your friend gets here," Ben said in as even a tone as he could muster, hoping to calm down Nikolai and buy himself a little time.

Nikolai just grunted.

Ben looked around the room and spied a folded up newspaper in one of the trashcans nearby. He could just make out the outline of a large Sudoku puzzle. A crazy idea blazed across his brain. His eyes returned to the knife. "So, what do we do now?" he asked.

"We wait."

"Do you mind if I do that Sudoku puzzle over there?" Benjamin pointed a quivering finger at the trashcan. Nikolai gazed at the trashcan and managed to look befuddled and irritated at the same time. "They help me relax," Ben added.

Finally Nikolai, who seemed to be preoccupied with thoughts of his own, nodded his assent. Ben retrieved the paper, thought for a couple of moments, then started scribbling numbers in the puzzle grid. Crude, he thought, but the best he could come up with under the circumstances.

Before he could write any more, the door opened and a man walked in. Ben recognized him as one of the anesthesia doctors from the hospital, but couldn't recall his name. He stared at Ben, sending a chill down Ben's spine. "So, this is the bugger who's playing with our computer. You're right, Nikolai. He doesn't look like a Fed, but looks can be deceiving."

He walked over to Ben. "What's this?" he demanded as he snatched the newspaper from Ben's hands. He studied it for a moment, his forehead creased in thought. "What the hell?" He shook his head and tossed it on the desktop.

The doctor turned Ben's chair toward him and leaned down, resting his hands on the arms of the chair so that his face was just inches from Ben's. He enunciated each word in a very serious tone, "Okay son, *who* are you and *what* are you doing here?"

"I'm Tony Jones," Ben said, "and I was trying to hack into your billing computer and zero out my bill." If he could just get them to turn the computer back on... "Look, I'll show you." Ben made a move toward the computer.

Nikolai grabbed both of his shoulders and pinned Ben back in his chair.

Doc stood up. "It's okay, Nikolai." His tone had softened. "I'll turn the computer on."

A surge of hope shot through Ben—perhaps he was buying the bogus bill story. Ben knew he could fake his way through this bill thing and secretly trigger the alarm in the process, if he could just get his hands on the computer. He held his breath as he watched Doc bend down and plug the computer and monitor back in. But Ben noted with horror that Doc didn't plug the cable modem back in. *Shit, he's smarter than I thought.* Ben knew that Soft Partner would regard loss of power as a Priority, Level 2 Caution and this would generate a warning message to the Bureau. However, with no connection to the outside world, the message would not be sent.

Doc powered up the computer, and Ben's heart sank even further. *Damn it!* He had left his flash drive plugged into the USB port on the keyboard—in plain view. It was supposed to be safely tucked away in his pocket.

Doc motioned to Ben. "Okay, Tony," he said, "why don't you show us that bill you're talking about."

Ben turned and reached for the keyboard and mouse, his hands shaking. With his right hand on the mouse, he opened the bill ledger and began scrolling through the outstanding bills. With his left hand, he casually picked up the Ethernet cable and got ready to plug the cable modem back in. Before he could complete this task, Doc slapped him hard across the face, driving him back into his chair.

"Hold on! What's this?" Doc yelled, pointing to the flash drive. "Hold him, Nikolai!"

As Nikolai's hands dug into Ben's shoulders again, Doc pulled up another chair and sat down at the computer. First he began to search the contents of the flash drive. Without taking his eyes off the screen, Doc said, "You don't want to fuck with me, boy!"

Ben knew the flash drive would register as empty—SoftPartner would never allow itself to be captured that easily. Ben's heart sank again. Doc was now initializing the computer, no doubt in preparation to perform a clean hard drive wipe, thereby erasing all contents of the computer. *Shit, this guy knows his computers.* But Ben knew that SoftPartner would most likely survive this maneuver anyway, having a 95% survival quotient depending on the sophistication of the wiping program Doc employed.

Doc plucked the flash drive out of the USB port and studied it carefully. Finally, he stuffed it in his pocket. He picked up the newspaper and re-examined it. "I don't like this." He shook his head. "I don't like it one bit." He thrust the newspaper at Nikolai and said, "Get rid of this." The Russian tucked the paper in his back pocket. Doc thought for a moment longer, then appeared to have made a decision. "I think we all need to go for a little walk. There are some things I want to show our young friend here, at the hospital."

Ben didn't like the sound of this and remained in his seat. "Look," he said, "I'm really sorry about sneaking into your office and using your com—" Before Ben could finish his sentence, Nikolai grasped his arm and yanked him to his feet.

The three headed for the door. Doc put his arm around Ben's shoulder, helping to escort him out of the room.

"Ow, you stuck me with something!" Ben cried out in surprise. He strained to turn his head far enough to see and managed to glimpse a little syringe in Doc's hand. "What did you do?" Ben shrieked. *God, not drugs—please, not drugs.* He tried to wriggle free but the two bigger men gripped him tightly.

"Just a little sedative, Tony—or whatever your real name is," Doc said. "Actually, Tony, you look a little peaked—maybe the flu, or maybe appendicitis is sneaking up on you."

"Good thing we are going to hospital," Nikolai added.

With growing horror, Ben felt increasingly weak and light-headed—the effects of the drug were getting to him already. He knew time was running out. "Look, hold on here," he said. "You're right—my name isn't Tony. I'm Special Agent Benjamin Harris of the FBI."

"You not look so special," Nikolai mocked.

"Agents are on their way right now," Ben added, trying to sound authoritative.

"We believe you, Ben," Nikolai said, and sniggered.

"Do they teach you guys to say that when you're fucked?" Doc asked. "I mean, it seems like they always say that when it's bogus. I'm just not buying it today, Benjamin. Sorry." Doc opened the door. "I'll go get a stretcher, Nikolai. You lock up."

Ben's head spun. Waves of intense nausea swept through him. He sagged on his feet and would've hit the floor, were it not for Nikolai holding him up. Nikolai led him to the doorway, where he paused to toss the newspaper in the trashcan and turn off the lights. Then the orderly half-dragged Ben into the hallway and twisted to lock the door behind them. Doc was coming up the hallway, pushing a stretcher. Ben's vision dimmed and began collapsing inward, like a tunnel. He wanted desperately to save the game here and replay this part—encounter with two drug-wielding hospital personnel—again.

CHAPTER TWENTY-THREE

Life just isn't fair, thought Gwen as she swung her Chevy Tahoe into a parking space in front of the Medical Arts Building at Swatara Regional. It was still dark out—the sun wouldn't be up for another hour. The parking lot was deserted. Gwen let out a big sigh as she shifted the transmission lever into park. What was the point of meeting the man of her dreams now, when he was already married? Not to mention, she was married too. How crazy was that? The only thing she did know for sure was that Rob was perfect for her. She realized that people who didn't believe in love at first sight simply had never experienced it. She figured most people didn't have a clue.

Gwen turned off the ignition, set the parking brake, and allowed her hemmed-in thoughts to run free. She imagined Rob holding her tight and stroking her hair. His hands were large but so gentle, and he knew just where to touch her. He would place one hand on the small of her back as he pressed her to him and the other hand would lose itself deep within her hair and cradle her head as he kissed her. To have someone be so into her sent her over the top.

She had never experienced the pleasure of a man so taken with her. She sighed again and checked her hair and makeup in the rearview mirror. Rob actually listened to her with undivided attention, seeming to hang on her every word. He said he marveled at her intelligence. This was new and exciting to her. He stared at her frequently—not in a freaky, stalker sort of way, but rather in a manner that radiated a mixture of love, desire, and admiration. And his eyes weren't roving all over the place every time some hot chick walked by. He told her he thought she was beautiful, really beautiful.

When he kissed her, she was in heaven. She had kissed many men throughout her dating days, before her husband came along. With most of them, it was so-so, take it or leave it. With some, like her husband, Jim, it was a physically pleasurable thing, like taking a hot shower or enjoying a nice meal. Or at least it used to be. But with Rob, it was much more than that—it was an emotional connection that transcended physical pleasure. She knew that sounded corny, bordering on an Oprah moment, and even though she had trouble describing it, she was very clear about one thing— she longed for more.

She reflected on the state of her own sad marriage. It had died long before she had met Rob. Jim had seemed just right at first—they were high school sweethearts and got married soon after graduation. He had been big man on campus, varsity football and baseball; she had been a cheerleader. They looked good together—he was ruggedly handsome and she was attractive. Everyone said they made a great couple. She would even have sworn she had been in love—but the bottom line was, they got married way too young and then compounded the mistake by having kids immediately.

Jim never wanted to waste time on college, preferring to bring home money right away working at his dad's Chevy dealership. He figured he was in line to take over the business after his dad retired and this would be their meal ticket. Gwen put her goals to go to college on hold while she worked as a billing clerk for the anesthesia department. She also had two children, a boy and a girl, in rapid succession. She longed for a more fulfilling career and some adult interaction. She believed she was an intelligent, sensitive woman who was wasting her talents.

Gwen checked her watch—6:00 a.m. Although the sun hadn't shown any signs of stirring, the eastern sky began to glow expectantly. She checked her cell phone to see if she had missed any calls or messages. She was hoping Rob could make it out of the house and meet her for coffee before work. Although they might have only thirty or forty-five minutes together, it seemed well worth the effort. Gwen shivered in anticipation as she imagined kissing and embracing him. Even his scent drove her crazy.

When the two kids were both in school, Jeff in kindergarten and Ashley in second grade, Gwen had taken some English courses at the local community college, HACC, and loved it. She dreamt of being an English teacher or perhaps a writer. Jim, of course, was very opposed to her going to school. He liked the control of having her stuck at home with the children and taking care of the household. But since Jim would leave early in the morning and work ten- or twelve-hour days at the dealership, he didn't really have much of a say. Many times she would already have the kids in bed when he rolled in at eight or nine in the evening.

Their relationship had actually unraveled quickly, but both were too young to realize it, much less do anything to safeguard the marriage. Jim seemed content to spend all his time at work. He would frequently go out with the other salesman at the dealership. He spoke of liquid lunches, and she knew it was a real good ol' boy's club. He got pretty familiar with some of the secretaries at the dealership and Gwen had had her doubts. But she was too busy holding down a job and trying to run everything at home to do much about it. In retrospect, she figured that Jim had traded the glory days of high school, where he was always popular, for the obscurity of the workplace. It was a lousy trade. He gravitated toward bad boy behavior, probably to reaffirm his masculinity.

But, Gwen didn't want any part of admitting to her family and friends that the perfect couple wasn't so perfect. Or that they had goofed, gotten married way too young and brought two kids into the world only to face a broken home. These were painful admissions better left unspoken. So Gwen soldiered on, figuring this was what married life was all about—the dirty little secret of genteel American society. People just put on good fronts for everyone else, so no one would have to admit their failures.

Gwen had always found solace in books, for which she had a great love, instilled in her by her father. Even though he worked as a mechanic, he loved to read. She recalled snuggling in his strong arms, feeling safe in his lap, hardly minding his scratchy chin as he read her bedtime stories. Although he frequently smelled of oil or grease, she wasn't bothered by it; in fact, she grew fond of these smells. Later on, as a teenager, she was especially drawn to love stories, preferring to lose herself in romantic fantasies and true love stories. She never actually believed they were anything other than stories—and she came to realize early on that characters in the world of make-believe generally enjoyed happier endings than people in real life.

Gwen knew her marriage was officially dead when she discovered indisputable proof that Jim was cheating. He didn't even bother to deny that the used condom she had found in the backseat of his car was his, but instead tried halfheartedly to put the blame on her. If she had done a better job of being a loving wife, he wouldn't have had to look elsewhere. Or if she had taken better care of herself and looked better, he wouldn't have been tempted. He had a ready-made excuse for everything.

Why didn't she just leave him? Gwen had asked herself this question a thousand times. Life was never black and white, though. She wanted to preserve the charade of an intact family for her kids as long as possible. Besides, Jim brought home a paycheck and kept a roof over their heads. And she wanted to get a college education so she had a prayer of supporting them. So she stood by her man.

She glanced at her watch again—6:20. She had to be at work at 7:00, so she knew time was ticking away. *C'mon, lover boy. Where are you?* She debated calling Rob, but she knew this would be foolish. He would call her the minute he was rolling—she had come to see he was very reliable in these matters. Something must've come up.

Gwen looked around the parking lot again and glanced over at the building. She was surprised to see the lights on in the billing office. She was usually the first one in to open up the place. A touch of fear passed through her. Did this have anything to do with her meeting Rob? Then she chuckled and forced herself to relax. This sneaking around stuff always made her a bit paranoid. Probably just the night cleaning crew.

Gwen settled down in her seat and imagined hugging and kissing Rob again. Having him stroke her hair and tell her how beautiful she was always made her feel better. She sat there for several minutes, immersed in her musings, before she sighed and sat up straight. A disturbing thought had brought the pleasant daydream to an abrupt end. Rob would never really leave his wife, would he? Sure, she knew he was smitten with her—you only had to see the way he stared at her with that childish grin plastered all over his face. That much she had no doubt about. He was hopelessly obsessed with her and had entered this out of control, reckless phase. She didn't mind—in fact, she loved having this power over a man. The funny part was, truth be told, she was slightly out of control, too. That lunch at the Golden Sheaf was ample proof of that. This part was new—never before had she fallen so deeply under someone else's spell.

But still, none of this meant he would leave his wife, the mother of his children. Her friends had all warned Gwen that they never do. It wasn't fair, though. Rob belonged to her.

Just then the lights went out in the office. She realized Rob wasn't going to get free this morning. Her thoughts quickly gave way to disappointment. No Rob. Time to go to work.

Not fifty feet away, the door to the Medical Arts Building opened, and out came two men in scrubs wheeling a stretcher between them. She could hear the wheels squeaking on the rough concrete. They were headed to the hospital via a short roofed-in walkway. She craned her neck to get a better view—but then she felt her paranoia return, in spades. This was definitely strange. The cleaning crew didn't push litters around. What was going on?

When she heard moaning from their direction and a muffled, "Noo..." she realized with a start that someone was on that litter. There were no patient rooms in the Medical Arts Building—it was strictly doctor's offices and business offices. This was highly unusual.

More moaning. She huddled down in the front seat, hoping to become invisible. They were coming her way and soon would pass within thirty feet of her. One man had his back to her, so she couldn't make out his face, although there was something about him that looked very familiar. Could it be Dr. Katz, her boss? The other, facing her, seemed to look right at her. A chill went up her spine when she recognized the man. He was a hospital orderly, but she couldn't recall his name. She felt a second chill, much stronger, as she feared she had been seen.

The litter quickly passed by her and vanished behind the opaque side panels of the walkway. Moments later she heard the hospital door slide open, then close, swallowing the squeaky wheels and the moaning.

What should she do? Her instinct said to follow them, but this was *way* too scary. Best not to get involved. Something very unusual was going on and it looked bad. Maybe she should call Rob? Suddenly, surprising herself, Gwen got a burst of courage. Desperate times called for desperate measures, right? She opened her door, hopped out of the vehicle, and quickly slipped her high heels off. She ran silently toward the hospital door where the two men and the litter with the groaning body had disappeared.

CHAPTER TWENTY-FOUR

Nikolai always hated being in the basement of the hospital—it was poorly lit, poorly ventilated, and just plain spooky. It was also uncomfortably warm. In fact, he could feel the temperature rising as he pushed the stretcher down the long, windowless corridor. Katz was at the other end, pulling vigorously. Nikolai started to sweat—he had never really made the transition from the cooler Moscow clime to central Pennsylvania. Or was it just his nerves?

Nikolai figured out where they were going and didn't like it one bit. But he also knew arguing with Katz was a bad idea. For starters, he worked for the guy and Katz paid him generously. Of course, he also supplied Nikolai with the fentanyl he was so fond of—all right, addicted to. But it was more than that. Nikolai didn't like to admit that he was scared of anybody—growing up in the street gangs of Moscow, where violence was the rule, had toughened him up plenty. But Katz was one of those guys you didn't cross—you never knew whether he'd laugh and pound you on the back for some slight offense or just as easily slit your throat.

They passed the huge laundry complex on their left, with its large wheeled laundry carts lined up in the hallway. Several of his aunts and uncles worked there. They were happy to have "real jobs in America." Nikolai could not believe that working in this subterranean sweatshop for meager pay signified success. Never a big fan of honest work himself, Nikolai had been determined to find something better when he arrived in the land of opportunity two years ago. But with no education to speak of, and his only skills being good in a knife fight and a pretty fair marksman with his trusty Makarov 9 mm pistol, he found himself working as a hospital orderly for minimum wage.

As luck would have it, after only six months, opportunity knocked. He had been playing around with his switchblade in the doctors' locker room early one morning, showing it off to one of the nightshift cleaning personnel, when several of the surgeons walked in on him and seemed pretty bent out of shape about the whole thing. But Dr. Katz had arrived just in time to smooth things over. Ever since that day, Katz had taken him under his wing. They established a business relationship of sorts: Katz supplied him with fentanyl and Nikolai pretty much did whatever was asked of him—like dealing with snooping federal agents.

Nikolai could just make out the little sign above the door up ahead: *INCINERATOR*. The door was a substantial metal affair, complete with bolted-on, heavy-duty hinges that extended halfway across the door for reinforcement. A small, thick-glassed window recessed into the upper part was so grimy, its usefulness was doubtful. He could, however, make out a streaky orange glow emanating from behind the door.

Katz opened the door and the noise level increased dramatically, riding out on a rush of hot air to assault them. An unmistakable burnt smell pinched at his nostrils. Katz held the heavy, spring-hinged door open with some effort and motioned Nikolai inward. Nikolai pushed the litter through the door, its wheels bumping over the uneven concrete floor. The kid groaned, barely audible above the incinerator's roar. Nikolai, who had avoided looking at the kid so far, glanced down in time to see him grimace and move slightly. Clearly, whatever Katz had injected him with hadn't killed him.

Katz entered the cramped room and the door slammed shut behind them. The heat and noise level intensified even further. The burnt smell became acrid and the hot air seemed to clog Nikolai's nostrils and burn in his lungs. There was only one bare bulb in a steel wire cage mounted on the ceiling. Although the

bulb was not very bright, the eerie glow from the incinerator il-
luminated the room.

The small room was decidedly messy. The concrete floor
was very dusty and littered with footprints. You could even see
the tracks the small wheels of the stretcher were making. Flat-
tened cardboard boxes of all shapes and sizes were strewn about.
Some had even made it into makeshift piles. A big steel cart with
wheels and a handle, loaded down with more boxes, was parked
against one wall. The litter and the two men barely fit inside the
room. The incinerator was a gargantuan furnace that took up
half the room. A large steel grate covered the opening, but flames
were visible through vertical slits in the grate.

"Open it," Katz yelled above the roar, motioning to the grate.

Nikolai walked over to the grate. The heat was frightening. The grate handle was a spiral of thick metal wire designed
to dissipate the heat. Nikolai grabbed the handle and instantly
snatched his hand back. "Shit—that fucker's hot." Shaking a hand
that still smarted from the burn, he looked around the piles of
junk for a rag or towel to wrap around the handle.

Katz walked up to the door and grabbed the door handle
without any hesitation. Nikolai watched with fascination, marveling that Katz's hand didn't seem to feel the burn. But then bits of
an old conversation came back to him, after Nikolai had walked in
on Katz in his office while he was chanting or praying in some unknown language—definitely not the stuff of Christianity.

* * *

"Sorry, Dr. Katz," Nikolai said that day. "I didn't mean to inter-
rupt you—whatever you were doing."

Katz was kneeling behind his desk with a black cloth draped
around his head, his hands clasped together. Candles burned on the
desk, flickering haphazardly in the air currents. Looking a bit startled, Katz quickly rose, composing himself. He removed the black
head cloth and pocketed it. "No problem. I was just, uh...praying."

Nikolai stood frozen in the doorway, unsure whether to enter or leave. Katz came over and put his hand on Nikolai's shoulder, as a father would to his son, and led him into the room. "Belief is a powerful ally, Nikolai," Katz continued in a kindly tone. "You must master it someday."

"Yes, Dr. Katz."

"Have you heard of the mighty firewalkers of India? Enlightened, spiritual men who can walk a hundred feet across a bed of coals in their bare feet and not get burned?" He swept out one hand to indicate the length of the coals as he said this.

"No," Nikolai conceded.

"Well, it's true—I've seen them. Their strong belief makes them impervious to the flames." Katz paused to study him. "What do you believe in, Nikolai? Tell me."

"Nothing, really," Nikolai replied quickly. However, after noting his boss's scowl of disapproval, Nikolai amended his answer. "Well, I do believe in the gods of money and fentanyl," he said, unable to keep a smirk from sneaking across his face.

Katz's scowl deepened and he dismissed Nikolai's answer with a wave of his hand. "You will remain weak without true belief." But then, as his eyes bored deep into Nikolai's, his tone became deadly serious. "Even the demons believe," he said, enunciating each word with finality, as if he had just shared the very secret of the universe.

Nikolai just nodded, and finally succeeded in putting a serious look on his face. He had heard Katz utter this particular saying before; he knew it was one of his favorites. Nikolai never really believed any of this. What Nikolai did believe was that Katz had been driven insane by the death of his son—Nikolai had heard all the stories but knew better than to openly discuss it. Truly, Dr. Katz was a man of strange beliefs—

* * *

Katz pulled on the handle and the cast iron door creaked open on its massive hinges, wrenching Nikolai back to the present. The interior of the furnace was a large circular affair, perhaps ten feet in diameter. Flames were present only in the center, dissipating to nothing around the outer half. Katz glanced inside, then at the outer housing of the furnace, searching for something. Finding a round control knob behind the door, he dialed it up from LOW to HIGH. Flames now erupted from the entire base of the furnace and the roar became deafening; the air being sucked in made strange noises, almost like howling.

Nikolai was now drenched in sweat—the temperature in the room seemed to have jacked up ten more degrees. Katz stared straight at Nikolai and nodded to the kid, then to the flames. He grabbed the kid under the shoulders. Nikolai latched onto the kid's ankles and the two men hoisted him up off the litter. Nikolai could feel the kid's legs squirm weakly in his hands, and he suffered a moment of indecision. Although he had little conscience when it came to robbing people or beating them up, even killing, if need be, this somehow seemed different. The kid was so young and defenseless.

Katz suddenly became motionless, the boy in his arms, staring at the flames. He stood there transfixed, eyes not really seeing, a strange look—a grimace, even—playing across his face. Maybe he was having second thoughts, after hearing the kid moan and feeling him squirm? He was only a kid, after all—couldn't be more than twenty. Nikolai realized this was probably wishful thinking on his part. Katz didn't really look as if he was hesitating—he looked like he was in a fuckin' trance.

"Dr. Katz, you okay?" Nikolai shouted. No response. Nikolai was breathing heavily, sucking red-hot air into his lungs that singed his air passages on the way down. Stinging sweat dripped into his eyes. The kid was getting heavy. If they were going to do it, they should just hurry the fuck up and do it. The kid was, after all, working with the FBI. "What you are waiting for?" Nikolai yelled.

Something got through to Katz. He ripped the kid from Nikolai's grasp and single-handedly, with almost superhuman strength, tossed the body directly into the center of the roaring furnace. Nikolai couldn't be sure, but he thought he saw the boy's eyes open just as the flames engulfed him. It looked as if he also tried to scream. Nikolai looked away.

Katz's face took on an extraordinary shade of dull red that was no doubt due to the exertion and from being half burnt, as well. He didn't back away from the opening. He was truly a scary sight: veins bulging out in his neck and forehead; face glistening with sweat, bathed in the flickering red-orange light. Dark shadows danced across his face, making him look otherworldly. He reminded Nikolai of a gargoyle standing there, like the ones sculpted on the roofline of the big cathedrals his mother used to take him to visit as a little boy in Leningrad. He remembered staring at those awful statues, wanting to look away but afraid to, lest they fly down and eat him. Nikolai's eyes were drawn back to the fire. He stood there, once again unable to turn his eyes away, watching with horrid fascination as the flames devoured the boy's writhing flesh.

It didn't take long for the flames to complete their work. "C'mon, let's go!" Nikolai yelled in Katz's ear.

Katz stood his ground, the grimace returning to his face. With arms outstretched toward the flames, he cried out in a voice full of anguish, "David, I'm coming. I'm coming, son."

Nikolai grabbed him, but immediately sensed the immovable nature of his body and realized the futility of manhandling him. Nikolai shouted louder, "We must leave—someone will come!"

Finally the glaze evaporated from Katz's eyes and his arms dropped uselessly to his sides. "Let's go," Katz said. "We must leave before we're seen."

CHAPTER TWENTY-FIVE

Gwen turned away in horror from the little window. She slid down against the wall, stomach churning, and began to gag. She couldn't believe they had actually thrown that body into the furnace. Even though she couldn't see clearly through the soot-streaked window, she would've sworn the body had moved slightly. That person had been alive, she was sure. She tried to listen, but couldn't hear anything above the roar of the furnace. Summoning her courage, she stood up and peeked back in. Eerily, after they threw the body in, the two men just stood there, motionless. Then one of them started yelling at the other.

Gwen shuddered and started to breathe again. She had seen quite enough—she needed to get away from these evil men. She ran back down the hallway, almost tripping over her own feet as she looked over her shoulder. She ducked down a side hall to the laundry and quickly hid between two full laundry carts when she heard the incinerator door open. She began shaking all over. The furnace roared momentarily, then the door slammed shut, muffling it. Heavy, determined footsteps echoed off the cement floor. They were heading directly toward her. She held her breath. The two men walked by, not slowing at all.

Ten minutes later, Gwen swiped her card to unlock the billing office door, her hand shaking so badly that it took her several tries. Closing the door behind her, she flipped on the lights and put one hand on the wall to steady herself. She was still trembling badly and her stomach was doing backward somersaults. Inhaling several deep breaths, she attempted to calm herself.

Feeling her heartbeat slow, Gwen turned and surveyed the room. Everything looked perfectly normal, no sign of a struggle. What should she do? Should she call Rob? She knew she should call the police—she could identify the hospital orderly. Could the other really have been Dr. Katz? She sat in the desk chair, eyed the phone, and took several more deep breaths. Then she snatched up the phone and punched in 911.

"Derry Township Police Department. How can I help you?"

Just then the office door opened and in walked Dr. Katz. Startled, Gwen slammed the phone down. Adrenaline raced through her, bringing back the shakes. She couldn't help but stare at him.

"What are you doing here so early, Gwen?" he asked.

"Just trying to get caught up from yesterday. We were so busy." Her voice sounded way too shrill. She manufactured a smile and tried to look relaxed, even though her heart was pounding and her palms felt clammy.

Katz went directly to the billing computer, ignoring her. He hit the power button and frowned. "What the hell!" he blurted. "Did you have any trouble with this blasted computer yesterday?"

"No, Dr. Katz, everything worked fine."

Katz knelt down under the desk. "Damn cleaning people— must've unplugged the damn thing." He grunted as he plugged several cables into the computer. "Don't worry, Gwen, I'll be out of your hair in a minute. I have to hurry and get to the OR." He played around with the computer for a short while longer, then printed something out. Finally he left, and Gwen breathed a sigh of relief.

She sat down in the swivel chair and ran her fingers through her hair. Dr. Katz seemed perfectly normal, obsessed as usual with the number of cases and up-to-the-minute billing informa- tion—he frequently liked to check their daily balance to insure the money was flowing in properly. Not at all like someone who had just committed cold-blooded murder.

Gwen reasoned that if she were wrong about Katz and called the police, she would certainly lose her job. She needed to think this through a bit more. Maybe it would be best to talk to Rob—he'd know what to do. Best also to go about her normal routine, not arouse any suspicion that she had been witness to a horrific murder.

As Gwen mulled over her course of action, her eyes fell on a folded newspaper sticking out of the nearby trashcan—a trashcan that should be empty, if the cleaning crew had done their job. Curious, Gwen fished the paper out and looked at it. It was open to the horoscope page, Word Jumble, and her personal favorite, the daily Sudoku puzzle. Someone had been working on the Sudoku, although they hadn't gotten very far. Gwen was about to toss it back in the can—she didn't have time for this—but something about the puzzle caught her attention. She had never seen such strange numbers in a Sudoku before.

6	-273	4	1	$\sqrt{-1}$	2
50		50		4	$86,400$
2	4	2.71	3	6.02×10^{23}	1
3.14	1		2.71	2	5
8.714	2		6	3×10^{8}	4
	6	1		5	2.71

Hmmm, what the hell was that? Very bizarre! Suddenly a strange premonition shot through her and she wondered if the puzzle was connected somehow to what had transpired that morning. Deciding to take a closer look at it later, she stuffed the newspaper in her purse. Maybe Rob could help her with this, as well.

Time to get down to work. Gwen reached for the computer mouse, but her hand froze in midair, and a chill ran down her spine. The white plastic housing of the mouse was streaked, as if a child had tried to color it with a piece of charcoal.

CHAPTER TWENTY-SIX

Jason Katz unlocked the door to his office and turned on the lights. He closed the door behind him and sat down at his desk, taking several deep breaths. He rubbed his eyes and ran his fingers through his sweaty hair. His soot-stained hands were reminders of the grisly events that morning. He leaned back in his chair and attempted to collect his thoughts.

His grand plan had almost been brought down by that twerp of an FBI agent—or whatever he was. Nikolai had saved the day; he felt his instincts about Nikolai had just been validated. It had been close, though. Bad luck? Katz didn't think so—he actually didn't believe in luck. He knew forces were at play in the universe and a larger battle raged, of which most people were completely unaware.

What bothered him wasn't that a federal agent had shown up on his doorstep, but that he hadn't foreseen this turn of events. Actually, foreseen was a poor choice of words. The truth was, he hadn't even had a glimmer of it. This was unsettling because normally he had a better grasp of situations and events. He was also irritated because the morning had brought back thoughts and feelings he thought he had left buried for good. But the fire, the screams—it all seemed so familiar, and it had stirred up painful memories.

He pulled out his wallet and opened it. There was a single photograph stored there, one he hadn't looked at in a long time. The picture, he noticed for the first time, was showing signs of age. The photograph of a much younger Jason Katz and his wife, Marie, with their only son, a grinning David, standing between them, was fading. The boy was twelve years old in the picture; in fact, they were celebrating his birthday at Hershey Park—he could make out the Comet roller coaster in the background. David looked as handsome as ever. Katz remembered that this picture used to bring tears to his eyes.

Not long after David's birthday came that fateful summer night that had changed everything, so long ago. He squeezed his eyes shut—he didn't believe tears were still possible, but just in case. He remembered the night with a vividness that defied all reason; he could still hear his boy's screams coming from the burning house.

Lord knows, he had tried to save him. The damned firefighters had grabbed him and wouldn't let him go in, but he had thrown them off and went into the inferno anyway. He had gone back into the house to get David, but the wall of flame upstairs had been too intense, the smoke too thick. His memory of being inside the burning house was vague, dulled by the passage of so much time, but he did recall two things vividly: pleading with God, and the expression on his son's face.

He remembered begging God with everything he had to spare his precious boy. He made every promise possible. The irony of it was that he actually believed, not doubting for an instant that God would come to his aid. His faith had never been stronger. Surely, God would listen to him—he had lived a good and righteous life for forty-plus years. He had gone to church regularly, believed in God and his son, Jesus Christ, and forgiveness and redemption. All of that used to make perfect sense in a world blessed by David. And all of that was turned on its head in an instant that summer night.

Katz had failed to reach his boy that night, suffering burns on 30 percent of his body in the process. Katz should've died in the fire, but the cursed firefighters, the very ones who delayed his entry into the burning house, saved him at the last minute. They dragged him out from the second floor where he had collapsed. But the firefighters didn't make it to David in time—he perished in the blaze.

David's body was actually untouched by the flames. He died of a combination of asphyxia and smoke inhalation. When they laid his body out on the dewy grass, his face looked completely angelic, although his expression was one of subtle surprise that to Katz could only, forever, mean, "Where's my dad?"

Katz had knelt on the grass beside his son and pounded the ground, sobbing—ignoring the firefighters' attempts to tend to his burns. His soul had been crushed. God, or rather that wretched creature who called himself all-powerful master of the universe, had just stood by and chosen to do nothing while his boy choked for breath. He cursed God over and over.

After his son's funeral, Katz sank into a deep depression that lasted for years, as he wrestled with God and the fairness of the universe. He saw a myriad of therapists, tried all sorts of antidepressants and tranquilizers, but to no avail. The damage was just too severe—nothing could heal the gaping, ragged hole in his heart where David should've been. His marriage disintegrated. Marie and he could never move beyond the blame game, so she left him. His faith crumbled. He couldn't get past the simple question: What kind of God would let an innocent little boy burn in a fire? A boy whose only fault was that he loved his dog too much. He developed a deep, burning hatred of God.

Another haunting question formed, crueler even than the first. How much precious time did the firefighters waste by dragging his own body out of the blaze? Could they have saved his son if they had passed over him?

One day, years after the fire, when it seemed he could sink no further and his life was a complete shambles, he awoke in what seemed to be a different universe—a parallel universe. His depression had lifted, he was free of its prison—in fact, he was free of everything. Rules bound him no more. Morality no longer applied. His conscience had been vaporized by the flames. He recognized that he was an aberration; he was not following the usual, slow descent into immorality, where one sin begets the next, until one creeps sideways into evil, all the while struggling to remain good. No, this was a phase transformation, like water to ice, where all at once, he awoke a different creature.

The freedom was exhilarating—perhaps, he noted with detachment, this was the only cure for his deep depression. Evil was suddenly natural and easy, and with no conscience to heap on guilt, he found it appealing. But beyond that, there was an unforeseen freebie and he savored the irony of it. Because he had been so steeped in the ways of religion and morality all of his life, he found he could easily pass himself off as a righteous man—a real, live wolf in sheep's clothing.

But again, it went deeper than that. Initially, after the transformation, as he liked to refer to it, Katz had feared for his sanity. But he soon realized his mind was whole and even his belief system was intact. The major players were all the same, he had just switched sides and was now playing for the other team. He gained a new understanding of the expression "Even the demons believe." Katz had received all of this in a vision of his new self.

Furthermore, Katz felt his new team had a good chance of winning the whole ballgame—the complete domination of mankind. Several genies had recently been let out of the bottle; the horses of the apocalypse ran loose and trampled many a soul underfoot. One only had to consider the multiple plagues that had been unleashed upon the earth. First, there was religious intolerance, pitting radical Islam versus Christian and Jew, leading to global terrorism, suicide bombers, and ethnic cleansing. Second, throw in the bloody struggle for oil, the proliferation of nuclear weapons, and the crisis of global warming. The world seemed to be spiraling out of control toward chaos and evil.

Katz also had determined that because the Dark Lord strongly covets the ruin of one so close to God, he also rewards him richly. That is to say, he bestows upon the fallen one powers normally reserved for his minions. The logic behind this was simple. There just wasn't that much celebration in Hell when a bad boy continued to be bad—no surprise there: everyone always knew he was a bad seed and expected the worst. The point being, he didn't fool any of the flock and wasn't a particularly effective tool.

But when a religious man went to Hell, well, then, Hell rocked—now there was real cause for celebration. This man could single-handedly take down dozens of righteous men. So the demons broke out the champagne and howled. Kind of like Hell's version of the prodigal son.

At first, Katz concentrated on his own life and worked on perfecting the art of lying. He remembered chuckling at the saying, "The truth will set you free." Untruer words were never spoken, he reasoned. He came to understand that only when one engages in total deception does one truly understand the absolute liberating nature of falsehood.

Soon he began to reach out to the people around him. He found pleasure in deceiving and taking other people down—in fact, he viewed these as acts of revenge against God. He was well versed in human weaknesses and how best to exploit them. He enjoyed tempting people and watching them struggle with their consciences while he nudged them toward the dark side.

Human faults were plentiful and it was so simple to take advantage of them that it almost seemed too easy, to the point of being unfair. For starters, there were greed and pride—common as dandelions. Plenty of men and women in his immediate vicinity sported huge egos, and these egos required large amounts of ready cash to continually fund their inflated images of themselves. The medical field was a perfect example of this. A doctor's path from idealistic compassion to materialistic obsession was all too often embarrassingly short.

Cultivating drug and alcohol addiction was also child's play. He had written prescriptions for friends for sleeping pills, knowing full well the potential for addiction. The pills would often stop working after a while, leaving the pill-taker in much worse shape. Again, he couldn't help but smile. What passed as a helpful gesture on his part was actually a hefty shove toward the precipice.

But his real trump card was adultery. Forbidden sex and love were as old as the hills, but still hadn't lost any of their power. In fact, one could argue that thanks to TV, Hollywood, and the Internet, adultery was on the upsurge. Katz smiled—this dog could still hunt. He thought back to his introduction of Rob Gentry to Gwen. This little romance was particularly sweet and he was very proud of it, the way a father beams over his son's first bagged buck in deer season. Acting only on instinct at the time, he had sensed the man's troubled marriage and knew Gwen's beauty could serve as the honey. This simple move was paying dividends now in spades as the two careened down the out-of-control adultery highway.

Katz's cell phone rang, jarring him from his thoughts. He recognized the number and frowned. "Hello," he said.

"Hi, it's me. Hey—any word on the timing of this thing?"

"Yes, I just got an email. I told you I'd call—"

"I know, I know. It's just that my schedule is tight and I wanted to free up some time."

Katz rolled his eyes. "It's going to take place Monday night. Do you think you can *make* it?"

"Yes. Who are these people, anyway? Are they really good for that kind of cash?"

So that's what this is really about, Katz thought, *the money.* "You've heard of the vast right-wing conspiracy? Well, I can't tell you anymore than that, now. I'll fill you in on the details later, but, yes, their funds are virtually unlimited."

"Wow. When do we get the money?"

"As soon as the deed is done, it'll be wired to our offshore accounts."

"Good."

Katz paused, debating whether he should mention the federal agent. "Listen, as long as I've got you on the phone, there's something else I need to tell you."

"What?"

"We've had a slight problem," Katz said matter of factly. "Somehow the Feds got wind of something and are sniffing around Swatara Regional."

"*What?*"

Katz noted with displeasure how quickly the voice on the other end became shrill. "Nikolai found one playing with the billing computer this morning."

"Oh, shit! Should we pack up?"

"Relax." Katz glanced down at his soot-streaked hands. "Nikolai and I took care of the problem already."

"Good. Wait a minute. How? What did you and that drugged-up Russian bastard do?"

"Look, there was no other way. And I won't tell Nikolai you called him that." Katz paused. "Don't worry, we left no trace."

"Well, I *am* worried, damn it. If he really was a Fed, don't you think it's possible he called for help? The place could soon be crawling with agents."

"No, we took his cell phone and disconnected the computer."

"Good. He didn't leave any notes, did he?"

"God, you're a piece of work." Katz took a deep breath and forced himself to remain calm. "He did put some strange numbers in a newspaper puzzle, but Nikolai took care of it," Katz said, starting to chuckle. "I think he probably threw it in the incinerator."

"Inciner—oh my God. Don't tell me any more. The less I know, the better. Listen, do you think we should close down anyway and get out of Dodge? We already have a lot of money."

"No. Remember, the mother lode is coming." The mother lode always got through to him. Big egos need big cash. "We've got to hold it together for one more score. Then we can leave the country, vanish into oblivion, and live the rest of our lives like kings."

"I still don't like it." But Katz could tell his resistance was weakening; he was undoubtedly imagining his palace somewhere. "Sounds dangerous. And I still don't trust that Russian thug of yours. What makes you think he won't turn around and double-cross us? We should never have brought him in."

"Look," Katz shot back, "without him, we'd already be in jail. He discovered the Fed today, for God's sake." He took several more deep breaths to keep his irritation in check. "Besides, I need him." Katz didn't add that he also held Nikolai in reserve to be the enforcer if certain partners got cold feet. "Don't go chicken on me. We can wrap this up on Monday."

"All right, all right. What about Daulton? You said he was snooping around last week after Mrs. Hinkle's case. Is he suspicious?"

"I don't think so," Katz lied. Of course, Daulton *was* suspicious—roaming around the hospital in the middle of the night and asking about fevers. "Look, just keep your eye out for the Feds, and I'll worry about Daulton. Hold it together till Monday—can you *do* that?"

"Yeah."

"All right, good." Katz hung up the phone and shook his head. People were so goddamned unreliable. Maybe it had been a mistake to bring him in. Just one more hurdle to get over Monday, and he could leave all this happy horseshit behind. The money would be more than he could spend in several lifetimes.

Katz had to admit he was mildly concerned about Daulton and Gentry. For some reason he couldn't quite put his finger on, he sensed the two of them together were dangerous for him. He opened the desk drawer and pulled out the 9 mm Nikolai had gotten for him. He examined the beautifully engineered pistol, checked to make sure the clip was full, then put it back in his drawer. The gun might prove useful.

Almost time to go to work. He looked at the picture of David one more time. Whenever he weakened or felt a tug of conscience trying to reappear, he would obliterate it in the fiery furnace of his mind. In fact, this was why he carried the snapshot of his dead son around in his wallet. The picture no longer had the power to make him cry. The immense lake of grief that had existed for fifteen years had slowly congealed into a putrefying swamp of bitterness, hatred, and anger.

He needed now to vaporize the stirred-up memories of his past. There was a twinge of pain where there should only be grim resolve. He used the picture as fuel for the furnace—the white-hot oven in his mind, where he continually hardened the steel of his agony and hammered it on the dark anvil of hate until it became transformed into the very sword of evil. He shut his eyes tight. There—almost complete. The boyish screams disappeared, replaced by the whoosh of air rushing through huge bellows, fanning the hungry fire, whipping the flames into a fiendish frenzy. He put the picture back in his wallet and pocketed it.

CHAPTER TWENTY-SEVEN

Friday, November 19, 4:45 p.m.

SoftPartner, version 3.1, came to life. The hard-drive erasure had failed to eradicate the virus, which had successfully replicated itself several thousand times during the process, in order to escape corruption. It was exactly twelve hours following installation and SYSOP Benjamin Harris had failed to enter the dormancy code. Normal programming dictated a twenty-four hour latency period, but three nearly simultaneous events had triggered the early wake-up. The zero-hour internal log contained the following flags:

flag ø, t=ø, installation

flag 1, t=.23 hrs, system loss of power, *LEVEL 2 ALERT

flag 2, t=.24 hrs, loss of internet connection, *LEVEL 3 ALERT

flag 3, t=.31 hrs, system power up

flag 4, t=.35 hrs, hard drive initialization, *LEVEL 3 ALERT

These events were fed through SoftPartner's threat/caution logic matrix. Flagged events 1, 2, or 4 taken individually would have yielded only low-level cautions, but taken together and factoring in their proximity in time, the matrix generated the highest level alarm.

****ALARM LEVEL 5 ALARM ****

Nature: Aggressive maneuvers aimed to neutralize SoftPartner 3.1

A LEVEL 5 alarm required immediate contact with the Bureau. However, there were two obstacles. First, SoftPartner detected that the Macintosh G5 computer on which it resided no longer had an operating system; it was a casualty of the hard-drive erasure. This was not a big problem. SoftPartner was equipped with multiple compressed machine language subroutines, enabling it to perform rudimentary computer functions such as Internet file sharing protocols and telecommunications. The second problem was much more serious—there was no intact link to the Internet; the primary source Ethernet cable was no longer present and the older computer lacked any of the newer broadband networking capabilities like WiFi, EDGE, 3G, or 4G. The virus searched for alternate pathways to the outside world:

Standard telephone line: negative

DSL line: negative

Cable modem: negative

However, SoftPartner did detect an external Bluetooth dongle, which would allow short-range radio frequency communication with Bluetooth-enabled devices. It scanned the area—no compatible devices were functioning in the normal user range of 3.3 meters. The virus boosted the internal signal strength to the max, thereby violating FCC regulations and effectively doubling the range. Still no compatible devices were located.

Next, the virus attempted to utilize the computer's power cord as an auxiliary external antenna and fed a regenerative signal down the two-meter line, further boosting transmitter range. Again, failure code was returned. SoftPartner had exhausted all its options and settled into a repetitive loop mode where it sent out a Bluetooth pinging signal every sixty seconds, intent on establishing some type of communication with the outside world.

CHAPTER TWENTY-EIGHT

"Follow me," Rob Gentry called back over his shoulder. "I know these roads from when I used to run the Chocolate Chase." His well-muscled legs pumped vigorously several times and his sleek racing bike accelerated smoothly, threatening to leave Luke in the dust.

"You're on," Luke yelled. He jammed down on the pedals of his Dick's mountain bike special, determined to show the older man who was boss here. Hershey Park flew by on the left and Wendy's on the right. They proceeded through the light at Hersheypark Drive and up the first hill of Sand Beach Road.

Luke was beginning to breathe hard toward the top of the hill and found himself struggling to match Rob's pace. Nonetheless, he was thrilled to be outside on this gorgeous fall day and finally riding with Rob—they'd been trying to set it up for months. Even though Rob was nearly twenty years Luke's senior, the two had hit it off since their first meeting in September at Kim's initial OB appointment. Only their busy schedules stood in the way of a more substantial friendship.

Luke crested the hill and saw Rob making a right turn about a hundred yards in front. Geez, that bugger was moving! He still felt sure it was only a matter of time before the older man would tire and Luke would be reeling him in.

He turned right onto Kieffer Road, giving it his all, then turned left onto Peffley Road, a choice that quickly led to a serious uphill. Luke shifted down into first gear, stood up on his pedals, and pulled on the handlebars for all he was worth as his bike lumbered up the steep incline. Fifty yards ahead, Rob seemed to glide effortlessly up the hill, then waited for Luke at the top. Luke was breathing hard. *So much for the age advantage,* he thought.

He began to reassess the match-up. He remembered being mildly amused when Rob had first shown up at his apartment all decked out in skintight biker shorts and shirt and sporting clipless pedals. Plus, he had a fancy Cannondale carbon frame bike that was light as a feather and had those ultra skinny tires; the bike actually seemed a bit too insubstantial to be a serious mechanical machine. Luke recalled glibly chalking it up to older doctor with money does new hobby thing. Perhaps he had been wrong.

Luke finally gained the summit. "You should try a road bike, Luke," Rob said, and grinned. "They're fantastic."

"I don't know if I could hack the shorts," Luke said between gasps for breath, then broke into a smile. He was sweating pro-fusely even though it was cool in the shade of the big oaks and pines.

"You'll appreciate this downhill," Rob said, and sped off down Swatara Road. He was hunched forward on his bike in an uncomfortable-looking tuck position.

Luke tried to catch his breath as he downshifted through the gears, accelerating on the flat. He gripped his handlebars tightly and pedaled hard, working his way down into twenty-fourth gear. The road soon dropped off precipitously, revealing a monster hill. He couldn't even see the bottom, due to a sharp curve. He con-tinued to pedal and his bike picked up speed alarmingly fast. The air roared around his ears, louder and louder. He leaned into the curve and hoped he didn't meet any cars or unforeseen obstacles. The sensation was totally exhilarating, yet scary at the same time; he felt the adrenaline rush with the pounding of his heart and the electricity crackling through his brain. One thing was certain—if he survived, he'd be back to this hill.

The road finally leveled out and then veered sharply to the left and went past one of the Milton Hershey homes for orphans. Up ahead, off to the side of the road, Rob had stopped and was leisurely drinking from his water bottle. Luke caught up to him, hopped off his bike, and was happy to stand up straight. His heart was still pounding.

"Glad to see you made it." Rob was all smiles. "Some hill, right?"

"Yeah! Unbelievable! How fast did you go down there?" Luke asked, knowing Rob's bike was tricked out with a speedometer.

"Forty," replied Rob.

"Why didn't you warn me you're a pro biker?"

"I'm not. It's just a hobby." Rob grinned some more. "What do you think of the route so far?"

Luke paused to catch his breath, squirt a drink, and take in his surroundings. Although he wasn't a pushover for scenic overlooks and such, he had to admit the view was striking. To the left, perched on top of a big hill, he recognized the Hotel Hershey with its distinctive twin turrets and flags flying. Swatara Creek was visible in the foreground to the right, meandering within its banks, with a rolling mix of farmland, small housing developments, and wooded sections beyond that. Although the fall foliage had peaked several weeks ago, most of the trees still hadn't shed their leaves and substantial color remained, albeit muted. He could just make out the roofline of Swatara Regional about two miles away. Beyond that, the lowlands stretched out to the Appalachian Ridge, about ten miles distant. The ridge was clearly visible on this crisp autumn day.

Rob was staring up the hill toward the Hotel Hershey. Several hawks floated leisurely in the blue sky, carving out perfect semicircles. Rob's smile had softened into a thoughtful expression.

Luke studied him. "What do you see?"

Rob didn't answer at first, but then slowly turned. "Nothing—just the hotel. You can see it for miles around, you know."

He shook his head and his next comment was garbled, carried away in a sudden breeze.

Luke thought he looked serious, maybe even sad, but had no clue what was bothering him. He took another gulp of water. The silence between them became awkward.

"Oh, I have something for you," Rob said. He pulled a piece of newspaper from a clever pocket in the back of his biker shirt. "I almost forgot."

Luke unfolded the paper. It was a clipping of a Sudoku puzzle. Some of the numbers were filled in. "I'm not very good at these."

"I thought you anesthesiologists were all experts at crossword puzzles and such," Rob said good-naturedly, and laughed.

"Right..." Luke drawled, ignoring him. He studied the paper more closely. "I've never seen numbers like this before. Where'd you get it?"

"Gwen left it for me with a note that said 'Please solve—urgent.'"

"That's weird."

"So, what do you think?" Rob asked. "Any bright ideas?"

"Naw, not really—other than the fact that my wife, Kim, is a freaking genius at this kind of stuff and she loves nothing better than a good puzzle."

"Great. Show it to Kim and get back to me." Rob took off his helmet and ran his fingers through his hair.

"She actually has an appointment to see you Monday."

"Super," Rob replied. He took another drink from his water bottle. "Hey, did you hear the rumor that Senator Pierce is coming in for gallbladder surgery Monday?"

"Yeah," Luke said, "good ol' Pierce is fierce."

"You realize how important his surgery is? I mean, control of the Senate is at stake."

"Yeah, I've heard," Luke said. "For the last two weeks, that's all they've talked about on the news."

"The Dems now have a razor-thin edge, with fifty Democrats, forty-nine Republicans, and one left-leaning Independent."

"Wow, that is close," Luke replied.

"If Pierce doesn't wake up from his surgery or has a fatal complication, then the Democrats lose a seat and it becomes a forty-nine-forty-nine tie. But—and here's where it becomes interesting—in Pennsylvania, the governor gets to appoint his replacement. Naturally, the Republican governor will appoint a Republican senator, giving the majority back to the Republicans. And even if the Independent votes Democratic, the Republican vice president can break any fifty-fifty tie."

"Luckily it's only his gallbladder," Luke offered, trying not to sound too uninterested. He didn't follow his politics that closely. "That's very safe."

"One would think so," Rob said. "When they thought it was his heart, the Republicans were frothing at the mouth."

Luke chuckled. "I think it's more than a rumor, though, about Pierce having his surgery on Monday. I heard Katz mention it yesterday."

"Really." Rob bent over to tighten the straps on his bike shoes. "And, speaking of Katz, how are you two getting along these days? Last I heard, he was riding you pretty hard."

"I'm doing okay." Luke wondered how much he should say. Rob seemed like a pretty easy guy to trust and Luke was drawn to him. But on the other hand, he had to admit that he didn't know that much about the man. "Actually, if you want to know the truth, he told me I was on probation after Seidle's C-section."

Rob's eyebrows rose. "Are you kidding?"

"No. He sounded pretty serious."

"Probation? For saving a patient's life?"

"Yup."

Rob shook his head. "Unbelievable. I told you to watch your step around him, right?"

"Yeah, you did." Luke studied his face, looking for clues. "What did you mean by that?"

Rob turned fully to face him. "Listen, Luke. Let me fill you in on a few things about Katz—I've known him for a long time."

"Okay."

"I knew him before his son died. Did you know about that?"

"I just found out about it last week. Sounded bad."

"Bad's not the word. It was a freak fire at their home—everyone made it out but the boy. The boy went back in—after a dog, I think. Katz was devastated—I mean *devastated*. I've never seen anyone go into a deeper, darker depression faster. He couldn't work, couldn't eat, couldn't sleep—couldn't do anything. It wouldn't have surprised me if he'd killed himself."

"Wow."

"Then one day, he snapped out of it—just like that. But, here's the thing, Luke. Katz used to be the nicest, friendliest guy around—a give-you-the-shirt-off-his-back type. Real religious, too—very active in his church. But something changed big time when he came back to work."

"What do you mean?"

"Well, it took me a while to see it, but it's there, all right. He became a prick—a hard-ass. I think something must've died inside him. He still talked a good game, so most people missed it. But underneath, he became a mean son of a bitch. Like that probation thing with you. Doesn't surprise me in the least."

Luke took another drink.

"You know what's ironic?" Rob asked.

"What?"

"Katz thinks he introduced me to Gwen."

Luke cringed and glanced away.

"He's wrong," Rob said. "I had actually already seen her in the cafeteria and knew from one look that she would be trouble for me. But Katz set up this meeting for me in the business office and, sure enough, Gwen was there. This is gonna sound crazy, but sometimes I think he tried to hook us up on purpose."

"On purpose to do what?"

"To wreck my life, of course."

Luke didn't know what to say. He disagreed strongly with

Rob on this point—Rob was making his own choices here, and if anyone was ruining Rob's life it was Rob, not Jason Katz.

Rob studied Luke for a moment, then said, "I'm thinking of leaving my wife."

Luke was stunned. "Are you crazy?" he blurted. Luke hated the idea of men cheating on their wives—he couldn't imagine cheating on Kim. He especially didn't care for the whole disposable relationship notion that seemed to be sweeping the country. "What about your kids?" Luke asked. He thought Rob was showing a large selfish streak here. Maybe it hadn't been such a great idea to open up to him. This guy had issues.

"I know, I know," Rob said. "It *is* crazy. And it's killing me. But I finally realized I'm in love with Gwen and I can't live without her. I haven't even told Gwen yet. I'm going to tell her Monday."

Luke could hear the anguish in Rob's voice and realized that maybe Rob's whole situation was more complicated than he thought. He also couldn't help being touched by the fact that the man was opening up to him.

Rob continued. "It goes against all my upbringing, all my beliefs and faith. I'm sure I'll go to Hell for it, if there even is one. I'm so mixed up, I don't know what to believe anymore."

Luke didn't know what to say. In a soft voice, he finally said, "I think it's wrong for a lot of reasons. One, there's your kids—what will happen to them? Two, you made a commitment. Stuff like that's supposed to mean something." Rob looked hurt and Luke hesitated, fiddling with his helmet strap. Preaching to Rob didn't feel quite right—after all, everyone had their issues, didn't they? Besides, despite their differences, Luke thought Rob was a decent guy. He tried to soften it up somewhat. "But I don't believe you'll be punished for it. I don't really believe in God. My dad taught me to believe in myself—he taught me this very well."

Rob cracked a thin smile, but clearly, it was a smile full of pain. "This is great," he managed. "The guy with no religion is counseling the guy with the crumbling faith. We make a great

pair, Luke—the blind leading the blind. Is your dad still an unbe-
liever? Sometimes age changes one's perspective."

"He's dead."

Rob grimaced and looked down. "How'd he die?"

"Heart attack—when I was eighteen." It was Luke's turn to
look away. He felt the familiar tangled mix of emotions associ-
ated with his father's death well up in him.

"That must've been very difficult," Rob said.

Luke didn't say anything.

"And it sounds like you still listen to him."

"You could say that."

Rob refocused on the building on the hill. "Luke, don't sell
love short—it's probably *the* most powerful force that drives human beings—stronger than lust or greed or hate." A new intensity lit up his brown eyes. "But beware. Love is also strange—like
a wild animal, easy to misread or underestimate."

Luke quirked one brow in query.

"I'll explain. But you'll have to humor me with this."

"All right," Luke said and took a drink from his water bottle.

"Imagine a full-grown Bengal tiger, reared from a cub in cap-
tivity."

"Okay..." Luke said.

"Without question the tiger's beauty is exquisite and its
fur is soft and cuddly. The tiger's trainer may *believe* that he has
tamed the beast, understands its behavior—he may even go so far
as to say that he has befriended it. But the tiger's mind is never
truly open to him, is it? The trainer may think he is in control,
but this is only an illusion—the tiger may sink his fangs into him
at any time when he least expects it."

Luke thought this was an odd description of love and wasn't
sure it was even directed at him, but he listened intently, nonetheless.

"Or," Rob continued, "there's the quote from the famous
French philosopher, Rousseau. He said—wait, let me get it right:
'Nothing is less in our power than the heart, and far from com-
manding we are forced to obey it.'"

"You've really given this a lot of thought," Luke said.

"Uh-huh," Rob said as he picked up his bike from the ground where he had laid it. He turned to eye Luke one more time. "Don't sell faith short, either," he said. "True belief can really move mountains, as they say. I hope to get mine back someday." He looked a bit wistful. "Both love and faith are more powerful than I think you realize."

"Maybe you're right." Luke wondered about what Rob had said as a sudden breeze came up and stirred the trees on the hill. Someday, he thought, he'd like to discuss the circumstances of his dad's death with Rob—but not yet.

The two men mounted their bikes. In short order, Rob was zooming down the stretch of straight road in front of them as Luke struggled to accelerate. Luke heard Rob's voice, carried back by the wind. "Try to keep up."

CHAPTER TWENTY-NINE

Gwen shut the front door behind her and heaved a big sigh. She tossed her purse and keys on the foyer table and walked through the narrow hallway into the family room. She had just dropped the kids off at her mom's in Enola. She had called her mother up this morning, frantic about a school project she had due tomorrow, and told her how she desperately needed some peace and quiet to work on it. Mom was a lifesaver and agreed to take the kids, last minute. The needing peace and quiet part was true; she had barely slept, the last two nights. She had made up the part about the school project, although she certainly did have a project of sorts, namely her life, to deal with. Thank God Jim wasn't here, either—he had gone into the dealership early to finish up some paperwork, or so he said.

Pacing the worn carpeted floor, Gwen ran one hand through her unwashed hair then gathered it in an elastic band, only to repeat the process a few moments later. What should she do? Thoughts too numerous to focus on and deal with whirled through her mind, making her head hurt. Images of that body being heaved into the furnace haunted her the most. Who was he, anyway? Why did they kill him? She was fairly convinced now that Dr. Katz had been involved. But why—she had no clue. Then, to add to her confusion, other thoughts, strange and compelling, floated into her mind—not at all clear yet, like storm clouds threatening in the distance.

And then there was Rob. She needed to talk to him. She really needed to be held by him. But—and this part made her want to scream—he was busy all weekend doing family things or riding bikes, for God's sake. He'd texted her that he would meet her Monday night at ten o'clock at the hospital, the earliest he could get away. He said he had something important to tell her. Maybe he was going to break it off with her again? Monday night might as well have been next year. She needed him now. Gwen resented the fact that it always seemed to be on his terms—whenever *he* had time, she should drop everything and run to him.

She had left that crazy Sudoku puzzle in Rob's mailbox at work Friday with a brief note. She wondered if he had gotten it. She still believed that the puzzle was linked somehow to the gruesome events Friday morning.

She had to make sense of it all somehow. Time was running out. Jim would be home soon. She stopped pacing for a moment and looked at the La-Z-Boy recliner—*his* chair. He spent more time in that chair than she'd have thought was humanly possible. He would come home and quickly park himself on the recliner and watch the game—it was always "*the* game," as if this one was somehow critical and more important than all the others before it. And of course he watched it on their new flat screen TV that they couldn't really afford. He usually popped a beer—she had come to doubt that it was his first of the day. He probably drank the beer to cover up any beer smell from work.

She noticed that Jeffie's artwork was still on the floor next to his chair, where Jim had tossed it. She recalled the conversation from Friday night:

"Look what Jeffie drew today." She handed him the crayon drawing on construction paper. Jeffie had traced his little hand and made it into a Thanksgiving turkey.

Jim took the paper, not meeting her eyes, and glanced at it so briefly that he couldn't have seen it. "That's nice," he said, tossing the paper aside, his eyes already returning to the TV.

"How was your day?" she persisted.

"Okay."

Gwen bent down and picked up the drawing that Jeffie had been so proud of. Such a cute little turkey. Sadly, she had actually learned how to decipher Jim's responses to her simple question, "How was your day?" "Okay" meant he was tired and didn't want to talk about it. "Pain in the butt" meant someone/something at work had pissed him off and he would soon get around to venting or ranting about it. When he was horny—although this didn't happen as much anymore—his answer was something crude, like "long and hard like my dick." She smiled wryly. And some people thought that romance was dead.

But she didn't dare say any of this. Sarcasm, let alone frank disagreement, would immediately trigger a fight—usually a loud one. She couldn't bear to subject the kids to this anymore. It wasn't that she was scared of him, per se. He had never actually hit her, although if push came to shove, she wouldn't put it past him.

It was funny, though. Early on, she remembered, she would engage in their fights with vigor and even match his yelling. That was when the marriage counted for something and she had some feeling invested in it. There was still some passion and something worth fighting for. Now, it just wasn't worth the effort. He wasn't going to change and she wanted desperately to shield the kids from any more ugly scenes. Better to play the game, keep up appearances, try to pacify Jim, and bide her time until things changed.

Maybe, when the kids were older and she got her bachelor's degree, the time would be ripe to leave him. She relished how she would tell him—calmly, matter of factly, with little emotion. She imagined the scene over and over.

She'd start off with, "How was your day?" as she always did. He'd respond with one of his stupid, brain-dead answers, it didn't matter which one. She'd say, "That's nice. By the way, I'm leaving tomorrow. The kids and I found an apartment in Dillsburg. Here's our new phone number." Just like that—and she'd hand him a slip of paper with the number.

Would he be upset, mad? Would he cry and beg her forgiveness? Would he finally haul off and hit her? Although Gwen couldn't predict what he'd do, she realized, sort of sadly, that she didn't care.

It felt good to replay the scene, though—it made it easier to slog it out in the trenches and carry on. Because the truth was, she wasn't ready to leave Jim. There was no English degree yet—it was still years off. And there was this little, nagging fear of plunging herself and her children into the unknown with no safety net.

Then Rob came along out of the blue and turned her world upside down. In fact, she hadn't realized how bad things were with Jim until she met Rob. He helped her crystallize some of her thoughts and feelings. For the first time in her life, someone actually cared about her thoughts and feelings. How different was that?

Furthermore, she could have discussions with Rob about issues other than football or baseball, or where the cheapest beer was to be found. He even read books, for God's sake, and liked to talk about them. They shared similar tastes in art and music—in fact, pretty much everything. She hadn't realized men like that existed. In a word, he was perfect.

Well, almost perfect. There was one little problem—this wife thing. Gwen didn't even know the woman, but she hated her. Cynthia—what kind of prissy name was that? What was her problem, anyway? Here she had life handed to her on a silver platter—a gorgeous, intelligent, caring guy like Rob—and she couldn't even make it work. She couldn't keep Rob happy. How hard would that be?

Gwen realized she was in love with Rob and that this was no doubt coloring her view of the situation. She was old enough to know that no one was perfect—everyone had their faults or imperfections. But she believed with every fiber of her being that she and Rob were soul mates, they were meant to be—destiny at work and all that.

Now, Gwen had a new scene that she liked to play in her mind. The one where she would welcome Rob into her arms and life. She would practically crush him with a big hug. She would smother any imperfections he had with her love. His imperfections would just make him human, after all. All she needed was one shot at this. This was a no-brainer—a win-win for all involved.

She thought back to their conversation that memorable day at the Hilton last week. What was it he had said to her? About how if his wife's plane went down, how much simpler it would make things. He obviously wished, like her, that his wife were out of the picture. So he'd be free to be with her.

Images of Rob and Jim and Dr. Katz and that poor man on the litter continued to swirl in her mind. But some ideas began to emerge from the chaos. Finally, for the first time in her life, she'd been dealt a hand with some high cards. She had a play to make here. Should she talk to Rob about it? Concoct some sort of lover's plan?

Her pacing had taken her back into the foyer and she reached for her purse. She took out a folded piece of paper. She opened it carefully, smoothing the creases down gingerly, almost reverently, and read the poem again for the hundredth time.

> *Gwen, you weave the softness of my dreams,*
> *Caress the essence of my mind.*
> *Love, from my body to yours streams*
> *By the fiery stars aligned.*
>
> *I long for the day we may be as one.*
> *Time moves slowly and yet it seems,*
> *Our love has scarcely begun.*
> *Gwen, you weave the softness of my dreams.*

She folded the paper and tucked it safely back in her purse. Her tears flowed freely. No one had ever written her a poem like that before. No one had ever written her a poem, period. So sweet, so tender. But she cried all the more when she thought about it. Because she knew, deep down, that Rob simply didn't have it in him to help her execute any plan—he didn't have a mean bone in his body. This was probably why she loved him so much—and this final irony was not lost on her. But dear Rob had never been pushed to her extremity—never had to live in her world of anguish and broken dreams. She'd have to go this one alone.

***

Gwen pulled into the parking lot of the Medical Arts Building adjacent to Swatara Regional. Because it was Sunday, the parking lot was deserted—just what she wanted. She had decided to take a closer look at the billing office when she wasn't so freaked out, searching for clues to the dead man's identity. If she got up enough nerve, she might even revisit the basement of the hospital.

After swiping her key card to gain access to the building, she walked down the hallway toward the elevator, opening her purse to replace her key card. At the bottom of her purse, her cell phone lit up as if it was about to ring. Strangely, it didn't. She pulled it out to take a closer look. The phone was dialing a number—a long-distance number she didn't recognize. That was odd. Had she bumped the phone when she got her card out? But how could she have entered such a long number? The dialing suddenly ceased. She wasn't sure what was going on, but she knew how to stop it. She pushed *END* and the phone went dark.

CHAPTER THIRTY

Kim Daulton maneuvered her Toyota Highlander smartly into a parking space at the Medical Arts Building, eliciting faint squeals from her front tires. She gazed at the attractive brick building of Swatara Regional Hospital. Sometime in the coming week she would be leaving that building with a newborn baby. Not just any baby. She would be cradling dear little Abigail, whom she felt she already knew, in her arms. It seemed strange, yet fearfully wonderful to imagine this—a dream come true. She and Luke would be mother and father, not just husband and wife. Kim practically shivered with anticipation and prayed that the time would pass quickly.

Kim was running about ten minutes late for her appointment because she had paused to let Colby outside before she left. Once outside, she hadn't been able to resist tossing him a ball a couple of times. Now she had to walk as briskly as her bulging belly would allow toward the building, not wanting to show up any later. She shivered a bit and regretted not bringing along her sweater. The weather looked unsettled; the sky was mostly cloud covered with just glimpses of blue. And without the sun, the wind was downright cool—perhaps the Indian summer was finally packing it in. She entered the building lobby and took the elevator up to the fourth floor.

The waiting room was crowded and noisy. Five other women, some obviously pregnant, were already seated about the room. Several had brought toddlers with them. One expectant mother had her hands full—a toddler at her feet and an infant on her lap.

The toddler was amusing itself on the floor with some toys while the infant squirmed in the mother's lap and looked like he'd be crying before long.

When Kim checked in, the receptionist informed her that the schedule was backed up because Dr. Gentry had gotten called away for an emergency C-section. Dr. Seidle was here seeing patients. Kim sighed and took a seat. She kicked herself for not bringing her book. She was reading *Marley and Me*, but had flown out of the house in such a hurry that she'd left it sitting on the kitchen table.

She was also sorry she wouldn't be seeing Rob Gentry today. It had been definitely tough switching to a new OB practice midway through her pregnancy when they had moved to Hershey in September. But Dr. Gentry had come highly recommended and, over the past several visits, she had built up a nice rapport with him. He had a very calm manner about him and made her feel comfortable and relaxed. He also seemed to know what he was doing. She knew this combination was hard to find in a doctor.

She was glad that Luke had gotten to go cycling with Rob on Saturday. Luke could certainly use a friend and, though Rob was somewhat older, the two seemed to share some of the same interests. Although she had to admit, she was a bit surprised when Rob pulled up in his fancy sports car and hopped out in his skintight biker duds.

People are funny, though, Kim thought. *You think you know someone or can categorize them or at least have a general idea about them, and you can be so wrong. It's not really that you're wrong, but you may have completely missed a whole other side of the person.* Rob seemed like such a dear in the office, caring and gentle. She could hardly believe it when Luke told her he was thinking about leaving his wife for another woman. What drove men, or women, for that matter, to stray, she didn't have a clue. Although she had never met Rob's wife, Cynthia, and hadn't heard glowing reports about her, she couldn't help but feel bad for her. She hoped that for their kids' sake they could patch things up. She would pray for them.

Her thoughts turned to her husband. Luke hadn't been himself recently—he was as lovable as usual, but something was clearly troubling him, and Kim was worried. She couldn't tell if it was the new job, the whole baby thing, or what. He was definitely having trouble sleeping, no matter what he said.

Did Luke have a side of him that she was unaware of? She didn't think so. She knew the two of them loved each other deeply and she felt she could trust Luke unconditionally. So why did she sometimes feel he wasn't telling her the full story?

Kim felt it had something to do with his father. As open and honest as Luke was, he had always been somewhat reluctant to talk about his father's death. She understood that Luke had a complicated love/hate relationship with his dad and it had to be tough, having him die at such a young age. She couldn't imagine losing her own father. But she also knew Luke's dad had been pretty hard on Luke and had placed a lot of expectations on him as a boy. As a result, Luke was always driven and had trouble taking it slow and relaxing. Kim helped him on that score, but it was a work in progress.

The infant across the room started crying in earnest and interrupted her thoughts. The mother, looking frazzled, rummaged around in her big purse or bag or whatever you called it; it looked like it could've passed for carry-on luggage. She found a small baggie with Cheerios and offered one to her baby. Kim wondered how she herself would stack up as a mother, or how Luke would do as a father. This whole parenting thing was a huge responsibility. Maybe she was overreacting; maybe it was just the stress of becoming a new father that had Luke on edge.

She clutched her crucifix and said a quiet prayer. She prayed for a healthy baby, a smooth delivery, and the strength to get through any unforeseen difficulties. She also prayed that Luke would receive the comfort he needed. She relied heavily on her faith as she went through life to help her through the tough times.

Kim felt unexpected tears come to her eyes as she thought

that Luke shared no such faith. She hated to become weepy in public—darn hormones. This was the only sticking point in their whole relationship. It wasn't like they never talked about religion. Just last week, she had come home from church, excited. She shared with him a passage from one of the morning's Bible readings; she hadn't given up on applying the art of gentle persuasion to help him overcome his agnosticism. The gist of the reading was that even the demons believe in the spiritual realm. Luke appeared to listen and said he had actually heard this verse before. But then he told her not to pressure him—he said he needed to arrive at this decision himself. She knew his lack of belief had no doubt been shaped by his father. Perhaps the experience of fatherhood would open up a spiritual side of Luke that she knew was buried in there somewhere

Kim glanced at her watch—she'd been sitting here for twenty minutes. God, she wished she had brought her book. Then she remembered the puzzle she had tucked in her purse—that crazy Sudoku puzzle Luke had given to her on Saturday. Ever since she had been a little girl, she always loved a good puzzle. She pulled the newspaper page out and unfolded it and reacquainted herself with the numbers. Again she was struck by an overwhelming sense that someone had put these strange entries in to send a message—it was not merely a botched attempt to solve the Sudoku. She decided to focus on just the inked-in numbers:

$-273/\sqrt{-1}/50/50/86,400/2.71$

$6.02*10^{23}/3.14/2.71/8.714/3*10^{8}/2.71$

Kim was determined to find out just what that message was—this was far more tantalizing than simply solving a difficult Sudoku. And it was a far better way to occupy one's mind, which would otherwise worry about all sorts of things. So Kim welcomed the distraction of the puzzle, but the screaming baby made it hard to concentrate.

Kim realized she probably wouldn't be able to give the puzzle her full attention here at her OB appointment. But, she also knew her brain was capable of multitasking and could work on this in the background while she went about her busy life. She just needed to lay the groundwork and load in the basic building blocks of the puzzle. Her brain would take care of the rest. She felt if she could get a quiet hour or two alone, she could crack this thing.

Just then, a nurse with a chart in her hand came into the waiting room and announced to the crowd, "Mrs. Daulton." She scanned the room with a blank look—clearly she didn't recognize Kim from Adam.

Kim stood up with the Sudoku in one hand, her purse in the other.

"You can come back now," the nurse said and held the door for her.

Kim wound her way through the toddlers to the nurse, careful not to trip on the toys strewn about the floor.

"Dr. Seidle will be seeing you today," the nurse added matter of factly. "Dr. Gentry is tied up doing a Caesarean section."

Kim already knew this and was resigned to the fact that in a busy OB practice there were no guarantees who you would ultimately see. Mark Seidle was okay, but he sure didn't have Rob Gentry's bedside manner. And, she had to admit, he wasn't nearly as easy on the eyes, either. In addition, now that Kim had the Sudoku on her mind, she would've liked to touch base with Rob regarding any background information about the puzzle that might help her solve it. Like for starters, why had he said it was urgent?

The nurse led Kim back to an exam room, where she got on the uncomfortable OB table. She despised the evil-looking metal stirrups, clearly designed by a man, and the stupid crinkly white paper. The nurse took her blood pressure and pulse, jotted the readings down, and asked, "Any problems?" She said it as if she was in a hurry and would really prefer if there weren't any problems at the moment.

"No," Kim said.

"Great," the nurse said, sounding a bit relieved. "Dr. Seidle will be in shortly," she added, already heading for the door.

Kim smiled to herself at the word "shortly." In the medical

realm, that word roughly translated into anywhere from fifteen minutes to an hour. She fetched the newspaper out of her purse and refocused on the Sudoku. Now that she was away from the screaming baby, maybe she could get somewhere. She began to run through several substitution algorithms in her head. Thinking about the Sudoku and her surroundings triggered a moment of déjà vu and she thought back to the square puzzle she had given Luke this past spring. She recalled those numbers easily: *25 63 24 25 49 19 61 19 64 00 !!*

It had taken Luke several days to solve it, but eventually he did. The puzzle was a basic alpha-numeric substitution affair based on the square of the letter's numerical value in the alphabet. The only tricky part was knowing how to split up the sequence to give all perfect squares. Thus, the correct bracketing was: {256} {324} {25} {49} {196} {1} {196} {400}

And the solution was:

$256 = (16)^2 = P$
$324 = (18)^2 = R$
$25 = (5)^2 = E$
$49 = (7)^2 = G$
$196 = (14)^2 = N$
$1 = (1)^2 = A$
$196 = (14)^2 = N$
$400 = (20)^2 = T$

She giggled when she recalled Luke's initial frustration and then his overjoyed reaction. He had been incredibly thrilled—he had hugged her tightly, danced around the apartment with her, and told her over and over how much he loved her.

Twenty minutes later, the door opened and in strode Dr. Seidle with the harried OB nurse. "Hello, Mrs. Daulton." He extended his hand.

"Hi, Dr. Seidle." Kim took his hand and shook it briefly. "Nice to meet you. Call me Kim, please."

"Okay, Kim." He paused for the briefest of moments, giving her the once-over before glancing back at her chart and mumbling to himself, "Breech presentation." Then he looked up at her. "So, I see your C-section is scheduled a week from today with Dr. Gentry."

"Right."

"Any contractions yet?"

"Maybe just a few minor ones."

"Good." Seidle scribbled something in the chart, then closed it. "I don't mind telling you, Kim—that husband of yours saved my bacon the other day. Did he tell you about it?"

"Yes, he did," Kim said evenly. She didn't add that Luke had also told her that he thought Seidle had kind of panicked and that if Rob Gentry hadn't come to the rescue, the patient might've died.

"He can give anesthesia for my sections anytime." Seidle smiled broadly. "Oh, I see you like Sudoku, too."

"Yes, I do." Kim felt oddly embarrassed that he might see the strange numbers, so she quickly stuffed the newspaper back in her purse. "Just something to pass the time."

"I love them. Now, I'll just need to examine your cervix to-day." All of a sudden his beeper went off loudly, making Kim jump. "Damn thing," he said. "If you'll excuse me for a minute."

He turned to the nurse. "Get her ready for an exam, and I'll be right back."

Dr. Seidle reappeared ten minutes later and snapped on a pair of exam gloves like he meant business. He sat down on a little padded stool and squeakily wheeled it into position. "Now, Kim," he said, "just relax and spread those legs."

Kim did as she was told, although the notion of relaxation in the face of cold steel and KY jelly was ridiculous. She hated the thought of yet another man examining her, but what choice did she have? She tried hard to zone out and imagine what Abi's face would look like.

"Hmm," Dr. Seidle murmured from between her legs. "Your cervix is beginning to dilate. I hope you make it to next week."

CHAPTER THIRTY-ONE

Senator Russ Pierce's limo pulled up in front of the white brick-and-mortar façade of the Hotel Hershey. The fortress-like structure was situated on top of a large knoll and surrounded by an army of mature oak, poplar, and sugar maple trees, effectively insulating it from the hustle and bustle of upscale suburbia that was the town of Hershey. *The view from higher up must be spectacular,* he thought, studying the twin turrets flanking the building, their triangular red flags flapping crisply in the November breeze.

Exiting his limo, Pierce and his entourage entered the turn-of-the-century charm and Moroccan architecture of the hotel. Stone archways gave way to high-ceilinged rooms, their walls lined with tapestries and wrought-iron fixtures. The place had a certain denseness to it that modern buildings just couldn't duplicate—even the air felt a bit heavy. The effect was otherworldly and out of time as well, and he felt a bit like royalty.

Fifteen minutes later, Senator Pierce gazed out the window of the presidential suite at overcast skies. He had just showered and was wearing his favorite cashmere robe with the United States Senatorial insignia embroidered on the lapel, and a pair of plush slippers that made walking a little tricky on the carpet's thick pile. The nice stretch of warm weather was finally giving way to cooler, more seasonal temps as a cold front marched across the state, bringing showers with it. Daylight was fading fast and wind whipped the tree branches about. It was downright gloomy

out, Russ decided, though he didn't let it put a damper on his
mood. He felt on top of the world right now.

Just several weeks ago, he had endured a brush with death.
When the intense, stabbing pains had hit, he thought for sure he
was having a massive heart attack, no doubt fatal, that would've
derailed his dreams for good. While lying there on the marble
floor of his campaign headquarters, with frantic staffers scamper-
ing around him and Wolf Blitzer buzzing in his earpiece, he'd had
a weird, out-of-body experience—a vision, or an epiphany. God
was speaking directly to him and what he said was really freaky.
He said he was finally punishing Russ for all of his misdeeds.

Pierce smiled now and shook his head to dispel these
thoughts. Wow, what a scare that had been. No fatal heart attack—in fact, the doctors said he had the heart of a thirty-year-
old. No cancer gnawing away at his insides. Just a run-of-the-mill,
rotten gallbladder. But the best part was, the spiritual revelation,
or whatever the hell it was, had all been a bad dream or hallucination; there was no divine retribution. *Amazing, the thoughts and
fantasies the stressed-out human brain is capable of.*

In fact, his pollsters said this gallbladder attack followed by
successful surgery would probably boost his approval ratings. The
conventional wisdom ran something like this: common medical
issues, so long as they weren't life threatening or immoral, like
drugs, alcohol, or sexually transmitted diseases, tended to hu-
manize politicians and gave people a way to relate to them. So the
surgery was folded into a new PR campaign—the only concession
was that they had scheduled the surgery late at night so the Secret
Service would have an easier job protecting him.

Pierce sipped a glass of wine and checked his watch. The
wine made the waiting easier. He was to have nothing to eat before surgery, but he *was* allowed clear liquids up to three hours
before, and surely wine was a clear liquid. And a few nibbles of
cheese probably didn't count as eating. Besides, rules were meant
for the masses, they didn't apply to him.

He began pacing, wine glass in hand, still gazing out the

window. No rain yet, but he believed he could just make out the peculiar smeared cloud formations over the mountains that signaled distant rain. Again he broke out a wide grin. He hadn't been this happy for a while. He felt on top of his game and in control of his destiny. This little gallbladder nuisance certainly wasn't going to stand in his way. He had waited a long time for his green ship to come in and had too much to live for yet. A simple hour of laparoscopic surgery and he'd be cured. *Let's get-r-done!*

Pierce checked his watch again. It was five o'clock—six hours to go before he had to show up at the hospital. The anticipation was becoming hard to bear. He smiled again—the Viagra was in full force and the jingle "Viva Viagra" played crazily through his brain.

A knock on the ornate wooden double door of the presidential suite made him turn. "Who is it?"

"Jensen," came the clipped military voice of his most trusted Secret Service agent, standing guard at the door. "Kiersten Page to see you, sir. Official business."

Pierce opened the door just far enough to let the young aide enter. She brushed by him and he got a whiff of some exotic scent and almost swooned. He pulled himself together and turned to Jensen. Jensen was a big man, six-three or -four, with an athletic build. Pierce had to look up to meet his eyes. "We'll be going over my post-op recovery speech. We'll need about an hour. Uninterrupted." He fixed Jensen with a stare just to make sure he understood.

"Very good, sir." Jensen patted his shoulder holster. "No one gets through this door." He smiled and added, "Take all the time you need."

Pierce closed the door. He liked Jensen and had come to rely on him heavily in these delicate situations. After all, trust was what this country was founded on, right? And favors—Christmas was just around the corner and he made a mental note to make sure the Jensen family would have a particularly merry one. This would fall into the money-well-spent category.

Pierce turned to feast his eyes on Kiersten—or Perky, to him—the young staffer who had shown such promise during the campaign. She had on a thick white terry robe with *Hershey Spa* emblazoned on it. The large robe seemed to swallow up her tiny body with those nice boobs. She gave him a big smile. "Have I kept you waiting long?" she asked.

"No, not at all," he lied. He was impatient, but didn't want to appear lewd. "Can I pour you a drink?"

"No thanks," she said sweetly.

He set his wine glass on the nightstand. "How was your massage?"

"Very relaxing." She untied the sash to her robe and started to loosen it, slowly, methodically.

This got his full attention and he decided to drop the refined approach and openly stare. God, her every move was fascinating. "You didn't wash the oil off, did you?" he asked, his voice beginning to tremble.

"No, of course not. It's a special Cuban nocha azula blend."

"Cuban? I like Cuban," he mumbled. He stood there, transfixed by her movements. His breathing grew heavier.

"Can you smell the jasmine?" she asked, working one shoulder free. The robe was now halfway off, providing him tantalizing glimpses of her full breasts.

"Yes, jasmine," he said weakly. He was mesmerized by her, but still managed to let out a little gasp when the robe finally flowed to the floor, revealing the tanned, hard body that only a twenty-something can have.

"You told me you like it that way," she said huskily and practically leapt into his arms, knocking him backward onto the king-sized bed.

CHAPTER THIRTY-TWO

There it was again—no mistaking it this time. A nasty little spasm, or ache, deep down in her belly that grabbed her attention. And then it was gone, leaving just as quickly as it had come. Maybe it was nothing. Kim shuffled around on the sofa, wondering if a shift in position might improve things. She snuggled closer to Luke. She didn't need to look at him to know he was asleep—his rhythmic breathing gave it away. *Such a lightweight,* she thought, and smiled. It was almost eleven and they were watching *King of Queens* reruns. Well, she was, anyway—Luke rarely made it past ten-thirty.

Her mind drifted back to earlier times. She had been comfortable with him from the beginning. She wasn't sure she believed in love at first sight, but it had been close, at least for her. Luke, on the other hand, had been a different story. It had taken a while to get through to him.

She was initially drawn to him because of his gentle nature and desire to help people. Well, that wasn't entirely true. She had also been attracted to his beautiful brown eyes, so expressive and kind, and his gorgeous smile. Overall she found him very attractive, even if he had seemed standoffish at first.

She quickly noticed that he was different. Luke had a gift, like she had a gift. She had seen this in action one day in the anesthesia basic research lab, shortly after she had met him.

* * *

Kim had walked up to the lab doorway and stopped to retrieve the latest PET scan data from a manila folder. Luke was sitting across the room at his desk. Immersed in his notebooks, he didn't look up. Before Kim could say anything, a lab tech, carrying a tray loaded with glassware, crossed the lab right in front of Luke. The girl seemed to be in a hurry. As she turned sharply to head for the sink, one of the beakers slid on the tray. In an effort to save the beaker, she quickly tilted the tray but overcorrected and the entire contents went off the other side, countless specimen beakers and flasks crashing to the floor. She cursed several times and stared at the mess on the floor, the empty tray hanging from one hand.

A look of horror and frustration flashed across Luke's face. Kim knew how driven he was to nail this research and she expected him to rant and rave like most med students would have. The tech had stopped to pick up the broken glassware. Kim watched with fascination as Luke went over to her and knelt down. "Don't use your bare hands, Janine," he said. "You'll cut yourself."

"A whole week's worth of experiments," Janine said, and began to cry.

Luke put his hand on her shoulder and fixed her with his brown eyes. "Don't worry—it's not so bad. We can repeat them."

"I'm sorry, Luke. I'm *so* clumsy."

"It's okay. I'll get the broom."

* * *

Luke's gift was to put hurting people at ease, and he reminded Kim of her father in this regard. What she had initially misinterpreted as standoffishness, she quickly realized, was his inner drive—he was obsessed with doing well in school. However, even though he was overworked in med school, trying to get good grades, he sometimes volunteered on weekends in the free clinic in Philadelphia. He had a strong desire to help people; she thought this was an unusual characteristic in a med student—scratch that—in a guy. Kim, too, was drawn to help people and volunteered at her church.

Once she finally got his attention, though, Luke's aloofness vanished. The chemistry between them was undeniable and the two came together naturally and vigorously. They shared everything together and talked endlessly. They especially enjoyed playing board games. Luke even said he liked losing to a girl, which was good because Kim proved to be the better gamer. Luke turned out to be more romantic than she would've thought possible, and their love blossomed rapidly.

That evening in May, when we went to the Accomac Inn to celebrate our one-year anniversary... She smiled, conjuring in her mind the historic colonial inn nestled between flowering dogwoods and azaleas alongside the swiftly flowing Susquehanna River.

* * *

"What are you going to have?" Luke asked that night, looking over his menu. His eyes sparkled and Kim could tell he was excited.

"Probably the chicken marsala or maybe the..." Kim hesitated.

"What?"

"Maybe the lobster," she said, grinning.

"Go ahead, get whatever you want. Tonight's a special evening."

"How about you?"

"Probably the roast duck. Yep, the duck." Luke closed the menu and groped around in his coat pocket. Out came his portable backgammon set, which he handed to her.

"What? You want to play now?" she asked.

"Sure, why not?" Luke picked up the wine list. "These fancy dinners can take forever."

"You're kidding, right?"

"No. Afraid you might lose?" He chuckled, but seemed a bit nervous. "Do you mind setting up the board while I pick out some wine?"

"Wine? Since when do you drink wine?"

"Since tonight. It's our anniversary, remember?"

"Okay, whatever you say." Kim opened the leather case. Mixed in with the brown and black backgammon pieces was a sparkling diamond ring. Kim gasped and almost spilled the whole set on the floor. "W-what's this?" she said, tears coming to her eyes.

Luke, who was now kneeling at her side, took her hand. "Will you marry me?"

* * *

Kim remembered something else from that evening almost five years ago—she'd surprised herself by saying yes. She had once thought that Luke's agnosticism was a deal breaker. Sure, he was a lovely guy and she thoroughly enjoyed his company, but she had never seen herself getting married and raising kids with a guy who didn't have any real spiritual commitment. What Kim hadn't counted on was how deeply and quickly she had fallen in love with Luke; she simply couldn't imagine spending her life without him. So she had said yes, hugged him tightly around the neck, and kissed him. Love conquers all, as they say. She then proceeded to spank him at backgammon.

Besides, deep down, she always thought Luke's personality didn't really fit with his lack of spirituality. He was too caring and concerned about other people—it just didn't add up. Most successful people she knew were pretty wrapped up in themselves. She had gotten hints that the answer might be somehow tied to Luke's past and his father. But on this subject, he was uncharacteristically quiet. She felt as if she didn't have all the pieces to the puzzle. But she vowed to solve this puzzle one day and bring her man to faith.

A stabbing pain wrenched her out of this pleasant daydream and back to her living room. *Shit, that was pretty bad. I can't be in labor yet.* She had just seen Dr. Seidle, and he said everything was fine—although he had mentioned that her cervix was beginning to dilate. Nevertheless, she figured these must be those pre-labor, Braxton Hicks contractions they talked about in prenatal classes. They should just subside.

The credits for *King of Queens* were rolling now on the TV. Colby lifted his head from the rug and eyed her curiously as if to say, *You okay?* She debated whether to wake Luke or not. He would help her get through this—as a support person, he excelled. But he had to work tomorrow and needed his rest, especially if this was just preterm labor. He had been having trouble sleeping recently, which was way out of character for Luke.

He had been having nightmares. Just last week he had awakened her by bolting upright, drenched with sweat, and screaming, "Dad, Dad!" over and over. When she had asked him about it in the morning, he looked away and said he couldn't remember anything. She doubted it. And it wasn't like him not to be completely truthful.

Another lancing pain put an end to her musings and forced a yelp from her lips. Kim was fully awake now and felt herself tensing up. She had thought she would've been spared the whole pain of labor ordeal because of having a scheduled C-section. She hadn't considered her labor starting early.

Finally, the pain subsided. In a flash, she got the whole nastiness of this labor thing that had plagued womankind since time immemorial. It wasn't just the pain, per se. God *knew* that was bad. It was more than that; it was the mind games the intermittent nature of it played on you. The horrible pain would retreat, but all too soon, you started counting the seconds until the next one would strike. This was what could overwhelm even the most stoic, stable minded of people—the relentless promise of future waves of pain.

Even though Kim was only in the early stages of labor, she grasped all this labor lore en bloc in the moments between contractions. Just as Luke had a gift, this was *her* gift—her mind was an ultra-fine tool, well suited for intuiting things. This was why all of her life she had been good at codes, computers, chess, and puzzles.

She also recalled there was a time when she had despised her gift; she had referred to it as the curse. She had been convinced that no guy would want to date a girl who was the fastest multiplier in high school. She remembered going to her father in tears one day. He'd hugged her with his big, hairy arms and told her not to worry—God had given her this gift for a reason and someday she would understand. He kissed her gently on the forehead and told her that the guys would wise up shortly. After all, she was a beautiful young lady and she'd soon have to beat them away with a stick, he had said. She remembered giggling through her tears at this silly image.

Dad proved to be right. By the time she was a computer science major at MIT, she was bombarded with male attention. So Kim eventually came to view her mind as a true gift from God, rather than a curse. Luke, of course, had helped her on this score as well. He constantly told her he loved her because of her mind, not in spite of it. Plus, it didn't hurt that he told her often how pretty she was and that he found her to be the sexiest creature alive.

She also knew it was time to wake Sleeping Beauty up.

"Luke, it's time," she said, even as the sweat beaded on her forehead. He groaned in response. She reached over and stroked his arm. "Honey, I'm having contractions."

The word contractions seemed to get through to him. He opened his eyes wide and shook his head. "Contractions?"

"Yeah, about five minutes apart."

"Shit, for real?" He looked at her with a mixture of sleepiness, concern, and cluelessness.

"Yeah, we gotta go." No sooner had she said this than she doubled over with the worst pain so far. She practically shrieked. *Control it, Kim. Don't panic.* Advice from her prenatal class instructor flowed unbidden into her mind. Concepts that had sounded so rational at the time, such as concentrate and focus and breathe through the contractions, now sounded absurd. It's hard for your mind to get a grip on anything once panic has greased your thoughts.

Colby got up and started pacing around the room, tail between his legs.

"Honey, are you okay?" Luke asked, staring at her helplessly.

"No," she gasped. "It hurts really bad. Can we go?"

Luke finally seemed fully awake. "Yeah, let's get you in there." He jumped off the sofa and took her hands. "Can you make it to the car? I'll drive. Where did I leave my keys?"

Colby stopped pacing and eyed them both intently, looking scared.

"Shit, nothing's packed!" Luke said to the air. "I'll throw some things together and meet you in the car." He ran back toward the bedroom.

Kim smiled for a second while she imagined what he might bring, but dread of the oncoming wave of pain quickly drained the humor from her. "Hurry, Luke," she got out, and headed to the front door. She turned and said in a gentle voice, "Don't worry, Colby—it'll be okay."

CHAPTER THIRTY-THREE

"Nice job, Stu," Jason Katz said, patting him on the shoulder. "Little different putting a United States senator to sleep, isn't it? Gives the old coronaries a squeeze, huh?"

Dr. Stuart Whitman exhaled deeply while taping Senator Pierce's endotracheal tube in place. "Thanks for your help." As he bent down, he got a whiff of a strange scent coming from the senator's body—eucalyptus or jasmine or something. *Strange cologne,* he mused, *for a manly man like the senator.* "I'm just not used to having Secret Service agents with guns in the OR."

"I know what you mean." Katz checked his watch. "You okay now, Stu? They should be wheeling Mrs. Daulton into the C-section room right about now."

Stu dialed up his anesthetic agent, adjusted the ventilator settings, and scanned his monitors; all was in order. "Yeah, everything looks copacetic—should be smooth sailing." He was a little reluctant to see Katz leave; it always felt reassuring to have a colleague in the room on a stressful case like this. He sat down and began filling out his chart.

Before Stu had gotten very far, one of the Secret Service agents on his right interrupted him. "How long you been doing this, Doc?" he asked in a conversational tone.

"About ten years now," Stu answered without looking at the agent. Stu was definitely on edge and recognized this fact.

"Okay to go, Stu?" came the general surgeon's voice over the drapes.

"Yeah, go ahead," Stu answered, but he was bothered by the senator's high end-tidal CO2 reading. *What's up with that?* Stu increased the vent settings and continued scribbling on his chart. He also noticed with dismay that the fentanyl he had given hadn't lowered the senator's pulse. In fact, the heart rate had sped up to 120 bpm. He gave more fentanyl.

"I thought about being a doctor, once," the Secret Service agent continued. "Your job looks pretty easy. How much do you get paid?"

Stu didn't answer. The first ten minutes were the most critical part of the anesthetic.

The agent asked a little louder, "How much money do you make?"

Stu sighed and turned from his monitors to face this guy. The agent's ID badge identified him as Mike Jensen and he sure was a big dude, but Stu didn't feel like shooting the shit with him. "Look, can we talk later? I'm kinda busy." Stu refocused on the end-tidal monitor and watched with disbelief as it climbed from 42 to 45 mm mercury, even after he had increased the vent settings. *How is that possible?* he asked himself.

"What's the matter?" Jensen asked. "Cat got your tongue?"

Stu chuckled nervously, but his eyes never left the CO2 monitor, willing it downward. He would've told the guy to shut the hell up, but he had to admit the gun was intimidating. The CO2 continued to climb. Damn!

Then it hit Stu like a ton of bricks—the horrifying thought of potential malignant hyperthermia. Was it possible? He had only seen it once or twice as a resident and had hoped to God he would never see it again. MH was so rare that you hardly ever thought of it—although Katz just had an episode of MH two weeks ago. He felt a wave of nausea sweep through him and his palms began to sweat. Still, the odds against MH were huge. The temperature would be key. He hadn't even gotten around to putting the temp probe in yet. He turned around quickly to get it from his cart and bumped into Jensen.

"Easy, Doc," Jensen said. "If I'm in your way, just say so—I'll move." The agent backed up a step. "You must make a hundred grand, right?"

"Not now," Stu said.

"Look, if you don't want to talk, why don't you just say so?"

Stu grabbed the esophageal temp probe and stuffed it down the senator's mouth. He tried hard to ignore the agent, who wouldn't shut up, and concentrate on the senator.

"I guess being a prick goes along with the territory," Jensen said. "I'm not sure I got what it takes in that category, if you know what I mean."

Stu hooked up the wire from the probe to the electronic meter box on top of the anesthesia machine. The needle jumped all the way to 38.5 degrees Celsius. *Holy shit!* They say if you *think* MH, you must treat it. MH rapidly becomes untreatable and fatal—50 percent mortality, at best. This just wasn't possible. Not the fricking senator!

Stu wanted to call Katz back to help, but he knew he was busy upstairs doing Kim Daulton's C-section. There was nobody but an anesthesia tech and that dimwit Russian orderly around, this time of night. A feeling of profound helplessness spread through him that threatened to immobilize him, sucking away his ability to react.

He had to pull himself together and think—the senator's life hung in the balance. No time to panic. Maybe it wasn't MH. A rotten gallbladder could cause a fever, which in turn could explain the elevated CO_2 and tachycardia. A blood gas would seal the diagnosis. But he knew he didn't have much time to waste. If he waited, fiddling with the diagnosis until it was clear, then it could be too late. Stu turned to the circulator and forced his voice to be as calm as possible. "Page the anesthesia tech. Tell her to bring me art line equipment, blood gas syringes, and dantrolene. And hurry!"

"Hey, Doc," Jensen chimed in, "you sound a little worried." He paused to look at the monitors as if he could actually make sense of them. "Everything going okay?"

CHAPTER THIRTY-FOUR

As he left the OR where Senator Pierce lay unconscious, about to have his gallbladder removed, Katz passed by one serious-looking Secret Service agent standing guard outside the room. Katz nodded to him and couldn't help chuckling. Sure, the man appeared formidable and his weapon looked just as deadly as the big guy's inside, but it really didn't matter. All the guards in the world weren't going to save the senator now.

Katz exited the main OR complex and reached into his pocket. His fingers brushed over the smooth metal barrel of the Makarov 9 mm pistol. He closed his hand lovingly around the knurled handle and was once again comforted by the reassuring weight of it. He was glad he had the gun; it gave him a sense of security and he drew strength from it. After all, he reflected, the weapon was a metaphor of his life. The Makarov was a beautifully machined and honed instrument, whose efficiency of design and diminutive size belied the destructive force contained within. The pistol was a marvel, surely one of his master's favorites—just as he was.

But Katz was no fool. He certainly had no intention of shooting it out with these professionals—that would be suicide. Thanks to his carefully crafted plan, he wouldn't have to. A well-thought-out scheme trumped brute force any day. Their physical prowess and firepower were virtually useless in the medical arena where he ruled. Kind of like taking a shark on, in the water.

Katz didn't head directly for OB, but rather made for his office. He still had a few minutes before the Daulton C-section and he had several pressing details to attend to. First he needed to send an urgent, encrypted message to his employers that all was proceeding according to plan. These people were sticklers for details and they wouldn't transfer the money unless he followed their instructions to the letter. After that, he would hurry up to the delivery room and tend to the Daultons. Only then could he relax—the fuses would finally all be lit and he could sit back and admire the fireworks.

The hallways were empty tonight and Katz smiled. The ruse was so simple, yet deadly effective. He had first demonstrated the technique on that lawyer's alcoholic wife several weeks ago. Adding a lethal amount of carbonic acid to one of her IV bags had quickly put her into acidotic shock. As her body struggled to metabolize the acid load, it sent her end-tidal CO_2 levels skyrocketing. He had chosen carbonic acid because it was a common compound found naturally in the bloodstream, so it wouldn't show up as a poison or drug on any tox screen.

But the real beauty was that high CO_2 levels and acidosis were the hallmarks of malignant hyperthermia. So it appeared for all the world that she'd died from a very rare, but very deadly, reaction to her anesthetic. There wasn't even any negligence or liability attached—Katz had made the correct diagnosis and administered appropriate treatment without delay. MH carried a 50 percent mortality, in spite of treatment. The only thing missing in the diagnostic triad of MH was the presence of a high fever. But he had addressed this as well. Only the illusion of a fever had been required. Nikolai had made sure the bogus temp gauge, which read four degrees higher than normal, was in the room and ready to go.

The test run had been very successful, if he did say so himself. Profitable, too. Although he had to admit that Daulton had almost spoiled the plan, driven by his damned desire to help. Luckily, he bought the phony temp gauge reading and the whole diagnosis of malignant hyperthermia. But Daulton had come back into the hospital later to sniff about, obviously suspicious about what had happened. He had even questioned whether the woman actually had a fever. How could he possibly have guessed that she didn't, in the face of overwhelming evidence to the contrary? That had been a little too close for comfort. Katz reminded himself that he had correctly foreseen that Daulton was trouble for him. So, he thought, having the Daultons involved with having their baby tonight was just what the doctor ordered—he needed to keep Daulton out of his hair just a bit longer.

Regardless of Daulton, this time Katz wanted the senator's death to be more believable—this death would be scrutinized to a far greater extent than Mrs. Hinkle's. No amateurish attempts here. The MH diagnosis had to stick. No questions about poisoning or murder or anything like that. His employers wouldn't pay for a botched job.

With this in mind, Katz had made two adjustments to the formula. First he had cut back the percentage of the carbonic acid solution in the special IV bag. Mrs. Hinkle's acidosis had been a little too severe to be totally explained by a metabolic process—even one as out of control and deadly as malignant hyperthermia. But you couldn't just go to the journals and look up the minimum lethal dose of carbonic acid—no one had seen fit to run these studies yet. So the downside of the reduced acid was that the whole liter would have to be infused to ensure a fatal outcome. And, this time, Nikolai would retrieve and destroy the tainted empty bag of IV fluid and replace it with a normal empty bag.

The second modification was sheer genius. He had added a trace quantity of reagent quality E. coli endotoxin that he had lifted from Micro. The lab used these standard endotoxins as control substances to check their sterility protocols on their equipment. This substance, when infused into a human in minute quantities of around 200 parts per trillion, was capable of rapidly producing a high fever as the immune system activated in response to a challenge by bacterial wall lipoproteins.

The bottom line: a perfectly mimicked episode of malignant hyperthermia. The carbonic acid would quickly put the senator in acidotic shock, producing high CO_2 levels and acidosis. And the pyrogen would provide the fever, so there was no need for the modified temp gauge they had used last time. An open-and-shut case of malignant hyperthermia.

He knew Stu Whitman was a serious play-it-by-the-book anesthesiologist and couldn't fail to reach the diagnosis. Once he started administering the dantrolene, the senator's fate was sealed. Not because the dantrolene itself was toxic and would kill him, but because it meant Whitman totally bought the diagnosis. Once you bought into a diagnosis, you stopped looking for other possibilities, your mind closed and you concentrated on treatment. Plus, there were a lot of steps in the mixing and giving of dantrolene—enough to keep several anesthesia personnel busy.

Katz entered his office, locked the door behind him, and sat down at his computer. While waiting for the machine to boot up, he leaned back in his chair, folded his arms behind his head, and let out a satisfied sigh—his plan was finally coming together. He marveled at the staggering immensity and sheer audacity of it. Although he had to admit, he had been wrong when he had made his initial list of human flaws and placed adultery at the top. There was one bigger weakness: the lure of political power—the naked lust for absolute power was the ultimate human weakness.

The computer came alive and Katz logged on to a special, anonymous IM service where there would be no record of the conversation and it would be completely untraceable. Just in case the NSA or CIA or Homeland Security had snooping capabilities Katz was unaware of, he also used a prearranged code. He knew his employers would be anxiously awaiting word from him.

Katz typed: PIE IS IN THE OVEN.

He didn't have to wait long for the reply: HOW LONG UNTIL THE PIE IS READY?

30 MINUTES.

GOOD.

Katz stared at the screen, practically holding his breath, waiting for more. Good? What about the fucking money! Shit, no mention of payment. He thought for a moment, calmed himself down, then typed: PAYMENT FOR THE PIE?

AS SOON AS THE PIE IS DONE, PAYMENT WILL BE SENT.

Katz banged his fists on the desk and howled. *Damn!* This was a deviation from the original agreement. A major fucking deviation! The money was supposed to be transferred to his offshore account upon initiation of the MH episode. That was now. That way he could verify receipt of funds before things were irreversible. *Damnation!* He jumped up from his chair and paced around the office. He sure hoped he wasn't being double crossed here. Finally, he settled himself down. *Honesty in business is so hard to come by these days.* The irony of this was not lost on him. He supposed they had a right to be cautious. Fifty million was a lot of money.

Just thinking about the money brought the smile slinking back to his face. He understood these people. They would do anything, say anything, and—here was the important one—pay anything to ensure political fortunes. This thing was paramount to them. Nothing else mattered. And they certainly had the money. He had finally tapped into the big one, the mother lode, and would exploit this for all it was worth. He'd be able to live out his life like a king, in the lap of luxury.

But monetary gain was only part of the equation. While immersed in the pursuit of happiness—rather, hedonism—he could forget all about little boys and fires. He could drown out the screams of his son with his own screams of ecstasy, fueled by an endless supply of women, drugs, and alcohol.

But even more than that, there was the bigger picture—all

of the havoc he could wreak with that kind of money. He could literally tempt, subvert, and harvest thousands of weaker souls. This was the ultimate reward, the kind of thing that could shift the very balance of power in the universe. His breathing quickened with this intoxicating thought until, utilizing his considerable self-discipline, he reined in his unruly imagination. Patience was a virtue—*this* one they got right. He didn't have the luxury of time to daydream; he had a date with the lovely Mrs. Daulton in the OB suite.

CHAPTER THIRTY-FIVE

"Okay, Mrs. Daulton," said Diane, the CRNA, "you can move over now."

"Call me Kim, please." Kim shimmied over to the cold, hard operating room table and looked around. She was not comforted by all the unfamiliar equipment, people, and lights. She felt like a bug about to be dissected. Thank God Luke was here. She couldn't imagine going through this by herself. He sat down to her left and held her hand.

"Okay, Kim," Diane said. "We'll hook you up to all the monitors and then work on the spinal. The anesthesiologist should be here in a minute." Diane busied herself slapping on some sticky EKG patches.

"What's going on downstairs?" Luke asked. "Where's Dr. Whitman?" He sounded uptight.

Then the next fricking contraction hit and she barely heard the OB scrub nurse's reply. "Haven't you heard? It's all over the hospital now. Senator Pierce is having his gallbladder out."

"That explains all the police cars and black Suburbans," Luke said. "Stu's really having a bad night." Luke looked at Kim. "You okay, hon?"

"Do I look okay?" Kim got out between clenched teeth. *What an asinine thing to say.* She felt like crying.

"Hang in there," Luke said meekly.

Just then the door opened. "Here's anesthesia," the scrub nurse announced. Kim craned her neck to see between the nurses.

She couldn't get a clear view of his face, but in a second didn't need to.

"Luke, Kim—how are you two doing?" came the unmistakable deep voice of Dr. Katz. "Sorry I'm late, but things are a bit crazy downstairs. Senator Pierce is having surgery tonight."

"Yeah, we heard," Luke said. "No problem." Luke was definitely tense—she could hear it plainly in his voice. He was also a bad liar.

"I helped Stu get started," Katz said. "It's a stressful case. There's a cast of thousands down there, including a bunch of Secret Service agents milling about." Katz chuckled easily as he walked across the room toward Kim. "And here's the lovely Mrs. Daulton."

"Kim, you remember Dr. Katz?" Luke asked her.

"Of course I do," Kim replied. She had met him at an anesthesia welcome dinner for Luke several months ago. "Hi, Dr. Katz." She held out her hand to shake.

"Call me Jason," he said as he took her hand in both of his and squeezed. His hands were warm yet powerful. "Now, I need you to curl up into a ball."

"Okay, Jason. It hurts a lot, though." Kim sniffled and her voice broke a little. "I'm not sure I'll be able to hold still."

"You'll do fine, Kim," Dr. Katz said as she curled forward as best she could.

"Perfect."

His voice was soothing, and Kim tried to focus on it and not think about the next contraction. She glanced over in time to see Dr. Seidle at the sink, scrubbing his hands.

"Is this your first child, Kim?" Dr. Katz asked as he began to prep her back with a cold liquid.

Kim shivered a bit. "Yes, it's our first." Luke squeezed her hand—she noticed his hand was cold and clammy. "Do you have children, Dr. Katz?" she asked.

"Well, I had one." The way he said this struck Kim as odd. At first she thought it was simply sadness—it sure sounded like he had suffered a loss. But it went beyond that—maybe more like bitterness. She wished she could see his face to help gauge his feelings. He stopped prepping her back momentarily and added, "It was a long time ago—doesn't matter."

Kim didn't know what to say. She realized she had inadvertently struck a nerve and regretted asking the question. Dr. Katz continued with the spinal and Kim barely felt a thing.

"There, all done, Kim," he said.

"My butt's getting warm already."

"That's a good sign, Kim," Dr. Katz said. "Now, I need you to lie down."

Dr. Seidle came into the room and got gowned and gloved.

"Hi, Mark," Luke said.

"Hi, Luke, Jason," Dr. Seidle said. "Kim, what're you doing here tonight? I thought I told you I'd see you next week."

He was kidding her, but once again she wished Rob Gentry were here taking care of her. "Sorry, Dr. Seidle, the contractions just started. But I feel great now—I can't feel those blasted things anymore. You ought to warn people about those." Kim turned to Luke. "I can't wait to see Abi."

"Me too," Luke said. She had relaxed a little now that the awful pain was gone, but she could tell Luke was still tight as a drum.

"You're going to be nice and comfortable, Kim," Dr. Katz said.

Kim zoned out for a moment, trying to imagine just how Abigail would look. It struck her as strange that she had been carrying this baby around for nine months and she felt she knew her intimately, but she had no idea what she looked like. The fuzzy ultrasound picture hadn't been a big help.

"Can you feel this, Kim?" Dr. Seidle said. "I'm pinching you with an instrument."

"Not a thing," Kim said. *Wow, this is definitely a weird feeling.*

"Okay, here we go," Dr. Seidle said.

Kim looked over at Luke, who was fumbling with her camera. He kept glancing over at the monitors. Dr. Katz had one hand on Luke's shoulder and was quoting a Bible verse, she guessed in an attempt to calm him down.

Dr. Katz's beeper went off. "Uh-oh," she heard him say. "I'm being stat paged to the OR—must be trouble with the senator. Diane, you take care of Mrs. Daulton here. The spinal seems to be working fine. I'll be back as soon as I can." Katz quickly left the room.

Kim was beginning to feel at peace. No more horrible contractions. The pain was gone. Dr. Katz had done a great job with the spinal—she hadn't felt a thing. The C-section was underway and she was nice and comfortable. She felt herself almost floating. The conversation around her drifted in and out.

Then something peculiar grabbed her attention and she snapped awake. She replayed Dr. Katz's last words. He had been quoting scripture from Romans. This, for some reason, sent her mind spinning and she recognized this feeling as a precursor to one of her lump intuitions or precognitions. And it felt like a big one.

In her mind's eye, numbers from the Sudoku puzzle danced and swirled about her—

$-273/\sqrt{-1}/50/50/86,400/2.71$

$6.02*10^{23}/3.14/2.71/8.714/3*10^{8}/2.71$

The disjointed gears of her mind whirred faster and faster, creating an almost uncomfortable sensation of pressure, or pain, in her head as the dissonance built. Then, just as suddenly, the gears slowed, aligned and came together with a loud clunk, meshing perfectly. She was suffused with a sense of release. She had come to love this feeling and described it as more exhilarating than sex.

She now held the key to the Sudoku puzzle before her. She relaxed and rode her wave of intuition.

Dr. Katz had provided the key when he mentioned Romans. She had completely forgotten about Roman numerals. Duh! The Sudoku puzzle was not at all complex. There was no complicated algebraic numerical solution like she had been focusing on. It was a code, a substitution code, pure and simple.

The two fifties were undoubtedly *L*s.

Kim was familiar enough with mathematical and physical constants to make some other connections here—3.14 were the first three digits of pi, the ancient geometrical constant; 2.71 were the first three digits of the base of the natural logarithms, otherwise denoted as *e*; 3*10^8 was the speed of light in m/sec, known in the physics world as *c*. So she had—

-273/$\sqrt{-1}$/L/L/86,400/E

6.02*10^23/PI/E/(8.714)/C/E

She knew she was on the right track. The puzzle had been composed by someone employing a physical constant substitution theme—someone undoubtedly with a math/science background. In short order, she deduced the rest: -273 degrees Celsius corresponded to absolute zero in degrees Kelvin or *K* in scientific shorthand. The square root of -1 was *i* in the world of imaginary or complex numbers. And 6.02*10^23 was the well-known Avogadro's constant from chemistry, abbreviated *N*. She locked briefly on the 86,400, but then recognized it as the number of seconds, or *s*, in one day. She wasn't familiar with 8.714, but quickly realized it had to be *R* of the famous ideal gas law of PV=nRT, for the puzzle to make sense. The substitution was complete:

K/I/L/L/S/E

N/PI/E/R/C/E

Rearranging, the puzzle was solved—

K/I/L/L

S/E/N

PI/E/R/C/E

This was amazing—way too coincidental not to be a valid solution. She must tell Luke. But when she tried to tell him, she found out she could barely move. "Luke," she cried, but heard only a whisper. "Luke!" she screamed.

"What is it, babe?" Luke bent down, his face next to hers.

"Can't talk." She saw him go ashen. "The puzzle—I solved it—forgot about Roman numerals."

"What are you talking about?"

"Su-do-ku." She was now speaking in gasps.

"Not now. Can you breathe okay?"

"It says 'Kill Senator Pierce.'"

"What?"

"Kill Senator Pierce," she repeated, in barely a whisper.

"Are you sure?"

She nodded because she couldn't speak.

"Can you breathe?"

"No," she mouthed, her panic rising.

"Diane, get me a tube!" she thought she heard Luke say before she blacked out.

CHAPTER THIRTY-SIX

Katz kept his mask up as he made his way out of the delivery room, afraid if anyone saw him they might notice the "cat that ate the canary" expression plastered across his face. He hadn't been stat paged back to the OR, but he did need to check that the senator was indeed heading south. He certainly didn't want to set foot anywhere near the OR and get tangled up with the authorities. Or get sucked into any resuscitation efforts. Nikolai would have to be his eyes and ears. He headed toward his office with a positive spring to his step. Amazing, he thought—things were working out better than he might've predicted.

The Daultons were busy having their blessed event—although with a little monkey wrench thrown in, courtesy of the total spinal he had just administered. No time for silly puzzles, now. Unforeseen just a few days ago, that both Mrs. Daulton and the senator would be here the same night, but actually there were some advantages. His master must've planned it this way—predestiny or something like that. And, he had to admit that Seidle had been right on this score, the reason for the panicky phone call Seidle had made this morning—

"Jason, this is Mark." Seidle had sounded very agitated. "Listen, she's got the fricking Sudoku! I saw it sticking out of her purse. I'm about to examine her."

"Slow down," Katz said. "What're you talking about? Sudoku? Who are you talking about?"

"Kim Daulton. I knew we couldn't trust them. What should we—"

"Get a grip, Seidle. You're not making sense. First of all, what the hell is a Sudoku?"

"The puzzle, you moron! She's got the puzzle with the FBI agent's writing all over it. The one *you* said you took care of."

Hmm, that is bad news, Katz thought. "How the hell did she get that?"

"I don't know—I didn't *ask* her that! I didn't want to draw any attention to the fact that I saw it. What matters is, she *has* it."

"Yeah, you're right," Katz said, trying to think. "Look, we don't even know if it means anything. The trouble is, I heard she's a frickin' math whiz and just might solve it."

"Exactly! So what do we do?"

"The senator's surgery is tonight. We just have to keep the two of them busy for a little longer." Suddenly, an idea hit Katz. "When is she due?"

"*What?*"

"When is she *fucking* due?"

"Soon—uh, next week sometime. Why?"

"Can't you induce her labor?"

"Well, I guess I could. But she's breech—she's scheduled for a section. There's no real indication."

"The *indication* is we need to stop her from working on the puzzle. Plus, if she comes into the hospital, you can keep an eye on her while I watch the circus in the main OR."

"Well, I guess I could apply some prostaglandin gel when I examine her."

"Excellent. Now you're thinking." Katz paused as another idea struck him. "Listen, Mark, we need a backup plan, just in case. Plan B, as they say. If we get wind that she figured the puzzle out and it has anything to do with Pierce, you must eliminate her during the section. We'll deal with Luke afterward."

"What? Did you say *eliminate*?"

"Yes, eliminate. Remember, Mark, this is for keeps—the big leagues."

Seidle didn't say anything.

"I'm counting on you," Katz said. Since when had he aligned himself with such a weasel?

"All right, I guess I could do that," Seidle answered weakly. "If I had to."

Katz shook his head at the recollection. Relying on Seidle had probably been a mistake. Giving him the gun may also have been an error. The stakes were too high with this one. Greed and ego were fine motivators, useful in their own right, but they only went so far. They didn't carry the emotional punch of love or hate or lust for power that might be required to push a man like Seidle to commit cold-blooded murder.

So Katz was proud of his little bit of improvisation back there in the delivery room—very creative. The timing had been a little hairy, but giving Daulton's wife a total spinal was a brilliant touch. That would definitely take Luke and Kim out of the picture. Kim wouldn't be able to work on the stupid puzzle, and Luke wouldn't get any heroic notions about helping with the senator's unfortunate case. When you want it done right, do it yourself, he always said.

Katz entered his office and locked the door behind him. He pulled out his cell phone and speed dialed Nikolai's number.

"Hallo," came the Russian's reply.

"Nikolai, are you still in the OR complex?"

"No."

Damn it! "Where are you?"

"In hospital, boss." Nikolai's voice sounded a bit slurred, and not just because of his thick accent. *Shit, he sounds like he's high.*

"I need you to go back to the OR and give me an update on the senator," Katz said. "All hell should be breaking loose by now. Call me back as soon as you can."

"Yes, boss."

Katz stabbed at the *END CALL* button with exasperation. *Fucking moron.* He thought he had made it clear to Nikolai to stay around the OR until he was sure the senator was toast. Another unreliable partner. Damn, now he'd have to wait for Nikolai's report. He sighed, sat back in his chair, and turned on the computer. Only when he was sure the senator was dying would they complete the money transfer. He would then exit the hospital and make good on his plans to vanish, leaving Seidle and Nikolai and Swatara Regional far behind. They'd all go their separate ways. But for now, all he could do was wait. He retrieved candles and the special picture of his son from a locked bottom drawer in his desk. He lit the candles and knelt at his makeshift altar and began chanting in the ancient tongue.

When Katz couldn't wait anymore—you could only chant for so long—he checked his watch. It had been almost thirty minutes. Why didn't Nikolai call? Fuck verification. The senator should definitely be fried by now. He quickly accessed the proper site and typed PIE IS COOKED. SEND MONEY.

Suddenly his cell phone vibrated on his hip. He assumed it was Nikolai getting back to him. Finally. He glanced at the caller ID and was surprised to see it wasn't Nikolai's number. It was a number he didn't recognize—though it looked like a hospital extension. Better take it.

"Hello," Katz said.

"I need to talk to you," came an agitated female voice.

"Who is this?" Katz demanded.

"It's Gwen Miller. I need to talk to you." Her voice was strained and she sounded slightly out of breath.

"Listen, Gwen, it's after midnight and I'm really very busy."

His computer beeped and a new message appeared: MONEY HAS BEEN TRANSFERRED.

"Gwen, you need to call me back—"

"Wait, don't hang up!" She was half whispering, but sounded a bit hysterical. "I saw you at the incinerator!"

"What are you talking about?"

"I saw you throw that man into it. I saw you kill him!" She was definitely breathing fast now.

Shit, unbelievable. Just when he thought he was free and clear. "I'm not sure what it is you *think* you saw, Gwen. Who have you told and why are you telling me this?" Katz took a deep breath and forced himself to slow down. Silence from the other end. He paused for another moment. "What is it that you want?" He understood full well how the human mind worked.

"I need something—I need a favor." Her voice sounded squeaky and she cleared her throat. "I need you to help me get rid of Mrs. Gentry." He heard her take a big breath. "In exchange for my silence. You make her go away and I'll never tell a soul what I saw down there in the basement. Okay? Do we have a deal?"

"Hmm," he said and paused. *So that's it.* He got the whole picture now very clearly. People are so predictable, but this stretched irony to the limit. After all, he had seen fit to introduce Gwen to the good Dr. Gentry. Just spreading goodwill at the time. Everyone in the hospital knew they were an item now, but he hadn't realized it had progressed this far. *Amazing—plant a seed and watch it grow.* "That's asking a lot, Gwen. Let me think—"

"Look, I saw you throw that poor man into the fire." Her voice was stronger now, becoming strident. "I *know* you can do it. I *need* you to."

Katz's mind was racing—she was threatening him, that was clear. No, blackmail was a better word. He couldn't suppress a brief flicker of admiration for Gwen's boldness—he approved of her technique. But it represented one more fucking loose end to deal with. *How many more will there be before this thing is over?*

"Look, Gwen, we shouldn't talk about this over the phone. Where are you? We should meet."

"I'm here at the hospital."

He thought he had recognized that number as a hospital extension. Unbelievable—here, now. Time for some more creativity. But he must be cautious—after all, patience was a virtue. *Does her being here have anything to do with the senator? Does she know anything about that?* "What are you doing here at this time of night?" he asked, trying hard to sound casual.

"I came in to talk to Rob—uh, Dr. Gentry."

That sounded legit—but it could also complicate things. "Is Dr. Gentry there with you now?"

"No," she said, "he had to go help with an emergency C-section."

What! How could this be? What was going on up there in OB? He had left just a short time ago. Was Plan B being played out? He wouldn't have thought that possible. "Listen, Gwen, I have some ideas. Meet me in my office in five minutes." *So much for things proceeding smoothly.* He blew out the candles.

He dialed Nikolai's number again as he headed out the door, back to Obstetrics.

CHAPTER THIRTY-SEVEN

"Mark, do something!" Luke implored. He watched helplessly as the suction canister filled up with his wife's blood, making a horrible gurgling noise.

"I'm trying, damn it!" Seidle poked the suction cannula around in Kim's open belly and the level in the canister continued to rise.

"Can't you stop it?" Luke was beside himself with fear and dread, and couldn't stand still. "Can't you deliver the baby?"

"I'm trying, Daulton." Seidle turned to the scrub nurse and barked, "Hemostat!"

"What's the problem? Can you at least tell me that?"

"Shut up, Daulton. Can't you see I'm busy?" He suctioned some more and then said in a grave tone, "I think the uterus might have ruptured."

Luke realized he wasn't helping the situation with his constant questions. Seidle needed to concentrate. Luke also remembered why he hated having family in the delivery room. When everything went smoothly, it was a wonderful, touch-feely, Kodak moment. But when the shit hit the fan, the docs responsible for life-and-death decisions didn't have time to deal with the raw emotions of scared shitless loved ones.

Luke needed to get a grip on his own emotions, even though he had never felt so helpless in all his life. He had just witnessed the horrifying spectacle of a total spinal on his wife. Luckily, he had recognized the symptoms quickly and had intervened. He and Diane had put Kim to sleep; he had intubated her himself. This had been bad enough, but now she was hemorrhaging profusely—maybe the result of the dreaded uterine rupture.

He stared down at Kim's face—her eyes were taped shut and an endotracheal tube disfigured her pretty mouth. Her lips looked so pale—she was bleeding to death right before his eyes. And Abigail's chances were dwindling rapidly as well. He turned to Diane and asked, "How long until we get the blood?"

"Ten minutes," Diane said.

Great, Luke thought. She needed the blood now. Luke paced some more but his mind kept returning to Dr. Katz. His suspicions of Katz were growing by the minute. After all, he had given Kim the total spinal. *Could that possibly have been an accident?* Luke strongly doubted it. But, what the hell was going on? And was Kim right about the puzzle? Was someone actually trying to kill the senator? Was Katz somehow involved in some bizarre plot? Or was it just a drug-induced hallucination? Who should he trust? It was hard to think straight while his wife bled to death in front of him.

The roar of the suction canister interrupted his thoughts. It now had over 1,000 ccs of blood in it—Kim's blood. He'd have to worry about Katz later. If the bleeding wasn't controlled soon, she would go into irreversible shock and then nothing could save her. The blood pressure machine beeped 60/40.

All of a sudden, a horrifying thought struck Luke—he stopped pacing as if he'd walked into a wall. *What if Seidle's mixed up with Katz?* His knees threatened to buckle as the implications of this hit him, and he reached toward the anesthesia cart to steady himself. *What if he's in on some plot to murder the senator? And overheard Kim solve the puzzle? And is killing Kim now to silence her? Dear God, what should I do?*

Luke turned to the nurse anesthetist. "Diane, do you see her pressure? Give some more Ephedrine or Neo!"

"I just gave a ton of it," she said, her tone defensive but

nevertheless laden with worry. "I'll give some more. The blood should be here soon."

Soon? She'll be dead soon. Luke resumed pacing, his footsteps becoming frantic as time slipped away. He had to know about Seidle. He had to figure things out. If Seidle was in on it, Kim didn't stand a chance—he was busy butchering her. But if Luke was wrong about him, he just might destroy the only chance Kim had of survival.

He banged his foot painfully into the wheeled base of the IV pole, making it rattle loudly. Suddenly, an idea blazed across Luke's mind—a way to pin Seidle down, perhaps. It had "bluff" written all over it, but bluff was the only card he had left to play. Kim and Abi were out of time.

"Mark!" he shouted across the drapes at Seidle. "Kim solved the Sudoku. It names you and Katz in the plot to kill Senator Pierce." Luke stared at Seidle, looking for a sign—for anything.

Seidle hesitated for the briefest of moments and his face reddened slightly, but then he quickly resumed his suctioning. "I don't know what you're talking about, Daulton. You're craz—"

But he didn't finish his sentence. Luke had jumped around behind him and now wrapped his arm around his neck. "Get away from her, you bastard!" Luke shouted as he manhandled Seidle to the floor. Seidle flailed with the scalpel and sliced Luke across his forearm. Luke ignored the burning pain and grabbed Seidle's arm. He smashed the hand clutching the knife on the floor over and over until the scalpel went flying across the room. Straddling Seidle, Luke punched him several times in the face. He could hear Diane screaming in the background.

"You're too late, Daulton," Seidle spat out between bleeding, crushed lips. "She'll bleed to death and you can't stop it."

Luke had heard enough—no more bluffs needed now. He whacked Seidle's head against the floor repeatedly until his eyes rolled back in his head. He instantly abandoned Seidle and jumped back up to the operating table. What he saw filled him with dread. Blood was everywhere. The gaping wound in Kim's belly was filled with blood. He couldn't see a thing. "Oh, shit," he mouthed. *God help me.*

Luke didn't know where to begin. Relying on himself only went so far—this was beyond him. He was out of his league. Anesthesia emergencies were one thing—he had been trained extensively for those. But obstetrical/surgical emergencies? He had no idea what to do. He had to rely on something bigger. *I need help. God, please help me.*

With these words, something opened up inside his mind, a door he had seen before but had never cared to open. Calmness flowed in—but more, knowledge crept in. This all took place in a fraction of a second, but to Luke it felt as if time stood still as many things washed over and through him. Multiple staggering revelations shook him, forcing the breath from him.

"Clamp," he shouted.

The scrub nurse just stood there looking at him, as if she had turned to stone. Her one hand twitched as if to do something, then stopped.

Luke grabbed a large Kelly clamp from her tray. He worked the suction catheter, hoping to clear some of the blood away so he could glimpse something recognizable and get his bearings. As fast as he sucked, more blood rushed in. *Shit, no good.*

"Pressure's 50/20!" Diane shouted. "And I'm losing the pulse ox."

"Give her some epinephrine. I don't know if I can stop the bleeding."

Luke reached in with his bare hands, searching for Kim's aorta, the main artery coming directly from the heart. He knew he must clamp her aorta to stop the bleeding. It was her only hope. He searched inside her belly. He felt the swollen uterus and realized it had a large gash in it—probably where all the blood was coming from. He tried to push the intestines aside but they kept slithering back. Everything was so damned slippery. *Shit, where's the aorta?*

Finally, after what seemed like ten minutes, his right hand

found a large, pulsing, garden hose-like object way toward Kim's back. He slipped the Kelly around it and closed it tight. There, that had to be good!

Now for the moment of truth. He suctioned her wound again. Her belly would either fill up with blood and she would die, or the god-awful pool would be drained and stay that way. He held his breath as he watched the suction canister fill up to 3,000 cc—over half her blood volume and probably past the point of no return.

Time seemed to slow down further. He could see her uterus now. The large gash was vertical, parallel to the muscle fibers of the uterus—this was not the usual horizontal incision used to deliver a baby. Luke realized it was clearly a surgical wound designed, no doubt, to mimic a uterine rupture. Seidle *had* purposely tried to kill her. The incision would have been quite lethal within a matter of minutes. But the abdominal cavity was remaining dry. At first he wasn't sure if this was just related to his altered time sense. He took a couple breaths to make sure time was passing. The blood was definitely not re-accumulating. The clamp was working. Thank God!

"Blood's here!" Diane said shrilly.

"Give the blood now," Luke yelled to her. "Skip the cross-match. Just give it."

"I'm spiking it now."

The scrub nurse spoke up. "What can I do to help?"

"We've got to deliver the baby, fast," Luke said, grateful for her help. Luke reached through the gaping hole in Kim's uterus and grabbed the baby. It wasn't moving. He maneuvered it out of the damaged uterus and then out of Kim's belly. The baby's skin was very dark, as though someone had rubbed charcoal all over it. This was a very bad sign—he wondered how long the baby's blood supply and hence oxygen had been compromised.

There was nothing more he could do.

Again, Luke felt that he was not in control of this situation. It was beyond his power to affect the outcome. *Self-reliance only goes so far, Dad.* He shook his head slightly. Perhaps there were other powers at work here?

Luke flipped the baby over and quickly clamped and cut the dangling umbilical cord. As he prepared to hand the limp body off to the neonatal nurse, something about the baby's still face caught his attention and he hesitated. He looked down into the most beautiful, angelic face he had ever seen. Abigail. She had light hair and the resemblance to her mother was striking. Luke stood transfixed, staring at her little face as powerful emotions roiled through him. He felt additional connections opening up to the spiritual world and realized the spiritual world had always been around him, just sort of translucent and not plainly visible in the harsh light of the living.

"Doctor!" the neonatal nurse shouted at Luke. She had her arms outstretched, motioning for the baby.

The little creature in Luke's hands startled at this noise and her eyes opened. She drew in a big, stuttering breath as if about to cry. A frown creased her forehead and her lips pursed together in a pout. Then she looked up at him. Her eyes spoke to him. She didn't cry, but took several more breaths and began to pink up.

Luke handed Abigail off with a renewed sense of wonder. As he turned to face the daunting task in front of him, he heard Abi gently whimpering in the background and he drew strength from her cries. Maybe he could pull this off after all.

He refocused on Kim's abdomen, but what he saw horrified him anew. The clamp had indeed worked to stop the bleeding, but at a fearful price—it also cut off the blood supply to the lower half of Kim's body. Kim's internal organs had blanched markedly, taking on a sickly white, mottled color. Clamping the aorta had only stalled the inevitable. Her internal organs would quickly die and she would sustain spinal cord injury from lack of blood, if he didn't release the clamp soon. But before he could release the clamp, he needed to repair the damaged uterus—something he had no clue how to do.

His calm evaporated. He heard the clock ticking as he debated what to do. He had brained Seidle, the only man in the room who could save Kim—he was now lying unconscious on the floor. Here he was for the third time in the space of minutes facing a challenge that was larger than he was—bigger than he could handle. His fledgling connection to the spiritual was being dealt a body blow, and he opened himself up to despair. *God, what's the point? Maybe Dad was right—if you rely on the void, you're left with nothing.* Kim would surely die at his hands and he would spend the rest of his life wondering what he should have done. And he would have to explain it to Abigail.

The cold metal barrel of a gun being shoved against his left temple cut short Luke's descent into despair. *What the hell?*

"Step away from her, Daulton!" Seidle's voice was gurgly.

Out of the corner of his eye, Luke saw the bloodied face of Mark Seidle glaring at him. He looked a little unsteady on his feet, but he gripped the gun tightly enough with two hands, pressing it painfully against Luke's head. "I said, get away from her!" Seidle screamed, and dug the barrel harder into Luke's flesh.

"She'll bleed to death." Luke tried to turn his head to get a better look at Seidle, but the gun barrel prevented him. "But I guess you know that."

"I'm gonna count to three and then pull the trigger," Seidle said. He spread his feet to take on a more stable stance. "One."

Luke frantically tried to decide what to do. If he left Kim, she would die. If he stayed, they would both die. Should he try to hit Seidle?

"Two!"

Luke figured it was over. At least, he consoled himself, he had saved Abi. That must count for something on the eternal ledger. Pretty soon he'd have his answer about the existence of the spiritual world. Was his dad right or wrong? A sudden blur across the table caught his eye.

"FBI! Freeze!" A pistol had materialized in the scrub nurse's hand, and she had it leveled at Seidle's head. "Drop the gun!" She sounded like she meant business.

"What the fu—" Seidle danced on his feet to get behind Luke, but kept the gun barrel pressed against Luke's temple. "I don't think so, lady! You drop yours or I'll blow his fuckin' brains out!"

"More agents are on the way," she said and edged slightly to her right to get a better firing angle on him. "You can't get away."

The delivery room door squeaked open. Seidle turned his head. Before Luke could comprehend what was going on, the room exploded with noise.

Two gunshots were fired in rapid succession, the reports deafening in the confined room. Luke turned in time to see Seidle crumple to the floor, gun still clutched in his hand. The door closed and Luke couldn't see who had opened it. The scrub nurse—make that FBI agent—stood with her smoking gun aimed at the door. *What is she even doing here?* Luke wondered. *Does this have to do with the senator?* Maybe the conspiracy theory wasn't so far-fetched.

Luke looked at Seidle. He wasn't getting back up off the floor this time—he had a bullet hole in his forehead and another through his left eye. A pool of blood was spreading across the floor from his head. Blood had spattered from the back of his head to spray across the far wall.

Luke's mind was reeling with sensory overload and his ears were still ringing. The acrid smell of gunpowder assaulted his nostrils. He struggled to process it all. Then he remembered Kim. Her life was still in the balance.

The door squeaked halfway open again. The FBI agent tensed and kept her gun aimed at the door. "Who's there?" she shouted. "FBI—come in with your hands up!"

"Don't shoot!"

Luke recognized the voice, shaky though it was, of Rob Gentry.

Rob came in slowly with his hands held high. "I'm Dr. Gentry—I'm here to help."

She turned to look at Luke, still training the gun on Rob. "Do you want his help?" she asked.

"Yes. Absolutely."

"Well, get in here, Dr. Gentry," she said, lowering her weapon.

"Holy Mother of God," Rob said as he walked by the body of Seidle and up to the OR table where he quickly gowned and gloved.

Luke stood there in amazement, blinking to make sure Gentry was for real. Up close, Luke noticed some red splotches on Rob's cheek. Was it blood? Or lipstick?

"Aortic cross clamp!?" Rob exclaimed as he examined Kim's open abdomen. "Nice move, Daulton. Her uterus looks like hell, though—not sure I can save it. Stitch! Give me a two-O vicryl suture."

Relief and hope surged through Luke. Maybe they could yet save Kim.

CHAPTER THIRTY-EIGHT

Luke was breathing hard as he raced down to the main OR complex on the second floor. It had been very tough to leave Kim and Abi, but Luke had grave concerns about the senator. This whole thing was deadly serious, if Seidle had been willing to murder to keep them quiet. A plot to kill the senator now seemed not only plausible, but likely. And then there was Katz. What had he said before he left? "Trouble with the senator." Luke wondered what kind of trouble—and hoped he wasn't too late.

Luke felt reasonably sure Kim would be safe with the FBI agent/nurse, and Rob. Mark Seidle was certainly no longer a threat. So much had happened so fast, he could barely make sense of it all. He couldn't tell if he was in shock or on cloud nine. Thirty minutes ago, Kim had almost died right before his eyes. And Abi, too. Not to mention facing his own death at the hands of that butcher, Mark Seidle. And now Seidle's brains were spattered all over the wall.

In spite of it all, Luke felt totally exhilarated that they had saved Kim and Abi. Thank God for that FBI agent—she had really come out of the blue. And thank God Rob Gentry had been at the hospital—presumably to rendezvous with Gwen. They always said God works in strange ways. Even all the God-talk didn't sound so weird.

Just as Luke got up to the main OR entrance, he saw Nikolai coming out.

"Nikolai, what room is the senator having surgery in?" Luke asked, out of breath.

Nikolai smiled widely but didn't answer. He looked drugged up, although, Luke thought, that wasn't uncommon.

"Nikolai," Luke said louder, grabbing his arm. "What room?"

Nikolai bristled. "OR 5." One of his hands slid into his pocket. He giggled and added, "Is going shitty in there."

Luke pushed by him and ran to OR 5. An armed guard was posted at the door. Luke briefly debated his course of action. He had to find out for himself if the senator was doing okay, but he had to feel out the situation carefully because he wasn't exactly sure who to trust. He didn't have time for a long explanation, and they wouldn't believe him anyway. All he had was a strange puzzle that his almost-deceased wife had solved. He pulled a slip of paper from his pocket and approached the guard. "I'm Dr. Daulton and I have critical lab values they need to see," he said, waving it in front of the guard's nose. He didn't wait for an answer but continued through the door.

Before he could make it over to Stu Whitman at the head of the OR table, he was tackled from behind and went down hard. For the second time that night, he felt a gun barrel shoved painfully against his head. The wind was knocked out of him and he could barely speak.

"Hold it right there, pal," a steely voice growled behind him. "Who the hell are you? And how'd you get in here?"

Luke struggled to look up. "I'm Dr. Daulton. I'm here to help," he said weakly. He twisted his neck around so he could get a look at the stern face of a large Secret Service agent. Stu Whitman looked very intense and was drawing up drugs and mixing drips frantically. "Stu, is the senator okay?" Luke asked.

"What are you doing here?" Stu asked, flashing him a baffled look. Stu turned to the agent. "Let him up, Jensen. He's my partner."

"Not so fast," Jensen said, although he eased the barrel off of Luke's head. "Anyone who comes busting in here like that is a suspect until I say otherwise. I'm responsible for the well being of the senator here."

"Luke," Stu said, "I'm worried that the senator might have malignant hyperthermia."

"Are you kidding?" Luke was incredulous.

"His temp's up, and so is his C02. I just sent a blood gas. I could really use your help."

Malignant hyperthermia! So, was *this* what Katz was up to? "I thought Katz came down here to help you. Where is he?"

"He *was* here—he helped me put the senator to sleep—but then he went up for Kim's C-section. I thought he was with you."

"He was. But then he left." Katz *had* to be in on the plot. It fit; he had been involved in every aspect, from Mrs. Hinkle's case just two weeks ago, to Kim's total spinal, and now the senator. Luke's gut feeling had been right all along. A flash of insight blazed across his mind. "Stu, what exactly did Katz help you do?"

"He started that big IV there," Stu said, pointing to the senator's right arm.

"Maybe you should get rid of that IV, Stu. You're not going to believe this, but I think someone's trying to kill the senator."

Luke suddenly felt a boot on his back, crushing him to the floor, and the muzzle of the gun returned to his head. "What the fuck are you talking about?" asked Jensen, his voice now threatening. "Did you say 'kill the senator'?"

"If you take your boot off me so I can breathe," Luke gasped, "maybe I'll tell you."

The pressure eased a little. "Go on."

"I believe there's a plot to kill the senator and I think Dr. Katz is involved. And I think Dr. Seidle was, too."

"Katz? Seidle?" Stu asked, still looking confused. "What do you mean, *was*?"

"It's a long story," Luke said, realizing he didn't know who he could trust. Could Stu be one of them?

Jensen, without easing his boot off Luke's back any further, turned quickly to Stu. "The senator's doing okay, right? Five minutes ago, you told me everything was fine."

Before Stu could answer, one of the circulating nurses walked over to Stu and handed him a piece of paper.

"Blood gas, Doctor," she said.

Stu held up his finger to keep Jensen at bay and studied the paper. The blood quickly drained from Stu's face.

"Well, *is* he?" Jensen shouted.

"No," Stu finally got out, his voice barely more than a whisper. "He's having a bad reaction to the anesthesia. It's called malignant hyperthermia."

"So, you can fix it, right?" Jensen asked.

"Maybe," Stu said. "It's potentially fatal. Somewhere around 50 percent mortality."

"Jesus Christ!" Jensen took his boot off Luke. He waved his gun about wildly, searching in vain for some elusive target.

"Stu, are you sure he has malignant hyperthermia?" Luke asked from the floor.

Jensen whirled and leveled his gun at Luke. "Not another word from you."

"Yeah, Luke," Stu said, ignoring Jensen. Stu bent down and showed Luke the blood gas report. "Look, his blood gas is shit—pH 7.12."

That's bad, all right, Luke thought, but his mind was reeling with conspiracy theories. Mimi Hinkle's Case One came back to him, and he remembered how her arm wasn't hot to the touch. Something had bothered him about that all along, even though she was acidotic as hell, too. An idea formed; he thought there was a chance he might yet be able to save the senator. "Stu, you gotta listen to me," Luke said.

"No he doesn't," Jensen fired back. "Look, pal, the senator's in deep shit and our man Doc Whitman needs to concentrate and fix it—not jaw with you about your crazy theories. Now we're getting you the fuck out of here." He grabbed Luke roughly under his arm while keeping the gun on him. "We can do this the easy way or the hard way," he said as he hauled Luke to his feet.

Luke caught Jensen's eye. "Listen, I'm trying to help. The

senator'll die if you don't listen to me." He could hear Stu in the background barking frantic orders to the anesthesia techs for dantrolene and ice packs.

Jensen froze for a moment, then something seemed to get through to him. Although he still maintained a firm grasp on Luke's arm and had his gun dug into Luke's ribs, he looked Luke in the eye and said in a low but deadly serious voice, "You got ten seconds, Doc."

"Stu, are you sure he's hot?" Luke asked.

"The temp probe's registering 39 degrees," Stu answered with growing impatience. "I gotta pack his body in ice now, before it's too late."

"Forget the probe, Stu!" Luke yelled. "At that temperature, his body should be red hot to the touch."

"Yeah, so what." Stu began packing the senator's head in ice.

"Touch him, Stu," Luke pleaded.

"You're not making sense." Stu paused to look at Luke. "I have touched him, okay? He's hot. Here, you touch him." Stu motioned to Luke and Jensen. Jensen nodded.

Luke touched the senator's forehead, which was dripping with perspiration despite his head being encased in ice. He quickly withdrew his hand. The senator's forehead was indeed burning up—the fever was definitely real. Luke was now totally baffled. Did that mean the MH was real and he was wrong about Katz? Was it all just a crazy coincidence? What the hell was going on?

"Okay, genius," Jensen said, "time's up." He shook his head. "That was your best shot? I'm no doctor, but I can read the fuckin' thermometer over there." He pointed to the temp probe, which now ominously registered 40 degrees Celsius. "The senator's burning up and Doc Whitman needs to fix that." Jensen started leading Luke toward the door. "You're outta here."

CHAPTER THIRTY-NINE

Katz rounded the corner into the third floor OB unit just in time to see two nurses wheeling Mrs. Daulton into the elevator. "Where are you taking her?" he asked, desperate to find out what was going on.

"To the SICU," answered Diane, her voice quavering. She looked pretty shook up—it must've been a rough case. Katz quickly assessed the situation. Mrs. Daulton was asleep and intubated and Diane was bagging her with an Ambu bag. An OB nurse he didn't know was at the foot of the litter helping with the transport. Blood was hanging and running into the patient's IV. He scanned the transport monitor—her vital signs looked decent, except her blood pressure was marginally low.

What the hell had happened in there? Things didn't make any sense. Why was Kim Daulton going to the SICU? The total spinal shouldn't have landed her in the SICU. Could this be the result of Plan B? No, he quickly reasoned. If Seidle *had* decided to take decisive action, she should be dead. Could it be just a coincidence that the C-section had gone bad in the delivery room, as they sometimes did? He found this hard to believe.

He did know that things were moving goddamn fast and threatening to unravel. He needed to tie up loose ends quickly here—Secret Service agents were crawling all over the place. And why the hell wasn't Luke Daulton with his wife? Something definitely didn't add up. Time to sort things out.

"Diane," he said, "it's a real mess in the OR. It looks like the senator is having a malignant hyperthermia episode." No time for secrets now.

"Wow, we just had one two weeks ago," Diane said as she maneuvered her end of the stretcher into the cramped elevator.

"Yes, I know," Katz said, working hard to control his breathing. "Why don't you go down there and help out. I know Dr. Whitman could use an extra hand."

Katz ignored Diane's pained expression and pressed on. "I think we got the situation under control, but when I heard Mrs. Daulton was having problems, I had to come see what had happened." Katz paused, trying to read her. "I mean, obviously the senator's extremely important and all, but Stu's got a good handle on things. The bottom line is, we take care of our own, right?" This seemed to have the desired effect. He got onto the elevator. "Listen, Diane, you go help Dr. Whitman, and I'll stay here and take care of Mrs. Daulton, personally." He put on his best caring smile and patted Kim's leg.

"Okay, Dr. Katz," she said reluctantly. "But did you hear what happened in the delivery room?" She was squeezing the Ambu bag a little too vigorously and her hand was trembling.

The OB nurse at the foot of the bed suddenly spoke up. "Diane, you go now. I'll fill Dr. Katz in on all the details." She stared at Diane and the two traded looks.

"Okay," Diane said, sighing with resignation. "I'll get right down there." She handed the Ambu over to Katz and got off the elevator.

The door started to close, but Katz stopped it with his foot. "Oh, Diane," he said. "Where's Dr. Daulton? I would've thought you couldn't pry him away from his wife."

"He said he was going to the OR to help with the senator. The two of you must've just missed each other."

"Thanks," he said. What the hell was Daulton up to? It didn't matter—he was too late to save the senator anyway.

The elevator door glided shut. Katz turned his attention to the OB nurse. He could now read her ID badge as Jenna Steele and it also identified her as a traveling nurse. He didn't know anything about her. Curiously, she was staring at him.

"Miss Steele, what happened in there? Did Dr. Seidle run into a lot of bleeding? Is the baby okay?"

Jenna continued to study him. Finally she said, "Yeah, there was quite a bit of hemorrhage. Dr. Gentry came in to help stop the bleeding."

So Gwen *was* telling the truth. Rob Gentry *was* here. "Where is Dr. Gentry?"

"He said he had to check on another patient," she replied.

Probably Gwen, Katz thought.

"The baby's fine," Jenna added.

Suddenly it hit him hard. Where was Mark Seidle? Getting info out of this nurse was proving harder than he thought. He didn't have all night here. "Where's Dr. Seidle?"

She looked him in the eye. "Dr. Daulton knocked him senseless after he realized Seidle was bleeding her to death."

Oh, shit! Katz could hardly believe his ears. *Plan fucking B! Amazing.* "What the hell are you talking about?" he said. Nurse Steele didn't answer but continued to stare at him.

Katz knew Seidle well. Yeah, he wanted the money badly, but he didn't seem to have the balls to kill someone. He must've had a really good reason to execute Plan B. What could possibly have forced his hand?

The elevator binged at the second floor and the door whooshed open. He looked up at the lit-up numbers above the door, and then it dawned on him—Kim must've solved the Sudoku. What else could it be? That would explain Seidle's drastic action. Perhaps it would also explain why Daulton wasn't with her. Damn that twerpy FBI agent! He deserved his fiery fate. And damn Daulton! Always trying to help, putting his nose in where it didn't belong.

They rolled into the SICU and entered the second room on the left. Katz quickly hooked Kim up to the ventilator to free his hands from the Ambu bag. Time was of the essence here, and he needed to take care of business.

"Listen, Jenna, I'll take it from here. You can go back to OB now. Take a break or something. I'll wait for the SICU nurse and give report."

"I promised Dr. Daulton I'd keep an eye on his wife," she said.

Unbelievable! It seemed this nurse had a backbone and was copping an attitude. Most nurses would've hightailed it out of there. "He obviously didn't know *I* would be here," he said, not bothering to hide his irritation. "I need to give her some pain medication."

He approached Kim. Jenna amazed him further by moving to block him. More than a *little* attitude. What was this bitch's problem?

"It doesn't really look like she needs any medicine, now, does it, Dr. Katz," Jenna said. She threw a glance over at Kim, who was sleeping peacefully.

Katz was momentarily dumbfounded. *What the fuck!* He felt his face flush. "Look, Nurse, are you telling me how to practice medicine? I said, I'll take it from here." He started to push her aside. "Now get the hell out of my way so I can do my job." Her shoulder felt a lot more solid than he would've expected.

"Let me make this clear, Doc," Jenna said, holding her ground, her face inches from his. "I'm not leaving her side, and you're not giving her anything." She glared at him. "I already saw this lady almost get killed. It's not gonna happen again."

"Who the *fuck* are you?" Katz snarled and pushed so hard that she gave up some ground. He pulled a syringe out of his pocket and readied it. Out of the corner of his eye, he saw her back up a step. Then her hand blurred.

"I said get away from her!" She emphasized her point by leveling a large-caliber, semi-automatic pistol at him. She pulled out a badge with her other hand. "FBI," she said.

Katz was stunned again. He backed away from Kim and returned the syringe to his pocket. He wished to hell he hadn't given Seidle the Makarov. He strained to think. *The fucking FBI. What're they doing here? Daulton couldn't have called them this quickly.*

As if to answer his question, she said, "Benjamin Harris sent me."

CHAPTER FORTY

Gwen paced nervously around Katz's office. The scent of burnt candles hung heavily in the air, and she found this odd, but dismissed it. Would Katz play ball? Where was he? She needed all her wits about her to pull off this meeting with him, but her unreliable, pathetic mind kept drifting back to Rob. Rob had sounded so serious on the phone earlier this evening when they had arranged to meet. What was it he had said? "I have something important to tell you." These words kept coming back to her, haunting her—the words she dreaded. She knew he probably wanted to break it off with her—again. She could read the writing on the wall, after all. Life just wasn't fair.

She thought back to their brief meeting in the call room earlier. They had barely gotten to say hello, and were in the middle of a good, hard kiss when that frantic OB nurse came barging in.

"Dr. Gentry, come quick!" the nurse had urged.

Gwen and Rob quickly disengaged, Rob looking sheepish, as he tried to wipe her lipstick off of his face.

"I'm sorry to *bother* you," the nurse added after sizing up the situation, "but it's Mrs. Daulton. She's dying!" She threw a sour look at Gwen as she grabbed Rob by the hand and pulled him out the door. "Dr. Daulton needs you!"

So, duty had called and Rob went to help with the emergency C-section on Luke Daulton's wife. Leaving her alone. Leaving her with his words echoing in her mind—*I have something important to tell you.* This had pushed her over the edge, this had driven her to take drastic action.

Gwen shook her head, trying to refocus on the task at hand—Katz. She studied his desk and noticed a framed picture that she had never seen before. It was a photograph of a boy of perhaps ten or twelve, smiling ear to ear, kneeling beside a dog. Nice-looking kid. Two adults were in the background, presumably the parents.

She bent over to take a closer look and realized with a shock that the man was Dr. Katz. He looked like a different person—much younger and happier—which explained why she didn't recognize him at first. In the six years she had worked for Dr. Katz, she had never heard him mention children. Although, come to think of it, there was a rumor about a fire long ago.

Gwen wrapped her arms around herself as she felt fear creeping in. Maybe calling Dr. Katz and trying to strike a deal with him hadn't been the best idea—dangerous, even. Katz was a monster now, capable of throwing a living person into an incinerator. She shuddered. She couldn't imagine a more cold-blooded murder. And anyone capable of killing someone like that could kill again—like kill her, for instance. But wouldn't it be just as easy to eliminate Mrs. Gentry?

This brought her full circle back to Rob and the "I have something important to tell you." She shook her head again and resolved to buck up, be tough. She was tired of playing the victim. She had been dealt some high cards and had a play to make here. Sometimes, you had to take risks. The ends justify the means and all that bullshit. The words flowed out easily enough and seemed to help, but nonetheless they had a hollow ring to them. Perhaps, she thought, sometimes you were just crazy in love. Love conquers all, right?

Gwen's phone rang and she jumped. She didn't recognize the number. "Hello," she said tentatively.

"Gwen, is that you? It's me." Rob's sweet voice.

"Where are you?"

"I just got finished with the section. They're taking Kim to the SICU now."

"It was nice of you to help." Gwen began imagining his arms wrapped tightly around her. "The SICU? Everything turn out okay?"

"You're not gonna believe what happened in there. Amazing. And I thought I'd seen it all." Rob was talking fast and sounded very excited. "Do *I* have a story to tell you. Hey, where'd you go, anyway? You said you'd wait."

"I had some stuff to take care of," Gwen said weakly. "I have a story to tell you, too." Her voice fell off to a whisper as she added, "About the incinerator."

"What? Did you say incinerator? Listen, meet me back in the call room. We can, uh, take up where we left off. And we can finish our little conversation."

Our little conversation. Great. Gwen's voice caught in her throat. "I'll be there in a few minutes."

"Okay, fine. I'll change out of these bloody scrubs and take a quick shower."

"All right." She bit her lip as she felt her emotions swirling out of control, getting the best of her.

"You okay? You don't sound so good."

"I'm fine," Gwen lied, then the tears started. She paused to wipe her face and snuffle, but the tears only got worse.

"Gwen, what's wrong?"

"I'm just not sure I want to hear the part where you can't see me anymore and you've gotta do the right thing and—"

"What're you talking about?"

"—and your kids would never forgive you and—"

"Gwen, listen to me. It's not like that."

She fetched a tissue out of her purse and blew her nose.

"I love you," he said. "Don't you know that?"

"Yes, I do. And I love you." This brought on a fresh wave

of tears. "But I get it. Love isn't enough. There are things bigger than love, like family and commitment. I get it."

"No, you don't get it!" Rob sounded like he was close to breaking up himself. "I wanted to tell you this in person, but—"

"I can handle it," she lied again.

"I'm leaving Cindy."

Again, Gwen couldn't speak. She snuffled loudly.

"Did you hear me? I said, I'm leaving Cindy."

"What?" Gwen croaked in a weak voice.

"I'm leaving Cindy to be with you. I love you. I can't live without you."

The words she had longed to hear for so long. Had he really said them? Gwen broke down crying afresh.

"Will you meet me now?"

"I'll be right up," she managed to get out between sobs, even as her heart began to soar. She could think of little else than hugging and kissing Rob. She hung up the phone and rummaged around in her purse for a mirror to check her makeup, which must be a shambles by now.

As she looked in the mirror, she couldn't help seeing that old picture with the smiling face of Katz staring back at her. Shit, what about Katz? What had she done? Had she really threatened him? Of course, there was no need now for drastic action if Rob was going to leave his wife. She must call Katz and tell him to forget about their little deal. It was all a mistake, a bad joke, nothing serious. She would never tell a soul about the incinerator.

Suddenly, she heard footsteps and whirled around to see Nikolai standing in the doorway. The makeup mirror fell out of her shaking hand and shattered on the floor.

"Where's Dr. Katz?" she stammered.

Nikolai smiled and entered the room. "He sent me to talk to you. He is very busy man." He closed the door behind him.

"Nikolai, I need to talk to him." Gwen's brain was reeling. Nikolai seemed spaced out and his speech was slurred.

Nikolai walked up to her. "Your makeup, it no look so good." He studied her. "You haf been crying." He reached out to touch her arm.

"What do you want?" Gwen asked, backing up a step, her voice shrill with fear.

Nikolai didn't answer, but she heard a metallic *pfft* sound that she couldn't quite identify. Then she saw the fearsome blade in his hand. Gwen screamed.

Nikolai lunged at her and clamped his free hand over her mouth as he drove her back into the wall. "I haf message from Dr. Katz." His face contorted into a fiendish grin as he buried the blade in her belly.

Gwen felt a sharp, tearing pain and she tried to scream again, but all she could do was moan. She felt Nikolai's sweat-soaked body pin her to the wall and heard him grunt with the effort of driving the blade farther into her. Her pain ratcheted off the scale and then she became strangely numb to it. She sensed that he withdrew the blade and took a step back, breathing heavily. She felt herself crumple to the floor in a heap. The rug felt comfortable and she noticed the subtle pattern in the nap for the first time. She could still feel some sensations in an odd, detached way—nothing sharp or painful. Her mind registered a warm feeling on her belly and she felt the front of her dress getting sticky wet. She felt bad that this would likely stain her pretty blue dress, and she considered what she should soak it in as a pretreatment. The room started to dim, and Gwen gazed up at the fluorescent lights.

Gwen also sensed Nikolai's presence above her, watching her. But she was too tired to look up at him. Would he stab her again? she wondered. A beeping sound roused her. She opened her eyes and forced her stubborn eyes to focus. Sounded like a text message. She saw Nikolai look at his phone.

Her head sank back down and she decided she was no longer interested in Nikolai. Instead, her thoughts turned to Rob and what he had just told her. He loved her and he was leaving his wife to be with her. Things were finally going her way. She loved him so much. She would rest here for a little and then go and be with him. Soon he would be cradling her in his arms. She just needed a little shut-eye so she could look her best. She always wanted to look her best for Rob. She closed her eyes and drifted down into the blackness, imagining Rob caressing her as she slept. She could feel his breath on her and heard him whisper in her ear that he would love her forever.

CHAPTER FORTY-ONE

Luke allowed Jensen to lead him out of the operating room without putting up any more resistance. His mind was reeling in shock from the events of the last two hours. Things were happening way too fast. He needed to slow things down and think.

Jensen led Luke to a chair in the hallway, then barked to the heavy-set agent standing guard outside, "Walker!"

"Yes, sir," Walker replied, coming to attention. Even though Jensen was much younger, he was obviously in charge.

"Don't fuck up again and let anyone in this OR. You got that?"

Walker's face reddened and he sputtered back, "But he said he was a doctor. I thought he was here to help."

"Yeah, he was a *big* help, all right," Jensen said, glancing at Luke. Then, almost speaking to himself, he added, "I can't figure out exactly *what* he's here for." Jensen turned back to Walker. "What we need is for you to think less and follow orders more. Can you do that, Walker?" Jensen glared at the older agent.

"Yes, sir." Walker studied the floor.

"Good, the senator's life may depend on it. I want you to detain Dr. Daulton here. I'm not sure how he's involved, but I want to question him when this is all over. Is that clear?"

"Yes, sir. I won't let him out of my sight."

Luke sat down, defeated. What the hell was going on? This much he knew—the senator was definitely burning up and his blood acid level was sky high. But Luke's gut still didn't buy the

MH diagnosis. What was he missing? What bothered him the most was that there were just *way* too many coincidences here. First, there had been a similar MH case with Mrs. Hinkle two weeks ago, and Katz had been the anesthesiologist. And now, he knew, Katz had been involved with the senator's anesthetic as well. Second, the mysterious Sudoku, when solved, certainly suggested a murder plot. And Seidle had tried to kill Kim right after she had solved the puzzle. And, of course, Katz had given Kim the total spinal in the first place. Suddenly, Rob's warning about Katz came back to him and seemed more telling than ever.

An ominous feeling descended upon Luke. Where was Katz, anyway? If Katz really *was* involved in a plan to murder a US senator, he wouldn't think twice about killing anyone who got in his way. Like Kim.

Luke thought furiously. Was Katz on his way right now to finish Kim off? Did Katz know about Seidle being killed? He needed to get through to Kim. But how could he? He was a prisoner. They even suspected him of being involved in the senator's fiasco. He had to get a message to Kim and warn her. He had to try something.

"Walker, do you have kids?" Luke asked.

"Yeah, we have two boys." Walker smiled. "Both play football at Central Dauphin."

"You must be proud. What positions do they play?"

"Derek plays center and Kyle plays linebacker."

"Nice. My wife just had a baby."

"When?"

"Tonight."

Walker's face softened and he smiled. "Congratulations, Doc."

"There were complications, though, and she's in the intensive care unit."

"Oh," Walker said. He seemed unsure of what to say. After an uncomfortable silence, he added, "Hope she'll be okay."

Luke looked directly at the man and thought he detected

genuine concern. "Walker, do you mind if I call the SICU to check on my wife?"

A frown appeared as Walker seemed to wrestle with the decision. "Sorry, Doc, no can do. No phone calls."

"I just want to know if she's all right. No funny business, I promise."

"Look, Doc," Walker said, his face taking on a pained expression. "You just heard me get reamed out, right?"

"Yeah," Luke admitted.

"I have to be careful, here. Jensen—he runs a tight ship."

Luke tried another tack. "Can *you* call them for me? Please?"

"Yeah, I suppose I could do that. What's the number?"

"It's 763-2126."

Walker dialed and held his cell phone to his ear for a while. "Sorry, Doc. No answer." He put his phone back in its cradle on his hip. "They must be closed for the night," he offered.

Shit. "The SICU doesn't close," Luke said. How could he get a message through to Kim? Several precious minutes passed as he pondered this. And then it came to him.

"Walker, can you do me one more favor and page my wife?"

"Page?"

"Yes. Call the page operator and tell her to page her."

"I guess so."

"Tell her to page Dr. Roman Daulton, Room 604, stat."

"That's a strange page, Doc." Walker frowned again and looked as if he was going to balk. "I dunno."

"Roman's her pet name for me. It has to do with a trip to Italy we took once. A love message, okay?"

Walker hesitated, looking uncertainly at Luke.

"It would mean a lot to her."

"All right."

"The words must be exact, though. Dr. Roman Daulton, Room 604, stat."

Walker made the call and the page soon went out over the hospital intercom.

"Thanks, Walker." Luke hoped Kim would get the message—and understand it—in time.

Suddenly the OR door burst open and Jensen stuck his head out. "Walker, get in here! The senator's going into cardiac arrest!"

Walker jumped out of his seat, drew his gun, and headed toward the door. Before he went in, he turned to Luke. "Don't go anywhere, Doc. I'm trusting you, now."

CHAPTER FORTY-TWO

Jenna struggled to maintain her self control as she trained her Glock 23 on Katz. This assignment had not exactly gone according to plan. She had already shot to death one of the physicians in the delivery room, and it didn't look like this fiasco was over just yet. Was this Dr. Katz one of the bad guys and aligned with Seidle? Or was he just one of the garden-variety, arrogant asshole doctors with a God complex? Hard to know.

She desperately needed more information. Good intel was critical in these situations and hers was spotty at best. For instance, how could it be that the fricking senator was here tonight having surgery? Coincidence? Worse—why she hadn't known about it? Communication between federal agencies, like Secret Service and FBI, still had a way to go. But, a bigger question remained—was the senator's presence here somehow related to the bloodbath in the delivery room? She reasoned it almost had to be.

Jenna knew the outcome of this night would likely determine the future of her career with the Bureau. She didn't want to overreact and be viewed as a trigger-happy newbie. Killing Seidle had been clear-cut—he had pulled a gun and threatened to use it. Not to mention, he had tried to butcher Mrs. Daulton and her baby. But, she couldn't tell if Katz was also trying to kill Mrs. Daulton with a lethal injection or if he was just trying to do his job. She didn't have the luxury of shooting first and asking questions later.

At the moment, Katz was fuming and looked like he was

perfectly capable of murder. Was he armed like Seidle? She couldn't be sure with his loose white coat covering his scrub suit. Should she cuff him? Or just call for backup?

Jenna recognized the first tug of uncertainty as the initial step on the path toward panic, just as they had taught her at Quantico. But, rather than give in to it, she chose to harness the energy. Other agents might have crumbled under the stress, but despite the ambiguity and danger of this current situation, Jenna felt more alive than ever. This was why she had left nursing, with its drudgery of bedpans and enemas, and joined the Bureau in the first place. She embraced the adrenaline rush and felt her body crackle with energy. She had dreamt of just these types of encounters.

The Glock, with its high-powered 40-caliber ammo, felt right as rain in her hand. After logging countless hours at the firing range, she could handle the gun like a pro. In repeated training scenarios over the past two years, she had also demonstrated a talent for killing the bad guys and ferreting out the non-combatants, often by making split-second decisions. She always scored well at the range and was told she had good instincts, but this was her first real-life test.

His face flushed with rage, Katz struggled to control his breathing. "What're you doing here?" he shouted.

"I'll ask the questions, Doctor," she replied. But, she had to admit, it *was* a good question. She had, in fact, volunteered to investigate when they had gotten the mysterious help call from Benjamin Harris's computer code on Sunday—her nursing background made her a perfect choice. Details had been scant and some pooh-poohed it as a joke or a computer glitch, but when Ben didn't return phone calls, Jenna knew something was up. Ben had more on the ball than most of the guys gave him credit for.

Besides, Jenna was looking for a way to distinguish her young career and to prove herself with the guys. Unfortunately, things were tight in the Bureau these days and manpower was limited, thanks to the Department of Homeland Security sucking up the lion's share of available resources. Money for tackling homegrown criminals just wasn't what it used to be. So she had been sent in alone and had just arrived on the scene tonight—the OB department had the only immediate opening.

She fumbled in her pocket for a pair of handcuffs, never taking her eyes off Katz or lowering her weapon. "Are you working with Dr. Seidle?"

Before Katz could answer, a young man burst into the room, practically running into Jenna. She jumped back a step, dropping the handcuffs, before turning her gun on the intruder.

"Hold it right there," she demanded.

"Whoa! Take it easy, lady," the young man said, raising his hands up high. "I cool."

"Get over there with him." She gestured towards Katz with her gun. The newcomer was a young man with Slavic features and an accent that was probably Russian. Could this be where Seidle's Makarov pistol had come from? Did these two have other weapons? Or was he just an innocent hospital orderly? She swung her head from side to side to try to keep an eye on both.

The man gave Katz a questioning look. "Do what she says, Nikolai," Katz said. So the older man was in charge here. Katz nodded and Nikolai moved over to stand beside him.

The two men exchanged glances, and Jenna worried they might rush her. "Don't think I won't use this gun," she said with as much no-nonsense bravado as she could muster. "Just ask your friend, Dr. Seidle. He made that mistake and he's got two bullet holes in his head to show for it." Katz looked vaguely surprised, but Nikolai appeared unfazed. Jenna wanted to keep them back on their heels, so she added, "And his brains are splattered all over the delivery room." There, that seemed to get the message across.

Protocol dictated that she call for backup now. Play it by the book. She pulled out her cell phone and looked down for a moment to dial it.

Pfft.

The noise came from across the room. *What was that?*

A nasty switchblade had appeared in Nikolai's right hand and he brandished it with glee. *Shit, a weapon!* The bad guys were multiplying, and her odds were worsening. She realized there was indeed something very rotten at this hospital and she was rapidly becoming outmanned. What had poor Benjamin gotten himself into? She hoped to God he was tied up in a back room somewhere. Jenna quashed these thoughts, hoping to tamp down the panic that was churning just below the surface. She resisted the urge to feel overwhelmed—or to feel anything. Emotions were not particularly useful in these situations. She refocused on her training and took several deep, calming breaths.

The presence of the knife didn't change her threat scene calculus. After all, the two men were five or six feet away. She still had the Glock and wasn't afraid to use it. She was in charge here. She just needed to continue to think clearly and control the situation. In fact, the knife clarified things. These two had revealed themselves as definite bad guys, justifying the use of deadly force. "Drop the knife!" she barked at Nikolai.

He just stood there, leering at her as he continued to make sweeping motions with the knife through the air.

"I said, drop the fucking knife!" She fired her weapon above him as a warning. Plaster bits from the wall sprayed down on top of Kim's ventilator. Nikolai lowered the knife and put up his other hand in a stop gesture. His smile faded, but he still didn't drop the knife. She needed to call in badly, but first she had to control this volatile situation. Should she cuff them and then call? Or should she shoot Nikolai?

The hospital intercom crackled loudly to life, startling her. "Dr. Roman Daulton, Room 604, stat! Dr. Roman Daulton, Room 604, stat!" Jenna took several more deep breaths and willed her pulse rate back down. She thought for a moment. Dr. Daulton? Wasn't he the brave doctor in the DR that tackled Seidle and delivered his own wife's baby? Talk about tough situations. Although, wasn't his name Luke?

Something about Nikolai's blade drew her attention. Was that blood on it?

Nikolai suddenly lunged at her. He moved awkwardly, with a surprised expression on his face, but with the knife still clenched in his hand. Jenna hesitated only a fraction of a second before firing her pistol twice. At this range she couldn't miss. She heard Nikolai yelp and saw his face contort in pain and disbelief as blood spurted from his chest, but he kept coming at her.

She quickly realized why—Katz was hunkered down behind Nikolai and was shoving him toward her like a battering ram. She sidestepped quickly, and Nikolai's limp body tumbled past her, thudding onto the floor. Katz swiped at her neck with his free hand. She kicked him hard, landing a solid blow to his ribcage that sent him stumbling to the ground.

She brought her gun back up and aimed it at Katz's chest. "Don't move!" she screamed, her heart pounding in her ears. She counted her shots—five, so far. That left her with eight rounds. Plenty.

Katz groaned and got to his knees.

"Move again and I'll shoot you," she said. He stayed put, huddled in the corner, staring at her. She slowed her breathing. *Okay, one perp down.* She had evened the odds and now it was one on one. Just like in the simulator. Her brain processed the distinct likelihood that Katz had actually pushed Nikolai toward her using him as a human shield. Talk about friends.

She touched the side of her neck where it felt as if something had scratched her. Her hand came back bloody. Shit! Had Nikolai managed to slice her with his blade? She didn't think so. She refocused on Katz and noticed he had a syringe in his hand. Was this the cause of the scrape on her neck? Things had moved so fast. She couldn't be sure of what had happened. "Did you inject me with something?" She waved the gun at him.

He nodded, and she thought she could detect a slight smile.

She wanted for all the world to shoot him right here and now and just fricking end it. But she resisted the temptation for the second time that night. She was, after all, one of the good guys. "With what?" she asked, trying to keep the dread she felt out of her voice.

"Just some mild pain medicine that I was trying to give to my patient, Mrs. Daulton—before you interrupted my care." He smiled innocently.

"Cut the bullshit! I know you were trying to kill her."

He eyed her closely, then glanced at the clock on the wall.

Bastard! All of a sudden, Jenna didn't feel so well. God, he'd drugged her. Was the damn gun already becoming heavy in her hand? She brought her other hand up to steady the gun. Now she felt totally overwhelmed and the panic that had been lurking nearby flooded into her. They hadn't covered this in the training manuals. The Glock was now so heavy that she needed both hands to hold it. She still needed to call for backup, but she couldn't even use the damn cell phone. This was not good. She tried to spread her legs into a more stable firing position, but her legs buckled beneath her and she went down hard onto her knees. Her legs felt like jelly and she wobbled miserably before they gave out completely. She fired in Katz's direction as she fell facedown on the floor.

Katz was on her in an instant, straddling her and holding her gun arm down. She struggled for all she was worth, trying to bring her gun into a firing position. If she could just get another shot off... But she couldn't overcome his grip. She twisted her neck to look up at him and saw a look of pure evil in his face. Something dripped onto her face and made her blink. Was that blood dripping down onto her—his blood? She prayed to God that she had hit the prick—and that it was lethal.

He pried the Glock out of her fingers. "You're right," he said, standing up. "I lied. I gave you a muscle relaxant, which explains why you're getting so weak. In about two minutes you'll stop breathing, and you'll be dead in four."

This time she believed he was telling the truth. She knew about paralytic agents. Four minutes wasn't a long time. She clung to the hope that she was in the intensive care unit of a hospital and that someone could still come by and save her. They had to have heard the gunshots. She began to gasp for breath.

"So long, Special Agent Jenna. Life's a bitch." He found her cell phone in her pocket and smashed it on the floor. Then he turned and headed toward Mrs. Daulton.

Jenna's air hunger was rapidly becoming unbearable and she no longer cared about Katz or Mrs. Daulton. *Please, someone help me!* As the room dimmed about her, she heard the intercom come to life once again. "Red Alert! Surgical Intensive Care Unit. Red Alert! Surgical Intensive Care Unit."

CHAPTER FORTY-THREE

Rob got off the bed and began pacing about the small OB call room. He checked his watch again for the tenth time. Where was she? She should be here by now. Rob couldn't imagine what was taking Gwen so long. She had sounded very excited on the phone and he thought she would be right up. He was surprised she had left in the first place. He dialed her number again. No answer.

Rob thought back to their earlier phone call. It wasn't exactly the way he had pictured the big conversation, the one where he professed his love for her and told her he was leaving Cindy. But he didn't see that he had had much choice in the matter. Her pain had cut through him and he didn't have it in him to keep her guessing any longer. He wanted desperately to hold her in his arms, squeeze her tight and convince her everything would be all right.

Something still bothered him about their conversation. What exactly had she seen fit to attend to in the middle of the night? He recalled that Katz's name had come up. How the hell did Katz fit into this strange night? What was that prick up to? He didn't have any hard evidence that Katz was involved with Seidle and that whole OB fiasco, but it would certainly come as no surprise if he was. He hoped to God Gwen wasn't mixed up with Katz. *Please Lord, keep her safe.*

It struck Rob as odd that he was still invoking God's name. *Old habits die hard,* he mused. After all, hadn't he written God off when he fell in love with Gwen? Surely, God wouldn't be listening to him now, or leastwise not be inclined to help him. He shook his head and sighed.

Rob peeled off his sweat- and bloodstained scrubs, tossed them in the circular hamper, and headed to the shower. He'd started the water and was just about to step into the stall when the hospital-wide intercom crackled to life. "Dr. Roman Daulton, Room 604, stat! Dr. Roman Daulton, Room 604, stat!"

Roman Daulton? How weird was that? What the hell did that mean? Rob shook his head, then stopped abruptly. The hospital only had four floors. There *was* no Room 604. Very odd.

He hopped into the shower stall, pulled the flimsy curtain closed, and stood under the weak stream. Rob was surprised how bloody his arms and chest were. He lathered up well and watched as the blood—Kim's blood—washed off him and went swirling down the drain in red spirals. He was glad he had been here in the hospital to save Kim. Such a sweet woman. The baby was adorable, too. Strange and big things were definitely afoot this night and fate seemed to be playing all its trump cards.

The hot water felt good rushing over his tired muscles, and he stood there for several minutes, soaking in the warmth. Although his body was exhausted, his mind was brimming with energy. He felt such a high, such exhilaration that it seemed his feet barely touched the floor. He recognized this as a symptom of being in love and smiled. He couldn't wait to see Gwen; hopefully she would be here any minute. He tried to listen for sounds of the call room door opening. Maybe she would even sneak up on him in the shower. He imagined her pulling the shower curtain aside and smiling at him. He would pull her into the shower with her clothes still on. They would stand there in the water kissing and holding each other.

The hospital intercom blared again, interrupting his shower fantasy. Sounded like a red alert. He strained to hear it, but couldn't make out the details above the rush of the water. Or perhaps it was a code blue being called somewhere in the hospital. In a busy hospital, patients were fighting for their lives at all hours.

All these thoughts about love and Gwen, God and Katz, and people dying reminded him of his recurrent nighttime plea to the universe—that either Cindy, Gwen, or he should die to put an end to his misery. Rob smiled wryly; he, of course, had no use for the gun of fate anymore. *Be careful what you wish for.* He had an uneasy sense about this and wondered if God was listening after all.

CHAPTER FORTY-FOUR

Kim regained consciousness slowly. What was that loud noise? What was going on? Had she imagined the noise? No, her ears were still ringing. Her torpid mind was very sluggish to respond. She felt so weak—all she wanted to do was sleep. She tried to open her eyes but they refused, as if someone or something were holding her eyelids shut. She noticed a very strange sensation in her chest. It was rising rhythmically even though she was making no effort to breathe. She then became aware of the horrible, plastic breathing tube lodged in her throat, and started to gag. She must be on a ventilator. She struggled mightily to coax her memory back to life.

She felt drugged. Wait, she had been drugged! In a flash, she remembered the whole ordeal—having contractions at home, Colby looking worried, Luke driving her frantically to the hospital, being wheeled into the C-section room—each memory linking to the next, like bridges connecting islets through a fog. Further, she recalled Dr. Katz giving her the spinal, which had put an end to those nasty contractions. After this, though, her mind drew a blank—the bridgework halted abruptly in mid-span. What had happened?

Then a horrifying thought struck her. Oh, dear God, what about the baby? Was Abi okay? She needed to wake up, get moving and find out. She tried to wiggle her feet but they didn't respond. Was she paralyzed? She suffered a moment of panic until she wiggled her fingers and found they moved normally. She remembered the spinal and reasoned it must be still working, explaining the numbness in her lower limbs.

Where was Luke, though? She tried hard to clear her mind, to get it working. For some reason she thought this was important. She focused on her other senses. She listened carefully and heard the beep-beep of a monitor over her head. Must be a cardiac monitor or a pulse ox. Again, she noticed the air being pushed into her by the breathing machine. Surely this wasn't normal—something must've gone wrong with the C-section. There was also a strange odor in the air that she couldn't identify. It reminded her of the Fourth of July, but she couldn't say why.

Suddenly, the hospital intercom came to life. "Dr. Roman Daulton, Room 604, stat! Dr. Roman Daulton, Room 604, stat!" Kim was amazed. *That's a weird page,* she thought. Very weird. Was she dreaming? A drug-induced haze? Roman Daulton? Room 604? What did *that* mean? She had an odd sense that the page was meant for her and that it was important. Her mind automatically set about analyzing the page, approaching it like any other problem.

This reminded her of the Sudoku puzzle. She remembered solving it and whispering the solution to Luke before she passed out. Kill Senator Pierce. Was this page related? Was Luke somehow involved? Where was Luke, anyway? It wasn't like him not to be here. Too many difficult questions. She felt so tired. The drug wave washed over her again and she sank into the incoming tide of drowsiness, surrendering to its power.

As she drifted down through deeper and deeper sleep levels, the loud noise returned. Then again. She awoke for a second time with a start. Now, her ears not only rang, but hurt from the noise. Were those gunshots? Suddenly Kim identified the strange smell as spent gunpowder and this sent chills down her spine. Something was desperately wrong here. Her instincts screamed. She needed to wake up. She shook her head back and forth, ignoring the gagging tube in her throat. And, there was something about that page that was vitally important. Roman Daulton? Room

604? She didn't know why, but she knew she needed to understand.

A familiar voice near her interrupted her thoughts.

"Ah, I see you're waking up, Kim. Good."

Kim nodded and strained to listen.

"You gave us quite a scare back there," the voice continued soothingly. "I've come to help you."

She recognized the deep voice of Dr. Katz. She felt him lean over her and remove some tape from her eyelids. She opened her eyes and the light poured in, temporarily blinding her. Soon her vision returned, although her eyes remained out of focus. She squinted up at him. He had a strange expression on his face.

"Don't worry," he said. "Everything's going to be okay."

She felt a bit relieved. She wanted to believe him.

Then the intercom blared again: "Red Alert! SICU! Red Alert! Surgical Intensive Care Unit!"

Something still wasn't right here. Kim struggled to move her head and look about the room, but her head felt very heavy and her vision rippled with dizziness when she did this. Something over in the corner of the room caught her attention, but Dr. Katz partially blocked her view. Was that a body there, in a heap on the floor? Her mind was slow to process the image. She craned her neck to get a better look, but succeeded only in triggering more waves of dizziness. And Dr. Katz seemed to shift his position to block her view.

Alarms were going off in Kim's head. There was definitely a body on the floor, lying in a pool of blood. Frantically, she fought to hurl off the effects of the damn drugs.

"Such a worried expression, Kim. Are you in pain?" Dr. Katz patted her arm. "Not to worry, dear. I have something for you. It will take care of your pain." He chuckled and added, "Forever."

Kim started to panic. Forever? She needed to focus. Room 604. Room 604. Roman Daulton. Kim's brain, nudged by an outpouring of adrenaline, kicked into overdrive. She felt the puzzle begin to unravel before her. Swatara Regional only had four floors. There was no Room 604. Roman numerals danced before her. In a flash, she had deciphered the coded message.

"My master has prepared a place for you," Dr. Katz continued and his eyes lit up as he spoke. "You will meet him soon." He turned for a moment to the supply cabinet behind him. She could hear him rummaging through the drawers. Kim seized the opportunity and acted on the message.

Seconds later, Katz returned to hover over her. Kim saw him inject something into her IV tubing. She tried to scream, but the endotracheal tube rendered any speech impossible.

CHAPTER FORTY-FIVE

Sorry, Walker. As soon as Walker left him alone, Luke dashed out of the OR and headed back to SICU. As he wound his way through the hospital corridors, the overhead intercom blared out, "Red alert! SICU! Red alert! Surgical Intensive Care Unit!" Some bad shit was going down in the SICU, like an out-of-control patient or family member. *Or a crazed, gun-wielding doctor on the loose. I hope I'm not too late!*

As Luke rounded the last corner to the SICU, he was greeted by a horrifying sight. Katz was at Kim's bedside, injecting something into her IV line. Luke sprinted toward the room, screaming, "Stop! Don't do it!"

Katz whirled. "You're too late, Daulton."

Luke launched himself at Katz, knocking him backward across the room, like a football player hitting the sled. The older man's head smacked against the wall. "You sick bastard! What did you do?"

Katz didn't reply; he was dazed but still conscious.

Two bodies were on the floor against the wall—Nikolai lying in a pool of blood with a knife in his hand and next to him was Jenna, who looked ashen in death. What the hell had happened?

Katz started to move, his hands rubbing his head. He focused on Luke. "I injected her with air," he croaked. "She'll die of a massive air embolus. A common complication following a bloody C-section."

"I'll kill you, you son of a bitch!" Luke wrapped his hands

around Katz's thick neck and began to throttle him. Katz struggled to free himself, but was too weak to offer much resistance. As Luke continued to squeeze the life out of him, he noticed the bullet wound in Katz's left shoulder, now bleeding freely.

Kim's monitor shrieked a piercing alarm. Luke looked over to see her EKG go flatline. He let go of Katz, who sagged to the floor, gasping, and rushed to Kim's side.

Cardiac arrest! Damn, I never should have left her. What should he do? Call a code and get help? Give epinephrine? Start CPR?

Luke ran over to the crash cart in the corner, over by Nikolai's body. He flung open the drawers, looking for epi. He also turned the defibrillator on and charged the paddles—even though there was no rhythm to shock. All the while, he knew it was hopeless—no matter what he did. There was no treatment for a massive air embolus, short of immediate cardiopulmonary bypass in the OR, for which they had no time.

Luke ripped open a box of epi and injected it into her IV port and ensured the IV was running wide open. He glanced at the monitor again, hoping for any sign of life—now, even her pulse ox failed to register. Was she dead already?

Luke felt the tears well up in his eyes as he injected a second syringe of epi. It seemed like he was standing in the living room twelve years ago, with his dad sprawled out on the floor. He could hear his dad's voice: *"Luke, what happens in life is up to you. There is no ghost world to rely on to do your work. Work hard and you will succeed. Misplace your belief in someone other than yourself and you will fail."* He always knew he was to blame for his father's death. And now he was responsible for Kim's death as well. What kind of God would let Kim die now? Surely not one he wanted to place his faith in.

He heard Katz stir behind him, but didn't care. Katz made his way to the door and said in a hoarse voice, "And to think I was worried about you and your wife. You're both pathetic and no match for me." He heard Katz stagger out of the room and down the hallway.

Luke began to weep as he put his hands on Kim's chest and prepared to do compressions. He stopped short when he noticed the bedsheet covering her arm was wet. There was a large wet spot, and it was growing—and it was blood-tinged. He quickly peeled the sheet back and realized with a shock that her IV catheter was lying loose in the bed. It was no longer in a vein and blood oozed from the site in her arm where it had been. Surely Katz hadn't pulled out the IV?

Luke was confused, but also couldn't stifle a ray of hope. He noticed the pulse ox probe was not on her finger. But that didn't explain the EKG flatline. He pulled the sheet entirely off her, exposing her whole upper body, and what he saw froze him. He saw one crumpled EKG pad with the lead wire still attached, clutched in her hand. No wonder the EKG had gone flat. He didn't dare to hope any further, but couldn't help himself.

"Please God," he whispered to the air. He was terrified to ask, but did so anyway. "Kim, can you hear me?"

No response.

He stroked her hand. "Kim, Kim, I love you. I'm sorry I wasn't there for you." Finally, after summoning additional courage, he bent down and put his face up to her ear. He could make out her unique fragrance, a tiny beacon almost lost in the overwhelming sea of harsh SICU smells. "Kim, are you there?" he asked.

Did her hand move in his?

"Kim," he said louder, his voice breaking. He squeezed her hand tightly.

She opened her eyes and looked up at him.

A rush of emotion swelled up in Luke. *Thank God,* he thought in utter amazement. *Unbelievable! Thank God.* "Are you okay?"

She nodded.

He kissed her on the cheek several times and squeezed her hand, his own hands trembling badly. He fought to control his breathing and settle his heart down.

Kim's eyes darted about the room, fearful.

"He's gone. Katz is gone."

She settled down and gazed up at him.

"You pulled the IV out, didn't you?" he asked, filled with admiration.

She nodded again, more vigorously this time.

"You got my message?"

More nodding.

Tears flowed from Luke's eyes. "Oh, I love you so much." He bent down and hugged her in spite of the ventilator hoses and kissed her again, smiling through his tears. "You're so smart." She had obviously decoded his message; 604 in Roman numerals was DCIV—medical shorthand for "discontinue intravenous line." She had also improvised and pulled off the EKG patch and the pulse ox probe.

Kim stared up at him, tears streaming out of her eyes.

He saw the question in her eyes and understood. "Abi's fine. The delivery was a little rough, but she's fine." He paused as Abi's angelic face floated across his mind. "I delivered her myself," he added with pride.

Again she smiled and managed to look beautiful in spite of the endotracheal tube.

"I'll explain it all later. Let's just work on getting you well. You need to rest, sweetheart."

Suddenly Kim's eyes opened wide, flashed a look of terror, then closed and her hand went limp.

"Kim, come back!" Luke cried. What was happening? Maybe she hadn't pulled the IV out in time and enough air had been injected to kill her? He snapped his head up to the monitor, but it was still disconnected and useless. "Oh, God, please, no."

A deep voice behind him startled him. "God's got nothing to do with it."

Luke whipped around to see Dr. Katz standing behind him, wielding a large pipe wrench. Luke barely managed to put his hand up in time before the wrench came down hard on his head and everything swirled to black.

CHAPTER FORTY-SIX

TUESDAY, NOVEMBER 23, 12:58 A.M.

Rob shut the water off, toweled off, and climbed out of the shower stall, his feet leaving water on the tile floor. He checked his phone on the counter—no messages. He dialed Gwen's number again and got her voicemail.

He checked his beeper out of habit—he wasn't on call tonight. He was surprised to see *2126 911*. This was the SICU number and the 911 meant stat. The time of the page was twelve minutes ago. Shit! Kim was in the SICU. He quickly wrapped the towel around his waist and dialed the SICU.

"Hello, SICU," came a breathless, shrill voice.

"This is Dr. Gentry. I was stat paged."

"Dr. Gentry—all hell's breaking loose down here. Didn't you hear the red alert?"

"I must've missed it. What's going on?"

"Somebody was shooting in Mrs. Daulton's room."

"Shooting?" Rob blurted.

"Yes."

"Is she okay?"

"I think so. The police are here now. You'd better get down here."

"I'll be right there."

Bad shit was going down out there and he still didn't know where Gwen was. Rob hopped into fresh scrubs, almost slipping on the wet tile floor. He put his sneakers on, not bothering with socks, and made for the door, then paused. He scribbled a note and left it on the nightstand: *Gwen, went to SICU. Call me if you get this note. I love you!!!*

Rob raced out of the call room so fast he bumped his elbow on the doorframe. As he ran toward SICU, he couldn't shake the eerie feeling that the gun of fate was preparing to mete out its judgment tonight.

There was a Derry Township police officer outside Kim's door, stringing yellow crime scene tape. Curtains were drawn across the door, partially blocking the view inside. Rob could just make out Kim lying in the bed in the center of the room—she looked unharmed.

"What happened here?" Rob asked the police officer. "I heard there were gunshots fired."

The bleary-eyed cop, whose badge identified him as Sergeant Markel, stared back at Rob without saying anything. He pulled a small dog-eared notebook from his back pocket and readied a pen. He cleared his throat. "And just who might you be, sir?" he inquired.

"I'm Dr. Gentry." Rob pointed at Kim. "*This* woman's obstetrician. Here's my ID."

The sergeant took Rob's ID and studied it for what seemed like a long time. He then looked up to inspect Rob. Not impressed, he showed no sign of moving aside.

"I need to examine her," Rob said, not hiding his irritation. He started to walk around Markel; politeness and civility be damned.

"Not so fast, Dr. Gentry." Markel blocked Rob. "My orders are to let no one in this room—not even Jesus Christ. The room is a crime scene." He pointed to the yellow tape for emphasis.

Rob looked past the man and saw blood on the floor—lots of it. There were footprints in it and scuffle marks indicating a struggle. Kim looked to be asleep with the ventilator breathing for her. Her vital signs on the overhead monitor appeared normal.

Rob sidestepped to see further around the rotund sergeant and gasped. Against the far wall, Nikolai, the hospital orderly, lay crumpled in a heap with what looked to be two gunshot wounds to his chest. On the floor in the corner of the room lay Jenna, the FBI agent/OB nurse. He couldn't make out an obvious injury, but she was clearly dead. And she had this haunting look on her face.

Rob reeled backward. What the hell was going on here? "What happened here? Where is Dr. Daulton, her husband?"

"We have several officers combing the building, looking for the perp," Markel said.

"The perp?"

"Husbands are always the number-one suspect," he added, with a knowing, almost smug expression. "We just missed them."

"Them?"

"Yeah, another fellow named Doctor...uh—" Markel consulted his notebook. "Katz. Katz was seen here with him. Perhaps the two are working together—you know, in cahoots."

So Katz *was* involved in this mess! Rob thought furiously while Markel droned on.

"We responded as soon as we got the call about shots being fired in Obstetrics. More officers are on the way. The Derry Township SWAT team is mobilizing—you know, long arm of the law and all that. Don't worry, we'll catch 'em."

Rob had a sickening feeling that this thing would be over long before Derry Township's finest got their act together. Homicides in sleepy little Hershey were rare. The urgent situation demanded action, but he wasn't sure which way to turn. If Kim were conscious, she might have a clue what happened here. "I need to talk to my patient," Rob insisted.

One of the SICU nurses hovering nearby came to Markel's defense. "She can't talk right now. She became agitated and I had to sedate her."

"What happened?" Rob asked.

"She was thrashing about violently when we came in—she even managed to pull her IV out," she said. "I was afraid she might hurt herself, so I had no choice but to sedate her."

"Fine." Rob tried to piece together the events of the evening, make some sense of it all. *First, Seidle tries to murder Kim. Then an undercover FBI agent shoots him dead. Now the FBI agent's dead and so is an OR orderly.* Plus, he learned that Katz was involved. This thing stank to high heaven.

Which brought him back to Luke. Where *was* Luke? He said he had to go to the OR to check on the senator. But instead, he showed up in the SICU. What was it Luke had said? Something about a puzzle and a crazy plot to kill the senator. Maybe it wasn't so crazy. Rob recalled a story he had read in last year's paper—about an anesthesiologist at Our Lady of Mercy Hospital in Lancaster getting mixed up in a murder plot in the OR. A couple of people were killed. His name was Landry, or something like that.

But for Rob, the bigger question remained—where was Gwen? He needed to find her. Something had prevented her from coming to the call room. She had said she would be right up. Could she be mixed up in this craziness? What else had she said? She mentioned she had some weird story to tell him about the incinerator—whatever that meant. Rob ran his fingers through his wet hair. This much was clear—he couldn't just stand here with Gwen and Luke unaccounted for, and a murderer running loose in the hospital. Things were happening quickly and he felt certain the local police would never sort them out fast enough. Time for action.

CHAPTER FORTY-SEVEN

FBI Special Agent Jared Smith walked silently up to the office door, gun drawn. His nerves were wired. What was it his boss had said? "Don't let the small-town setting fool you—some bad shit's going down at this hospital. Figure it out, okay? And Smith—don't fuck up and get yourself killed." *Thanks for the pep talk, boss.*

Jared had been dispatched from the Harrisburg branch office just after midnight when Special Agent Jenna Steele had failed to call in. He hadn't been thrilled to take the call, but he knew Jenna and this made it personal. They had started working at the Bureau at about the same time—Jared after fifteen years in the army, Jenna right out of nursing school. He didn't think she graduated, but somehow had grown disenchanted and made a career change. She was young and bright—not bad looking, either. A bit too in your face for his tastes, but what the hell. The brass liked her and that's what counted. She was headed for a promising career—her nursing skillset a bonus for the Bureau. He didn't know the other agent, Benjamin Harris, but the word was, he was a complete computer geek.

Unfortunately, Jenna's cell phone had gone dark and so had Harris's, making it difficult to pinpoint their locations. So the boys down at IT had triangulated on the cell phone signal that was the origin of Harris's computer distress call. This led Jared to the Anesthesia billing office, which was deserted. So Jared proceeded to the next logical place.

The sign on the door read *Chief of Anesthesia: Dr. Jason Katz*. Jared tried the handle—it was unlocked. He took a deep breath, flung open the door, and burst into the room, finger poised on the trigger.

Holy shit! A woman lay crumpled on the floor in a pool of blood.

After checking to make sure the room was clear, he rushed to her. At first he thought she was dead, but up close, he saw she was breathing very shallowly. He checked her pulse—weak. He rolled her onto her back and ripped open her blouse. He recoiled at the jagged abdominal wound, probably knife-inflicted. The woman had lost a lot of blood—a whole lot of blood!

Jared had been a corpsman in the Gulf War so was familiar with battlefield trauma. The fact that she was still alive after receiving no treatment was a good sign. It meant she was unlikely to have suffered a penetrating heart or lung wound, or major blood vessel transection, as these would have killed her in minutes. He believed they could save her, but they needed to get her to an OR immediately. Jared radioed for help.

The woman was moving her lips. Although her eyes remained shut and she was probably delusional with shock, she was trying to say something. Jared bent down close to her face. She was very beautiful, even under these circumstances. He also caught a whiff of her perfume. She was whispering something—repeating something over and over: "Rob, I love you."

CHAPTER FORTY-EIGHT

Tucked in a little-used hallway between the SICU and the OR was the freight elevator. As far as he knew, this elevator was the most direct route to the basement. Rob hopped on the dingy car, which smelled musty and was clearly not intended for public use. Hoping the thing was still functional, Rob pushed *B*. The old elevator lurched and ground noisily into its descent.

Rob noticed droplets of fluid on the cracked linoleum floor of the elevator. He crouched down to take a closer look. Was it blood? It was hard to tell in the dim yellow light thrown off by the single bulb recessed in the ceiling. The elevator reached the bottom with an alarming jolt, and the door opened hesitantly amidst more loud grinding noises. He was glad to get off the thing.

Out in the better-lit hallway, he saw more red droplets on the floor. No question about it now, it was blood. Not a lot of blood, just enough to leave a few drops every few feet. His heartbeat accelerated as he followed the blood trail. The hallway cut through the center of the laundry complex. The air was warmer here and more humid. Laundry carts were parked along the wall and the smell of institutional detergent and bleach hung heavily in the close air. The trail of blood led Rob through the laundry to a door at the end of the hall. An orange glow emanated from its small window. The incinerator room.

Rob's heart began to pound and his throat went dry, as a deep sense of foreboding gripped him. He approached the door and peered through the grime-streaked window. What he saw made his blood run cold. Dr. Katz was pushing a wheeled cart toward the furnace—and there was a body on the cart. And the large grated door to the furnace was wide open.

Rob ripped open the heavy door and screamed at Katz, "What are you doing? Are you crazy?" He wasn't even sure Katz could hear him above the roar of the furnace.

Katz spun to face Rob. "Get away! You can't stop me!"

"The hell I can't!" Rob shouted back. He ran over and jumped between the cart and the furnace, glancing down at the body on the cart—Luke. He had a wicked gash and a large goose egg on the side of his head. Rob immediately bent over and shook him, hoping for any sign of life. Luke moaned.

Katz rammed him from the side, knocking him away from the cart—both men went down hard. The two men grappled on the dirty floor, all the while moving closer to the grated door of the furnace.

Rob broke free and regained his footing, breathing rapidly. Katz stood up and the two men squared off against each other, looking for an opening. Rob shot a look at the furnace—it had a way of commanding your attention. The control knob was set to low, but it still seemed frightfully hot. Rob snapped his eyes back to Katz and noticed the older man had a gunshot wound on his left shoulder that was oozing blood. Apparently oblivious to his injury, Katz threw several vicious punches. Rob put his arms up to protect his head and absorbed the blows. He launched two quick jabs himself—the first one just missing Katz's head, the second landing solidly on his injured shoulder.

Katz grimaced and backed up a step. "Guess you don't know about Gwen," Katz spat out.

"What're you talking about?"

"I know she's here."

Rob was breathing hard. The room was ungodly hot and he was drenched in sweat.

"She came to see you," Katz said.

"Make your point!" Rob shouted back.

"She made a big mistake tonight. She called me and tried to blackmail me."

Rob swung again, but Katz deflected the blow with his good arm.

"She wanted me to kill your wife," Katz said.

Rob felt as if he had been sucker punched. Nausea washed over him and the room started to spin. "That's absurd!"

"Is it?" Katz circled, putting Rob between him and the grated door. "Is it so far-fetched?"

"Gwen would never—you're lying, damn you!"

"Don't underestimate the power of love, Gentry."

"You're lying!"

"I can prove it." Katz began to advance. "Want to see her number on my cell phone?"

"No!" Rob backed up. Sweat burned his eyes and he wiped at them. "That doesn't prove anything. "I don't believe you."

"It was a *big* mistake to threaten me."

"If you laid a hand on her, I'll kill you."

"*I* didn't touch her," Katz said.

The heat from the open door was becoming painful on Rob's back.

"But that crazy Russian," Katz continued, "you never know what *he* might do. He was a drug addict, you know."

"I swear to God, Katz, if anything happened to her, I'll kill you!"

"Swearing to God, now. Don't you know that's a sin, Gentry? Where's your faith now, when you need it the most?"

"You know nothing of faith, you bastard."

"That's where you're wrong—dead wrong. My faith has made me strong. Don't you know that even the demons believe?" His smile was grotesque. "And to think I used to worry about the two of you." He snorted derisively and gestured to Luke. "He's already done for. As for you, with your precious faith in tatters, you are no match for me. The only chance you had was to take me on together. You missed your chance. I taste victory already."

To emphasize his point, Katz locked onto Rob's shirt with a steely grip and began to push. Slowly, inexorably, Rob was forced backward. Shit, Katz was strong. How was that possible for an older man? How was that possible for an older man with a gunshot wound?

Would Gwen really have considered murder? This crazy question ricocheted about his head, sapping his strength as he felt himself being pushed ever nearer to the open grated door. He could feel the temperature rising as he got closer and closer to the flames. Finally, his feet collided with the bottom of the grated door. He threw his arms out, frantically groping for the doorframe to keep from getting pushed in. The frame was red hot and burned his hands. Rob yelped in pain, but didn't let go.

"It's over, Gentry. You've lost. You surrendered your faith for that whore, and now she's dead!"

She couldn't be. "You're lying!"

Katz sneered at him and breathed into his face. "Nikolai gutted her like a sheep! He showed me the bloody knife blade. I have it."

This seemed to ring true. Was Gwen really dead? This dreadful question consumed Rob's mind, quashing all other thought. If Gwen was dead, he *was* beaten. Rob felt some of the fight go out of him.

Katz must've sensed this as well, as he released Rob with one hand and dug into one of his pockets.

As the pressure eased, Rob quickly adjusted his footing and repositioned his hands for better leverage. This was all he could manage.

Katz produced an evil-looking switchblade stained with blood. "Do you want to smell her perfume on it, lover boy?"

Rob turned his head, refusing to look at the knife.

Katz shoved the blade in his face. Although faint, Rob could detect Gwen's scent. He howled with anguish and felt all of his remaining strength flow out of him. Maybe Katz was right—maybe he *had* lost and had nothing left to live for. His body sagged precariously inward toward the flames. He readjusted his hold on the edge one more time. His back was beginning to blister and the odor of burnt flesh assailed him. He glanced down at Luke, who would go into the furnace next.

"Gwen told me all about the incinerator," Rob shouted at Katz.

"What're you talking about?" Katz demanded and again the pressure eased up a notch. "Not that it matters. She's dead and your time is limited."

Arching his back away from the heat in a mostly futile gesture, Rob continued. "She also called the FBI. You'll never get away with it." He tried to play the bluff for all it was worth. It was all he had.

Katz hesitated. "You're a bad liar, Gentry. Care to take some lessons?"

The pressure increased again. The bluff had failed. It was over. Suddenly, a new thought occurred to him—radical and unexpected.

Rob released his hold on the edge of the incinerator door, and in the same motion grabbed hold of Katz with his half-burnt fingers. Rather than resisting anymore, Rob pushed backward for all he was worth with his biker legs, catapulting them both into the incinerator. As Katz's outstretched hand struck the doorframe, Nikolai's blade dropped to the ground. Rob blocked out all else and focused his mind on thoughts of redemption.

Katz screamed as the two men tumbled into the flames.

CHAPTER FORTY-NINE

Luke slowly regained consciousness. Something was digging uncomfortably into his back, so he shifted position. God, it was hot and noisy. Where was he? What had happened? He opened his eyes and instantly, lightning bolts of pain shot through his skull. He quickly shut them. He had seen enough to know that he was in some sort of incinerator room—the source of all the heat and noise. And he was lying on a wheeled cart.

What the hell was he doing here? And what was that horrible stench? Luke tried valiantly to reconstruct his memory, but it was a total blank for recent events. The last thing he remembered was driving to the hospital for Kim's C-section. Kim! Where was she? Was she okay? He had to get moving.

Luke rolled onto his side and, with considerable effort, managed to sit up. He opened his eyes again. His head thumped miserably in protest and the room swam around him, but he forced himself to endure until his vision stabilized. He cradled his head in his hands; he felt as if a large spike had been driven deep into his skull. When he gingerly probed his right temple, he felt a huge tender swelling, and his fingers came back bloody.

He looked around the small room as he tried to muster the energy to stand. The grated door to the furnace was half open, revealing flames behind it. A can of fuel oil and a shovel were over against the wall. Footprints were plainly visible in the dirt on the floor, as were signs of a scuffle. There was also blood spattered over the floor. *Whose blood?* he wondered. His pulse quickened, but this only intensified the throbbing in his head. He needed to wake up faster, but the image of blood seemed to be hugely important. He concentrated on the blood for a moment and another big chunk of his memory fell back into place.

There had been the fiasco during Kim's C-section—the pool of blood in Kim's abdomen. Seidle trying to bleed her to death. Luke delivering his daughter Abi out of this pool. The FBI agent shooting Seidle dead. Seidle lying in a pool of his own blood. Rob Gentry appearing from nowhere to save Kim.

Luke sat on the side of the cart and massaged his sore head and eyes while he tried to coax the rest of his memory back to life. There were still too many unanswered questions. Where was Kim now? Why was he here? And what in God's name was that overpowering, nauseating smell? One thing was clear—he must find Kim—now.

Drawing a deep breath, Luke rose to his feet. As he did, he saw stars and the room began to spin. Shards of pain again lanced through his skull, but he remained standing. He grabbed the handle of the cart to steady himself. No time for weakness now.

He hobbled toward the door to get out of this hellish room, but a loud creaking noise behind him stopped him. He spun in time to see the grated door to the furnace swing wide open. Luke's breath caught in his throat as a gruesome figure emerged from the fire. *That's impossible*, he thought. *No one could possibly come out of there.*

The figure spoke. "What's wrong, Daulton? You look like you've seen a ghost"—a spasm of raspy coughing interrupted—"or a demon."

Luke gasped. The creature's face was hideously burnt beyond recognition, with one eye just a blackened socket, but Luke recognized Katz's unmistakable voice. Luke stood staring, barely able to breathe, as his battered brain struggled to comprehend this. He now realized that the stench was burning human flesh.

"It's me, all right," the Katz creature uttered.

The sight of Dr. Katz caused the remainder of Luke's stubborn memory to come flooding back. Of course—Katz!

"And I've come for you," Katz said in a gravelly voice.

"What were you doing in there?" Luke asked, perplexed. He was treading water, desperately trying to buy some time while his mind came online. He still couldn't think straight. Was this all just a dream? This seemed entirely possible because his mind kept returning to: no *real* man could climb out of that inferno, could they?

"Taking care of business," Katz said cryptically.

Luke glanced at his watch. Roughly thirty minutes had elapsed since he had last seen Kim. What had happened *after* he was knocked out? A suffocating cloud of dread began to descend on Luke. Surely Katz would've finished Kim off while Luke had been unconscious. After all, Katz had access to Jenna's gun and Nikolai's knife. For God's sake, all he needed to do was disconnect her ventilator tubing—she was a sitting duck. And he, Luke, had failed to save her.

A further horrifying thought occurred to him. Had Katz thrown Kim into the furnace? Was that the source of the foul odor? He was terrified to find out. Luke swallowed hard and said, "It's over, Katz. You're done for. Secret Service and FBI are all over the place." His words sounded hollow and he knew it—he was the one who felt like it was over. Life without Kim would be unthinkable.

Katz laughed in response, a hideous gurgling noise. "Brave words, Daulton, but it doesn't matter. It's just you and me. No one knows we're here."

"Then I'll take you, myself," Luke said, removing his hands from the cart's handle. He noted with horror he was still unsteady on his feet.

"I doubt you're up to it, my boy. It looks like you can barely stand." Katz took several steps toward him. "Your buddy Gentry, who was much stronger than you, didn't make out so well."

"Looks like *you* didn't make out so well, either!" Luke fired back.

Katz gestured to the furnace. "Can you smell him? Now it's your turn to join him in the hereafter. That door is the portal."

Luke recoiled at the thought that this stench was all that remained of Rob. But his mind, becoming unhinged, clung to the thought that at least it wasn't Kim. At the same time, the thought of Rob dying at this bastard's hands reignited his anger. He could feel it burning brightly inside him and he drew strength from it. "You'll be the one going through the damned portal." He lunged at Katz, ignoring his wobbly legs.

Katz easily dodged Luke's clumsy attack. "You're no match for me, Daulton."

Luke stumbled past him and went down hard, skidding on his knees until he was just several feet from the mouth of the furnace. The heat was pouring out of it and threatened to cook his face. He clambered to his feet and turned to face Katz. "We'll see about that," he shouted, the sweat now dripping off his forehead. God, he wished his legs would steady and his head would clear in time to make this bastard pay.

Katz appeared to study Luke. "I sense something different about you."

"That's right—I'm going to kill you this time," Luke said.

"You're beginning to believe—to have faith. How did this happen?"

"You wouldn't understand," Luke replied, returning Katz's stare.

"Oh, really." Katz tried to smile, but instead produced a hideous oozing from his burned eye socket. "You're placing your belief in the wrong one, Daulton."

"What're you talking about?"

"Your side is going to lose. The human race is hurtling toward destruction and nothing can stop it—certainly not *your* God. He deals in phony, feel-good crap and cuts and runs when the going gets tough."

"You sound like my dad—rely on yourself."

"Your dad was an idiot! I never said rely on yourself," Katz said angrily. "My master is trustworthy—"

"That's a hoot!"

"—when he says he'll give you power, he means it."

"My father was wrong—and so are you. He never saw what I saw." Luke wiped the sweat from his eyes. "I delivered my daughter from a pool of blood. One look at her convinced me there is more out there than meets the eye. Clearly, she was saved by something beyond me."

"Very touching, I'm sure. But it's not enough—your fledging faith will do you no good. My faith is mature, tried and tested in the furnace, so to speak. How do you think I survived that?" He pointed again to the furnace.

Luke shot a glance over his shoulder. The furnace's gaping maw was only two or three feet away. Despite the intense heat, chills ran up and down his spine because he had no answer to Katz's question.

"My master gives me strength," Katz said.

"What a joke! You have no real faith. You believe in the father of lies."

Katz growled, then came at Luke, locking onto his arms. The two men, as if welded together, pirouetted about the small room, bumping off the grimy walls. Luke smacked his knee painfully on the heavy cart. As they struggled, he felt himself being slowly maneuvered backward toward the furnace. *God, he's strong.* Luke thought of Rob burning to death in the incinerator and fought back harder.

"Even the demons believe!" Katz shouted and stood up straighter, thrusting his chest out and looking upward.

"I know that verse!" Luke cried out. "You're a fool. Once again you deal in half-truths and lies. You left out the most important part!"

Katz paused, cocking his head.

"It reads," Luke continued, sucking in air as he tried to catch his breath. "Even the demons believe and they *shudder*!"

Katz's face contorted and his grip weakened.

Luke pushed him back a foot or two, away from the god-awful furnace.

But Katz recovered quickly. "Your cheating friend Gentry *shuddered* when I tossed him into the hellfire! He died trying to save your sorry ass." Katz put his head down, tightened his grip, and started pushing Luke backward again. "His faith was as weak as yours, and I crushed him like a bug. You're next. The only chance you morons had was to take me on together. My master warned me of this."

Luke felt his feet slipping backward on the dusty floor. If only he could get his hands around Katz's thick neck and complete the job he had started in Kim's room.

"Your wife also shuddered when I killed her!" Katz shouted in his face.

Luke felt like he had been stabbed in the heart and his body sagged. There it was, plain as day—he *had* killed Kim. Despair filled Luke, all hope now extinguished. He barely felt the intense heat on his back.

Katz eased up the backward pressure for a moment, although his hands never released their grip. He stared into Luke's face. "The air embolus touch following a bloody C-section was brilliant, don't you think? A natural fatal complication. Almost as good as MH. No one will suspect." Katz, obviously relishing the opportunity to rub salt in Luke's wounds, continued, "You should never have left her side, Daulton. *You* doomed her!"

This was too much for Luke to bear. His anger flared anew and he cried out through his pain, "I'll kill you!" Freeing up one hand, he landed a couple of solid blows, one directly to Katz's burnt face. Katz looked vaguely surprised, but the blows didn't seem to inflict any damage; the Katz-creature appeared impervious to pain. As Luke's anger intensified, he fought back even harder, but he still couldn't overcome the man. Katz's strength was unreal, inhuman.

Katz grunted and again began pushing him slowly, relentlessly toward the furnace door. Luke's feet slid back until his heels bumped up against the bottom of the furnace doorway. A strange thought intruded on Luke's mind. Did he say *air embolus*?

Something didn't quite fit here. Luke was missing something vital and he desperately needed to understand this.

"Time to go through the portal," Katz said, slowly ratcheting up the pressure. He seemed to enjoy prolonging this part and watching Luke squirm.

Luke let go of Katz and braced himself with his outstretched hands against the doorframe. The hot metal frame burned his hands, but he ignored the pain. In a time measured in microseconds, the following thoughts raced through his mind: Luke knew Kim had survived the air embolus—she had pulled out her IV in time; he had talked to her. Was it possible that Katz didn't know this? Did he think he killed her with his injection of air into a bogus IV?

Luke thought back to his last vision of Kim. She had closed her eyes and her hand had gone limp in his. Had she perhaps seen Katz approaching behind him and played possum as her only possible last defense?

"What's wrong, Daulton? Where's your precious faith now? I watched your wife flatline."

Amazing! That didn't fit either. Wouldn't a guy like Katz, who prided himself on the brilliance of his plans, see fit to taunt Luke, if indeed Kim had survived his first attempt—the injection of air—only to have Katz realize it and kill her anyway? And would he really have taken the time to restart her IV and inject more air, when he could've easily killed her in so many other ways? Plus it made no sense that Katz would brag about administering a fatal air injection, if he *had* killed her by some other means.

Maybe Kim is alive!

"You bastard!" Luke shouted, but almost smiled. An enormous feeling of love swelled in his heart. The possibility that Kim might be alive reenergized Luke more than all the anger in the world. His despair vaporized and he fought back vigorously with everything he had. He managed to push free of the hot doorframe and broke Katz's grip on his arms. The two stood facing each other again. Two could play at these mind-game things. "You know the senator is still alive?"

"What're you talking about?" Katz demanded.

"I know about your stupid plot to kill the senator. I know the MH was a fake."

"Nice try, Daulton, but you can't lie any better than your dumb, dead friend, lover boy. Doesn't really matter now, does it? You'll never live to tell a soul."

"You made one stupid mistake, you moron."

Katz looked irritated. "And just what might that be?"

"My dad did teach me one thing that's true. Never send a boy to do a man's job. Your stupid Russian flunky was too busy getting high to finish the job."

Katz hesitated before replying. "It doesn't matter. The plan was foolproof."

"Maybe. But not idiot proof." Luke was on a total roll here. "I helped Stu save the senator." He had no clue whether the senator had lived or died. In fact, he thought it most likely that he was dead. But he could see the bluff was definitely rattling Katz, so he persevered. "The first thing we did was take down the IV bag you started."

"That's enough!" Katz came at him again. With unbelievable strength, Katz latched onto Luke and drove him back against the hot doorframe. Luke barely got his arms out in time to keep from getting pushed in. His hands were once again being cooked on the doorframe. Frantically, he looked around the room for anything he could use as a weapon. He saw a shovel across the room. It would do nicely, but since it was out of reach, it might as well have been on the moon. An orange glint caught his eye, the flames being reflected from some shiny surface on the floor. Luke glanced down and saw the blade of a knife, a blade he had seen before—Nikolai's switchblade. But Luke needed both hands to resist the inexorable pressure of Katz shoving him backward. If he let go with one hand to try to retrieve the knife, it would be over—he would go in. What could he do? He couldn't hold on much longer.

Suddenly a vision of Abi, angelic Abi, came to him. Maybe this was a defense mechanism, his mind offering the illusion of being cradled in love to give him peace before his own death? He relaxed a bit, ignored the scorching heat on his back and hands, and immersed himself in the vision, concentrating on Abi's face. She seemed to be speaking to him. Abi meant so much to him. Saving her life had been the key that unlocked his faith. Wait—Abi was trying to tell him something.

And then it dawned on him.

Luke pushed back from the doorframe with all his might. "I also know about your son," he lied. "Rob told me everything. How he died in the house fire and you were consumed by guilt."

Katz straightened up again and the pressure eased. "You don't know shit about what happened." Katz glared at him with his remaining good eye.

"I do know one thing," Luke said, returning the glare. "You failed to save him!"

"I tried, damn it!" Katz shouted, spittle flying into Luke's face. "God knows, I tried."

"Do you still hear him scream?"

"No, of course not," Katz answered too quickly. Katz got a faraway look in his eye, as if he were listening to something only he could hear. The pressure eased further.

Luke carefully removed one seared hand from the doorframe and moved it slowly to search the floor, not daring to look. "You talk about my faith being weak," he said, his hand desperately continuing the search. "It sounds like *yours* was weak!"

"No, that's not how it was! God knows I tried to save him." Katz was snarling. "It was God who screwed up!"

Luke never took his eyes off Katz, meeting his stare, but his groping hand connected with something hard and metallic on the floor—the switchblade.

Katz continued his rant. "The fucking master of the universe couldn't save one twelve-year-old boy! God must pay for betraying me. I'll make him pay. You'll see. Souls are mine for the taking!"

"I doubt it." But it seemed that Katz had reignited his anger with his fresh hatred of God, because the pressure ratcheted up once more. With only one hand to resist him, Luke knew that he only had a few more seconds. He cut his finger badly on the sharp blade as he frantically tried to locate the handle.

"I'm done playing with you!" Katz grunted and pushed hard.

Luke finally found the smooth handle of the switchblade. Grasping it tightly, he swept it up in an arc, ramming the blade deep into Katz's chest with all the fury he could muster. Katz screamed and his hot blood gushed out, running down Luke's knife hand. Luke hugged Katz tightly, and they swiveled like a dance pair doing the tango, completing a 180-degree turn with the blade still buried in Katz's chest. Blood was now also running out of Katz's mouth, but he held on to consciousness, anguished moans emanating from deep within his throat. Luke stood up straight and withdrew the blade, watching new blood spill forth from the chest wound. Katz tottered on his feet and looked like he might fall. Luke delivered a powerful kick, sending him tumbling backward into the furnace.

Katz shrieked, sounding like the inhuman wraith that he was, as the flames engulfed his body. Luke grabbed the can of fuel oil, uncapped it, and dumped it all over Katz's burning body. "Burn in Hell!" Luke slammed the door home and latched it. He spun the furnace control knob to max and the flames roared like an angry beast. For good measure, Luke grabbed the shovel and wedged it in the door mechanism, jamming it tight. "Let's see you climb out now!"

EPILOGUE

Luke beamed with pride as he pushed the wheelchair down the hallway. Kim rode in the wheelchair with a neatly wrapped bundle in her arms—Abi. Luke was filled with an enormous sense of relief and gratitude that he was leaving the hospital with the two most important people in his life—alive and well. Things could easily have turned out differently. He also realized on some gut level that his future happiness would forever be tinged with bittersweet memories.

Senator Pierce had survived his gallbladder surgery, although was still in the SICU recovering. Stu Whitman had indeed taken down the acid-laced IV bag after Luke had been forcibly removed from the OR. This action had been life saving and allowed Pierce's resuscitation. However, Pierce had suffered a stroke during the operation, probably due to a combination of acidosis and low blood pressure. Time would tell to what extent he would recover his mental faculties and whether or not he would retain his Senate seat.

Gwen was also in the SICU, recovering from abdominal surgery. The surgeons had found massive liver and spleen lacerations and she had required whole blood volume transfusions to keep her alive. Had she been found ten or fifteen minutes later, she probably wouldn't have made it. But thanks to her youth and good health, she now had an excellent chance of making a full recovery. Except, Luke knew, she was being treated for severe depression, which had gripped her ever since she had learned of Rob's death.

In his debriefing with the FBI, Luke learned that the skeletal remains of three different bodies were pulled from the incinerator. In addition to Rob's body and Katz's, a third body —FBI agent Benjamin Harris—was also retrieved. Luke didn't know Benjamin Harris, but was informed that Ben's quick thinking under duress had not only produced the Sudoku puzzle, but also summoned help—before he had been roasted alive by Katz. Luke shuddered when he thought how close he had come to suffering a similar fate. Ben was to receive the Medal of Valor, the FBI's highest award for bravery, posthumously.

Luke was also deeply saddened to learn that Jenna Steele— the OB nurse/FBI agent, who had saved his life during Kim's C-section and helped deliver Abi, was also dead—killed by Katz. In addition to shooting Mark Seidle to death, they told him that Jenna had also shot and killed Nikolai Andropov and had wounded Katz. In fact, they speculated that the blood loss from Katz's shoulder wound had probably weakened him, helping Luke to overcome him in the end. Jenna would also receive the Medal of Valor.

The FBI said they had uncovered evidence from Katz's computer of a murder-for-hire ring operating at the hospital. Luke provided them with some additional details about Mimi Hinkle's suspicious death in the OR. They thanked him and said they were already on it—Katz's phone and bank records had led them to investigate two prominent local attorneys, Bart Hinkle and Kyle Schmidt.

The FBI also mentioned they were attempting to follow the money trail from Katz's bank accounts to identify and apprehend whoever was behind the attempt on Senator Pierce's life. But this was proving a tougher nut to crack. So far, the bad guys here—no doubt well-connected political operatives—seemed to have done a much better job covering their tracks, and the trail was obscured by many false leads and dead-ends. The investigation was ongoing, but likely to be drawn out, as it was already getting bogged down by political headwinds and outright stonewalling.

Luke thanked the FBI for their continuing efforts and for the service and sacrifice of agents Benjamin Harris and Jenna Steele, both murdered in the line of duty by that bastard, Katz. Luke realized he owed his life to them. The thought of Katz made Luke's fists tighten. The memory of their fight to the death in the incinerator room would haunt him forever. He could only hope that Katz had been wrong about his dire predictions for the human race. And he couldn't help but wonder how many more Katzes were loose in the world. He was glad he had sent that unholy demon straight back to Hell, where he belonged.

And that left Rob—the tough one. Luke still had to choke back tears when he thought of him. Rob had saved Kim's life, as well as Luke's, in an unselfish act of bravery and sacrifice. Luke literally owed him everything. He missed Rob already and mourned the friendship they never had a chance to develop.

Luke parked the wheelchair next to the entrance to the hospital chapel. There was a beautiful wooden carving of Jesus on a pedestal, in a little alcove to the right of the chapel door. The door also had a lovely stained-glass window in it. Kim looked up at him.

"Do you mind if we stop here for a minute?" Luke asked.

"Of course not." Kim blinked several times and he could see tears glistening in her eyes. "Take your time."

Luke went inside, knelt down at a pew, and started praying.

Twenty minutes later, he came out of the chapel to find Kim absorbed, staring peacefully at their daughter's face. She looked up and asked, "How'd it go?"

"Fine," Luke answered. "I got some stuff off my chest that's been there a long time—it felt good. I also passed along some long overdue thanks." He heard his voice break.

She reached out with her free arm to comfort him.

Luke returned her sad smile and the two looked into each other's eyes without saying anything more. "Let's go home," Luke finally said in a stronger voice, and began nudging the wheelchair forward.

"Sounds good," Kim said. "This one's going to be hungry soon."

Luke paused just before reaching the main entrance. "There's something I have to tell you."

Kim turned and took his hand and squeezed it. "Go ahead," she said. Abi looked up at him.

"It's about my father."

Luke took another step forward and the automatic glass doors whooshed open. The new family headed out into the bright, sunlit morning.